SO THIS IS LOVE

Sheridan Adams, young, attractive, but saddened by disillusionment, is totally unlike the fat, smiling, middle-aged housekeeper Richard Hayden has in mind when he advertises in the local paper. A young widower, left alone with his small son Dick, he badly needs someone to look after his home. Sherry, though she may not be quite the person he has pictured, suits the post admirably. Having found a home for herself and her little daughter, Anne, she is able to forget her troubles for a time. But her tranquillity is short-lived and it is only after many misunderstandings that Sherry ultimately finds true happiness.

cabvi
Central Association for the Blind and Visually Impaired
live your vision
Mid York
LIBRARY SYSTEM
The Power To Imagine

For
Mother and Isobel

So This Is Love

by

Patricia Robins

Dales Large Print Books
Long Preston, North Yorkshire,
BD23 4ND, England.

British Library Cataloguing in Publication Data.

Robins, Patricia
So this is love.

A catalogue record of this book is
available from the British Library

ISBN 1-84262-143-2 pbk

First published in Great Britain 1953
by Hutchinson & Co. (Publishers) Ltd.

Published in Large Print 2002 by arrangement with
Claire Lorrimer

Dales Large Print is an imprint of Library Magna Books Ltd.

Printed and bound in Great Britain by
T.J. (International) Ltd., Cornwall, PL28 8RW

CHAPTER 1

It had had a strange beginning – this friendship between Richard Hayden and his young housekeeper Sheridan Adams. Sherry's few friends said it was an amazing coincidence. Richard's little son, Dick, called it 'jolly lucky'. Sherry herself felt it to be the first decent break life had offered her for ages.

It had started one Friday when she had picked up the local paper and looked through the 'Domestic' column to find her advertisement. She had phrased and rephrased it so often that the printed words were unfamiliar after her pencilled efforts on sheet after sheet of paper. Then she caught sight of an ad. so similar to her own that it attracted immediate attention.

WANTED. Capable housekeeper to take complete charge; widower with child aged six. Nice home for right person.

Then – and here, perhaps, was the coincidence – followed her own ad.

WANTED. Post as housekeeper by capable lady with child. Could take complete charge.

One above the other, they seemed already joined by their joint requirements.

'It's too good to be true,' Sherry had thought, excited in spite of herself. For a moment, the grey-green eyes clouded as she thought: 'He won't want Annabel if he has a child of his own. She would be relegated to the kitchen – the staff quarters. She'd grow up in a position which wouldn't be fair to her.'

'Why be so pessimistic?' Susan, her dearest friend, had replied when Sherry told her about the ads. over lunch. 'He may be fond of kids. He may be glad that Annabel is old enough to keep his child company. He's probably terribly rich and will end up marrying you and having to advertise for another housekeeper!'

Sherry had laughed, her beautiful almond-shaped eyes lighting with humour and her wide, generous mouth curling upwards. Glancing at her, Susan sighed. It was really a shame that a girl as beautiful and sweet natured as Sheridan Adams should have had such a raw deal from life – should be forced into taking a job as a cook-general – for that's what it really amounted to. At twenty-eight, with her education, background and looks, Sherry should be having a wonderful time as Bob's wife, entertaining for him in his huge country house, hunting, dancing, holidays abroad – lacking for nothing financially or spiritually.

Instead, Bob had had to be killed in that terrible hunting accident and left Sherry at twenty-four a widow with a baby only a few months old.

Bob, being Bob, had left no will but, as his next-of-kin, Sherry inherited everything – the gorgeous old house, his large private income which, even after death duties had been extracted, still left enough for her to live a life of comparative luxury. His death might not have been such a ghastly tragedy if it had not brought to life an episode in Bob's past that was to alter completely Sherry's and Anne's future.

Bob de Lage had been a handsome, gay, irresponsible, young man with more than his fair share of good looks, charm and wealth. Perhaps it was those very things which had made him so irresponsible. Susan was not in the least surprised when Sherry, quiet, home-loving, sensitive, humorous, was swept into marriage after a crazy whirl-wind courtship. Susan felt Bob could have swept *her* off her feet if he'd ever tried. Every woman loved him – but none other so whole-heartedly as Sherry. Susan, who had known Sherry since childhood, was fully aware that it was the first serious love-affair in Sherry's life and that with her nature, generous and impulsive beneath the quiet thoughtful exterior, it must always be all or nothing. With Bob, it had been all her heart and her heart had been broken not so much by Bob's death, for she might always have treasured his memory, but by the astounding piece of information that came from Bob's solicitors: *Bob had been married before* – and Sherry was not legally his wife.

'But who was she? Why didn't we know about her?' Questions had poured from Susan's lips when she arrived at Bob's home in answer to Sherry's telegram.

Sherry, white faced with deep shadows beneath her eyes, but unnaturally calm and untearful since her one outburst of crying the week Bob had been killed, said in a whisper: 'She is a French chorus girl. Bob married her one week-end in Paris, the day after he had met her. They spent a fortnight's honeymoon on the Riviera and then Bob left her. He's been sending her money all these years. Apparently, he realized he had made a mistake but she wouldn't divorce him. The solicitor told me he isn't sure whether it is because of Bob's money or because her religion forbids divorce. But it doesn't matter. What matters is that Bob knew he was committing bigamy when he married me. I could have forgiven him if he had told me. I might have ... oh, what does it matter what I might have done?' Her voice broke, and she continued in a whisper, 'I loved him. But what I shall never forgive him for is – Anne.'

Annabel, Sherry's infant daughter asleep in her pram in the beautiful grounds of Hardley Manor – Anne, with no right to her father's name – and Sherry had been so wildly happy when the baby was born. Susan had visited her in hospital and Sherry, starry-eyed and proud, had vowed there was nothing more she wanted from life – unless it were Bob's son – later.

Gradually the dreadful tangle had sorted itself out. Bob's parents who lived in London, had wanted to buy the French girl's silence. They minded only because of the scandal attached to Bob's name. They admitted his blame but could not concern themselves with what was past. It was the future that counted and they were afraid of what people would say. They had tried to persuade Sherry to stay on at Hardley Manor – or else close it temporarily, and go to their London house. To them, Sherry *was* Bob's widow, but to Sherry, facts were facts. The French girl was Bob's wife – his heir – and none of this belonged to her – the house, his money, his name. Only Anne was hers; and her pride. Steadfastly, she refused to be pitied or cajoled by her erstwhile 'in-laws', or persuaded by the family solicitor to 'go on as if nothing had happened'. How could she, when her heart as well as her life was broken into irreparable pieces?

She had packed only her own personal belongings which she had brought with her when she was married, and together with Anne, she had gone to London to live with Susan. Anne was placed in a crèche, and Sherry got a job selling clothes in a fashionable store so that she could pay her own and Anne's way. The staff at Hardley Manor were given notice and Sherry told Bob's parents that she intended to start life again and that since she would rather forget everything to do with Bob and the past two years, she would prefer not to see them again.

'They didn't care about seeing *me*,' she told Susan rather bitterly, after her final interview with them. 'They only cared about Anne – said she was Bob's child and all they had left to live for. I'm afraid I was a little cruel. I told them that Anne belonged only to me and I would rather she grew up to know nothing whatever about the man who was her father. I had to be cruel – for Anne's sake. As to – Bob's – wife – they can do as they please about her. I never want to see her and the money doesn't interest me.'

Susan had admired Sherry's attitude even while she wondered if she would have had the courage to do the same thing in her friend's place. After all, money *did* matter, and Sherry, who, even before she was married, had been used to a reasonable standard of luxury, was finding it extremely hard to pinch and scrape. The long hours of standing at her job took two stone off her weight and she was far too thin. Her cheeks were hollowed and there were always violet shadows under her eyes, for, when she got home, there was still Anne to be coped with – Anne's night and early morning bottles, then, as she grew older, wakeful nights teething. She never had enough sleep, and if it hadn't been for Susan who did all the cooking, she wouldn't have had enough to eat.

What had happened to Hardley Manor, Bob's wife and his parents, neither she nor Sherry knew for, true to her word, Sherry refused to see them or even correspond with them. That phase of her life was past and she lived now only for Anne; was friendly only with Susan and the girls she worked with, dropping her old acquaintances of her 'married' life and leaving Bob's family to make what excuses they chose for her disappearance.

Susan, who knew Sherry better than anyone, understood what her friend suffered, how low were her spirits when she grew tired, how much it worried her to have to leave Anne always in the care of strangers; having no real say in her upbringing, none of the real joys of her babyhood. Anne's first words, her first steps, her gay happy laughter occurred in the daytime. By six o'clock at night, when Sherry collected her from the crèche, Anne was sleepy, sometimes irritable and wanting little but her cot and a warm drink.

'I'll have to change my job,' Sherry had said finally, when Anne was four and practically a stranger to her mother. 'I must see more of her. If I got a job – say, as a housekeeper, she could be with me all the time.'

'A housekeeper!' Susan had echoed. 'But you'd hate that, Sherry dear – cooking, cleaning, counting the laundry!'

'I wouldn't hate anything if I had Anne with me,' Sherry said, glancing down at the sleeping child. Anne, at four, was oddly unlike either of her parents. She had Sherry's dark, wavy hair, and the blue of her eyes was Bob's colouring, but the shape was different. Her nose was tip-tilted, unlike Sherry's which was longish and straight, and her mouth a childish rosebud, showing no signs of her mother's wide, generous lips. Sherry was glad that she wasn't like Bob. Three years had helped to soften the blow, as well as the memory, and she could even forget him for weeks at a stretch until some mannerism of Anne's brought him back to mind, and all her suffering with it.

'I could always pack the job in if I didn't like it,' Sherry said, continuing their conversation. 'But I think it would be best from all points of view. You've been terribly good putting me up so long, Susan. It isn't really fair on you, especially now there's Gerald. You have every right as an engaged couple to have a bit of privacy and a fat lot of chance there is at the moment with either Anne or me barging in at the wrong moment! Oh, I know you are far too nice to admit it, and so is Gerald, and I don't want you to think it's because of you both that I'm going. I've been considering it for ages and it's for myself. I *must* see more of my child.'

Susan hadn't argued, partly because she knew Sherry could be very obstinate once her mind was made up, partly because it was true that she and Gerald never had two moments alone together. If Susan were really going to settle down in some job, they might even get married. They could afford it if Gerald got the rise he expected in the new year.

So the advertisement had been composed and sent in. And here it was in print, directly above one from a widower wanting a housekeeper. It really was a coincidence.

Sherry had taken a day off from the office and gone down to the address in Buckinghamshire to see the 'widower and child'.

They lived in a very large, rambling modern house on the side of a hill overlooking the Vale of Aylesbury. The house was not particularly attractive, nor unpleasant to look at, but the surroundings were perfectly beautiful and, as Sherry came to know later, belonged mostly to the National Trust.

Sherry was shown into the drawing-room by what was obviously the 'daily help' and asked to wait. While she studied the furnishings, which were tasteful if somewhat shabby and uncared for and lacking any feminine touch, a small boy came into the room and studied her carefully.

'Are you the vicar's wife?' he asked after a while.

Sherry judged his age to be five, though she knew from the advertisement that he was a year older. This must be the 'child'. He was a small but sturdily built little boy with sandy hair and freckles and a rather over-serious expression that was not in tune with his humorous little face.

'No!' she said smiling. 'I've come in answer to your father's advertisement for a housekeeper.' She wondered if he knew about it.

'Oh, so you're one – a housekeeper, I mean. Daddy said you'd probably be middle-aged and very fat and smiling. You're not a bit like that.'

Sherry smiled, but it was a little ruefully. If

that was the type of woman his father wanted to employ, she wouldn't get the job. She wished she hadn't worn her new suit and that absurd, if smart, little beret. She should have dressed down and not up to the part.

'I'm afraid I'm not,' she said. 'Will your father be coming soon?'

'No!' the small boy said, and then, seeing that more was required of him, he went on: 'Daddy said I wasn't to ask him to come in until I'd made up my mind. You see, if I don't like you, I don't have to have you.'

This time Sherry laughed outright. She had an intuitive picture of some tall man saying to the small boy, 'You don't have to worry, old boy, if you don't like her, we needn't employ her. You can take a quick look at her and make up your mind. She'll probably be middle-aged and fat and motherly.'

'Why are you laughing?' the child asked.

Sherry bit her lip.

She knew from experience that children don't like to be laughed at, so she said:

'Oh, I just like laughing. I have a little girl, you know. She's younger than you, but we always laugh a lot. It makes us feel happy.'

The little boy considered this gravely, then said:

'I laugh sometimes, but not very often. My mummy used to laugh a lot. But she's gone to live with Father God, you know. I think it was jolly unkind of her to go off like that without taking Daddy 'n me too. Daddy says we'll go and live there too one day, but goodness only knows when.'

The unconscious pathos touched a weak spot in Sherry's carefully rehearsed armour. She had meant to judge this job and its prospects so unemotionally. Emotion always brought pain and this time she had meant to be hard-headed, level-headed. Instead, she was forcing herself not to put her arms around this pathetic little figure as she knelt on one knee beside him and took his hands, saying:

'If I came to live here, we'd laugh a lot, just as you used to do. My little girl, Anne, is very funny. She'd make you laugh, too. What's your name?'

'Dick! Is your little girl like you?'

'To look at? No, not very. She's not like anyone, except herself.'

This made Dick laugh.

'Well, you're always like yourself, aren't you? I mean, you've only got to look in the mirror! I'm not like my mother either. Nor my daddy. He's ever so tall and I'm only three foot six, cause we measured me last night on the nursery door, so I know that's right. I growed five inches last year.'

'Then you're heaps taller than my Anne. But she's only four. She's a real tomboy. She likes climbing trees and she keeps a snail she found in Hyde Park in a matchbox.'

'Gosh! I've got a beetle in my box. Goodness only knows why – or that's what Mary says. She's the "daily", you know. She opened the front door because Daddy said it would make a good 'pression. What is a good 'pression?'

Sherry fought back another smile.

'Well, it's what I hoped to make when I came here. I try to look and behave my very best so that you and your daddy think you would like to have me here.'

'But why do you want to come here? Mary says the stairs are a death-trap, but I haven't seen any traps. Daddy says the house is far too big with just us and there's absolutely nothing to do all day. Of course, Daddy goes to work. When I'm grown up I shall go to work, too. Daddy calls it the "Old Bind" and that's what I call school. I like school. It's fun there, and there are lots of boys my age to play with. We do lessons, too. I can read and write, you know. Can your little girl?'

Sherry was about to answer when the sitting-room door opened and a tall man in his late thirties came into the room. He was frowning slightly and looked harassed and worried. Sherry noticed that the sandy hair was touched at the temples with grey, and that his face was long and thin with an unhappy mouth.

Dick turned to his father and grinned.

'I thought you weren't coming till I called, Daddy?' he said, ignoring, or perhaps unaware of the embarrassment on his father's face.

'Well, you were such a long time, old chap, and I thought Mrs Adams would be wondering–'

'Oh, we were talking,' Sherry broke in quickly, feeling a fraud at the sound of her maiden name with 'Mrs' before it. But she had no wish to explain her private life to strangers and it seemed the easiest way since she would not again take Bob's name.

'She's ever so nice, Daddy,' Dick said, clinging on to his father's hand and jumping up and down. 'She's got a little girl called Anne who's got a snail like my beetle.'

'That's nice, old chap! Now run along up to the nursery, or else go to the kitchen and tell Mary to get some tea sent up there. We'll be up in about ten minutes.'

'Are you going to view her now?' Dick asked as he went obediently to the door.

His father shot a quick, agonized look at Sherry but, seeing her smile, his face seemed suddenly to relax its tension and he smiled too.

'Children!' he said. 'They can be very embarrassing.'

'But refreshing, too,' Sherry said. 'As your son would put it, goodness only knows what we'd do without them.'

'He's picked that up from Mary. Heaven knows what else he's learnt from her. Still, she's fond of him – and kind. Won't you sit down?'

The tension was back in his voice and Sherry realized that this interview was as much a strain for him as for her; that he was wretchedly embarrassed, if not shy. Like a lot of Englishmen, he was clearly out of his *métier* in domestic affairs. To put him at ease, Sherry said:

'Dick has already told me that I am not what you expected. I'm afraid I also omitted to tell you on the phone last night that I have a little girl – she's four. I shall quite understand if you feel, therefore, that I'm not the kind of person you wanted.'

Dick's father handed her a cigarette and lit it before replying. His face was turned away from hers when he spoke and was reserved and thoughtful

'To be quite honest, Mrs Adams, I wasn't sure what to expect, and when you telephoned, I hadn't made up my mind what I wanted. You see – my wife – she only died last year. My son went to his grand-parents for six months and I went abroad. Since we both returned here, we have made do with Mary.' He looked at her as if apologizing for the obviously inadequate arrangements. He continued in a low, jerky voice, filled with acute suffering which Sherry recognized only too well. 'My wife's sister wanted to come and keep house, but I felt – that I didn't want anyone around – just Dick and myself. He didn't care very much for his aunt though she's quite a nice girl. Still, that's getting off the point. The idea was that we'd live here just during term time and Dick would go back to his grand-parents for his holidays. But he said the other evening that he didn't want to go away from me. Naturally, I don't want to part with him. It was only for his sake – so I realized I'd have to make better arrangements than Mary. Dick will need to be properly looked after during the holidays and so it seemed that a housekeeper was required. I had in mind a–'

'Plump, motherly woman, about middle age,' Sherry finished for him. He met her eyes and his face lightened for an instant into a smile. 'Yes!' he agreed. 'I thought that would be best for Dick.'

In one of her impulsive moments, Sherry identified herself with this worried, harassed father and forgot her own interests in the situation.

'That type of person is very hard to find these days. They were the now almost extinct breed of Englishwomen reared to domestic service. They started at the bottom and worked up to the trusted, respectable position of housekeeper. Well, they are all too old for work now, and the new generation didn't go into domestic service. The war changed that. They wanted something better – more exciting, better paid. You'll only find such types as war widows who are forced to take a job to keep themselves and their children, untrained and for the most part unreliable. I'm sure it would be better if you changed your idea and got someone young for Dick – someone who would still be adaptable to your way of life and – and…' she broke off, the blood rushing to her face, as she realized it was someone like herself she had the temerity to recommend to him! What must he be thinking of her. 'Look – I wasn't trying to force myself – force you – I mean, I wasn't considering myself when I spoke just now. I'd forgotten I was even here – oh, dear – I really think I'd better go.'

This time it was he who broke in. His eyes were lit again with that curiously gentle smile, and the sadness had momentarily gone.

'No, *I* think you'd better stay. I think you're right! And I know you weren't thinking of yourself just now. It's perfectly obvious that you are far too young to have had such a job before – if any job, come to that. You spoke from your heart and I appreciate your consideration for Dick. Maybe it is better for him to have someone young around the place – someone – similar in outlook, background, behaviour – to – to his mother. It never occurred to me that I might find anybody like yourself. Will you tell me more about yourself? Our conversation on the phone was very brief last night and I felt a little confused. I don't even know if I told you my name.'

Sherry had recovered her composure while he spoke and now she could smile again as she shook her head.

'Then I must introduce myself. My name is Hayden, Richard Hayden. Dick is my only child.'

'My little girl is called Annabel – Anne it has become now. She's just four. Her father died in a hunting accident when she was a few months old. Since then I have been working in a large shop in London selling clothes. I didn't mind the hard work so much, but I hated being parted all day from my little girl. So I thought I'd try to get a job as a housekeeper. It may sound a little presumptuous, but I feel sure I can do the job. After all, I ran a house with twelve servants for two years when I was first married.'

If Richard Hayden was wondering why, as a wife, she had been financially well off, yet, as a widow, forced to work, he did not mention it. He remained silent for a moment, trying to sort out his conflicting emotions.

Dick obviously liked this girl – for she wasn't much more than that. She was their own class – to use a word that was outdated. She was pretty and sensible, and she must know about children since she had a child of her own. Would it work out? He could afford to keep Mary on to do the rough work and cooking if this girl were willing to do everything else. Why shouldn't he engage her? The house was large enough for her to have her own suite of rooms. They could live their separate lives and Dick could run between the two of them; have the child for company during the day and his father at night – it might work, and he could stipulate a three-month trial period.

He put the proposition to her, adding:

'If you think it would work out from your point of view, Mrs Adams, I suppose we ought to discuss the financial aspect. I am a little vague on such things. Perhaps you would tell me what kind of salary you would expect?'

They discussed salaries with some awkwardness and embarrassment on both sides. At length, it was decided that Sherry would get three pounds a week and her own and Anne's keep. She should have three rooms on the second floor of the house, furnished as a bedroom each for herself and Anne, and a sitting-room of her own.

'You are being very generous,' Sherry said

finally, accepting the cigarette he offered her. 'Believe me, I shall do my best not to let you regret it. I shall do everything for young Dick that I would do for my daughter and try to make him happy.'

Richard Hayden leaned forward in his chair and his face became suddenly young in its eager boyishness.

'That is what really matters to me, Mrs Adams. He hasn't been very happy since – since his mother died. She was – very beautiful, and very gay. Dick adored her. It was a great shock to him when – when it happened. I had hoped he might settle down with his grand-parents but now I shall be glad he did not do so. I'm devoted to him and I hated the thought of being parted from him.'

'I fully understand your sentiments,' Sherry said quietly. 'It is because I felt I must be more with my little girl than my job allowed me that I decided to take this kind of job. I never imagined I should be so fortunate as to find such a congenial position so soon. If it hadn't been for our advertisements–'

'It was strange, wasn't it?' Richard Hayden broke in with his swift smile. 'It seems as if Fate intended us to find one another…' He broke off as if aware that his words were not perhaps usual for an employer interviewing a prospective employee. But then, the whole situation was unusual. Obviously this girl came from a good family. She was simply but smartly dressed and everything about her spoke of good taste and quiet simplicity. She might have been one of his wife's friends… 'Oh, June, June, my darling!' The thought was wrung from his heart as he realized yet again the vastness and finality of his loss. 'We had everything, you and I. So much to live for.' Now there was nothing left in life – except Dick, his son *her* son. 'I'll take great care of him, June; wherever you are, you will hear what I'm trying to tell you. He shall be happy, I promise you–'

'I think I hear Dick calling us,' Sherry broke in on his reverie. She had been acutely aware of the trend his thought had taken. Tragedy and sadness were written across the man's grave face as he stared past her into the fire. He was looking into the past, remembering the young wife he had lost; remembering as she had promised herself never to do. But there was bitterness among her memories and there was none among his – only the pain of lost love. Her own heart ached in sympathy and she was glad when the little boy's cries gave her an opportunity to bring him back to the present.

'Dick? Oh, that will mean tea is ready. If you don't object, we'll have nursery tea. It's always more friendly and cheerful up there.'

Sensitive to his mood, Sherry could not help guessing that this sitting-room where once, no doubt, his wife had poured tea for him in friendly affectionate intimacy was not easily lived in now that she was dead.

'We will help you to banish the past,' she thought as she stood up with her easy graceful movements. 'Dick and Anne and I. You will hear laughter when you open the door at night and there will be at least two pairs of childish arms to welcome you and wave to you when you go in the morning.'

'How soon do you think you could come?' Richard Hayden was asking as they went out into the hall.

'I shall probably have to give a fortnight's notice at my present job,' Sherry said. 'Then I could come as soon as you like.'

'The sooner the better!' the man said quickly. 'Shall we say two weeks from today?'

Sherry looked up and met the pleading in the blue eyes. She had expected to take a few days' holiday, somewhere alone with Anne, before taking on a new job, but she could not refuse that look. And in her own heart, she felt an eagerness to start this new life with the Haydens – to prove to herself and to them that she could make a success of it. She would be happy here and so would Annabel. Richard Hayden was charming and considerate, and the fact that she would be a 'glorified servant' as Susan had put it, worried her not in the least, with such an employer.

A smile lit her eyes for a moment as she said:

'I expect you would like references. I will ask my present employer and my bank manager to send them to you.'

Richard Hayden coughed to hide his embarrassment.

'I'm sure it isn't necessary, Mrs Adams, but perhaps I should take your advice on such matters.'

'I know you should!' Sherry laughed openly now. 'For all you know, Mr Hayden, I may walk off with the family silver.'

'If that is all references are needed for, then I'm sure I don't need them,' came his courteous reply, but Sherry said:

'I'll have them sent to you anyway.'

'Do-o-o hurry up,' came Dick's voice from the landing above them. 'There's buttered toast *and* crumpets and the butter is melting.'

The two 'grown-ups' looked at each other and smiled.

'They make life worth living, don't they?' said Sherry quietly, as she followed Richard Hayden up the stairs.

CHAPTER 2

'Why joo keep calling Mummy Mrs Adams,' Annabel asked Dick as they lay side by side on the rug in front of Sherry's sitting-room fire, doing a simple jig-saw puzzle while Sherry tackled the huge pile of mending she had found to do.

'Well, what else am I supposed to call her, silly,' said Dick scornfully. 'She's not *my* mummy. My mummy's dead.'

'What's dead?' Annabel asked, chewing her middle finger and staring round-eyed at her new young hero.

'That's – well, being dead means you've gone to live with Father God,' Dick replied. 'And Father God, case you don't know, is a sort of Jesus, only He's not a baby.'

Sherry smiled at this rather inaccurate religious explanation and thought, 'I must suggest to Mr Hayden that the children go to Sunday school.'

'I'm not a baby. I'm four!' Annabel announced somewhat irrelevantly.

'Well, I'm six and I shall be seven next,' Dick retorted. 'What will you give me for my birthday?'

'A doll!' Anne said promptly, voicing her

dearest wish.

'Boys don't play with dolls, darling,' Sherry put in quickly, fearing for Dick's *amour-propre*. It was important that the so-far perfect alliance between the two children should not go awry! 'I expect he'd rather have a cow-boy outfit or–'

'A cap gun!' Dick broke in grinning. 'That's what I want most of all. I wonder when my birthday is. Do you know, Mrs Adams?'

'I shall have to ask Mr Hayden,' Sherry thought and, at the same time, she realized that Anne was right. Dick couldn't go on calling her 'Mrs Adams'. It was too formal for the friendly 'motherly' relationship she had established already between them. Dick was in no way a problem child and had a boy's natural affections. He wanted to be loved and needed to have someone to run to, to turn to if things went wrong. In the past year, he had turned to Mary or to his father when he was home, but Mary was usually busy or else incapable of coping and his father away so much. Sherry, always friendly, always interested, always ready with the right word of condolence and tactful enough to wait for Dick to make the first moves, had soon won her away to his heart though it was only just three weeks ago that she and Anne had moved in.

'It's working out right!' she thought

contentedly as the children chattered between themselves. 'The house is beginning to look cared for and I'm rapidly getting the linen and Dick's clothes sorted and mended. I'd like to catch up with it all before spring cleaning. Mary will be a great help then. She's a good girl, willing and not the least resentful of my coming. She might have felt her erstwhile freedom was being curtailed.'

Instead, Mary was an ally in all respects and, with a little tact and guidance from Sherry, she kept the large house spotless and shining.

'Do you think Daddy would let me have a pony, Mrs Adams?' Dick broke in on her thoughts. 'That's what I'd like most of all. I'd let Anne have a turn now 'n again if she wanted.'

'You'll have to ask him, Dick,' Sherry said, thinking that if Mr Hayden could afford it, and they could manage between them to look after it, it would be a lovely idea for the children. It was good for them to grow up with animals. If they didn't have a pony, they might get a dog.

She looked at her watch and saw that it would soon be time to put Annabel to bed. Usually, about this time, Mr Hayden arrived home from work, tired, cold and in need of a drink. It had become her custom before she ran Anne's bath, to go downstairs and make sure the drawing-room fire Mary had lit after tea, was blazing cheerfully and that she had not forgotten to put out the whisky decanter and soda water. Dick would go down for an hour with his father before it was time for him to go to bed. Sherry never disturbed them at this time for she felt that Richard Hayden would like to have his son to himself.

There were the week-ends, of course, when Dick could have his father to himself, but lately, instead of Dick going down to join his father, they had both come upstairs to the nursery to join Anne and herself. Anne adored Dick's father and flirted with him in the manner of a four-year-old, smiling up at him from her large, round eyes, climbing on to his knee and completely ignoring her mother. Sherry had been grateful that Richard Hayden was so patient and affectionate with her child. He made no difference between her and his own son; if he brought home a present for Dick, there would be one for Anne, too. She had mentioned the fact and he had replied:

'I never noticed *you* making any difference between them either!' which was true enough.

Later that evening, the children asleep, Richard Hayden sat facing Sherry across the dining-room table. He had suggested the day she arrived that she had dinner with him 'to save Mary carrying trays and things', he had said. In fact, although this reason was true at first, he had found that he looked forward to the companionship. Since June had died so suddenly and unexpectedly of double pneumonia, he had become accustomed to dining alone. That is to say, it had become customary although he had never really accustomed himself to doing so. He had been too grief-stricken to wish to entertain and as to dining at the club or in town with friends, if he were to do so, it would mean forfeiting his brief hour with Dick before the boy went to bed.

How lonely and silent it had been there alone at the table with only Mary's chatter – mostly village gossip – as she dumped plates in front of him. The meals, not very tastefully served (though beautifully cooked, for Mary was talented in this respect only) failed to tempt his not very voracious appetite and he had lost a lot of weight.

Already, he felt sure, he must be putting on weight again. Somehow or another, his 'housekeeper' had found fresh flowers for the table. Mary appeared in a crisp, white apron. The tablemats and napkins were white and fresh-looking, the glassware and silver shone brightly. It looked as it had once looked when June saw to these things for him, and he was immensely grateful to Sheridan Adams for restoring the household standards.

There had been big improvements in other ways. His socks were darned, his shirts had buttons on them, a warm fire greeted him in the evenings and the whisky and soda which was his habit before dinner and bed. In Dick, also, there was a difference. No longer quiet, subdued, almost cowed as he had become, he was once more the noisy, mischievous, energetic little boy he had thought would never return. Mistakenly, he had put Dick's quietness down to the shock and loss of his mother. But children were oddly callous little devils. Now he seldom spoke of his mother and when he did it was without tears or a tremor in his voice. While he wondered a little, Richard Hayden was immensely glad that the boy was no longer grieving. It amused him to listen to Dick's account of his day's activities and he had learnt a lot about his new 'housekeeper' (though he seldom thought of her as such) and the little girl. Dick spoke of little else – what they had done and planned to do. Gradually, he had been persuaded up to the nursery to join them at weekends and discovered for himself why Dick was so pleased with life these days.

Studying Sherry covertly across the table, Richard Hayden paused to wonder if the new arrangement suited her as well as it suited him. Was she happy here? Did she find the work too hard – the rewards too few? Did she wish she had never come?

It was hard to imagine she had not settled down and found life to her liking. The pallor and the violet shadows had gone from beneath her eyes and her face seemed younger, gayer, more youthful. She was a very attractive young woman! Richard thought suddenly. And somehow the thought disturbed him. Until this moment, his relationship with her had been easy, unstrained and always dignified. Above all, completely impersonal. She had just been 'the girl who had answered his advertisement and become his housekeeper'. Now, suddenly, she was a person in her own right. He found himself wondering about her – about the kind of man her husband had been, whether he had been killed in the war, if she grieved for him. She was almost as reserved as he was himself and he realized he knew nothing of her private life. Her bank manager, he recalled, had said the usual things about her – that he could place every reliance on her honesty, etc., etc. Her employer had spoken of her as an excellent, tireless, conscientious and sober worker. He remembered being amused by the 'sober' and had made Sheridan laugh when he told her about it. It was strange how he thought of her, not as Mrs Adams, but as Sheridan. The Mrs Adams sounded too round and complacent and homely. It did not suit her.

Sheridan – really a boy's name – seemed to suit her rather enigmatic nature to perfection. She had a boy's slim, tall figure and a man's directness of approach. Yet she was feminine, too, dainty, fastidious, graceful…

He broke off his train of thought with a sudden rush of colour to his cheeks. What must she think if she could have read those thoughts.

'What that damned old tittle-tattle of a doctor's wife had thought, no doubt,' he told himself ruefully. Outside church, where he had accompanied young Dick last Sunday, the doctor's wife had waylaid him to say: 'Such a charming young woman, your housekeeper, Mr Hayden. Such a pleasant companion for you, I'm sure! She tells me she has come as a housekeeper?' The statement was barbed, he felt certain and was angered at such malicious behaviour in a woman who ought to have been above it. Nevertheless, it was highly probable that the village people were talking. After all, the girl was young and he wasn't very old! Mary went home to sleep and they were alone in the house except for the children. Nasty-minded gossips had plenty to chew over, damn them! It made the position very awkward. He wondered if the question of their living unchaperoned had crossed her mind and felt sure that it had not. 'I'll broach it later on this evening,' he thought. 'I am responsible for her and she ought to know.'

Over coffee, the question of what Dick should call her came up between them.

'He was saying tonight that "Mrs Adams" doesn't suit you, and I'm inclined to agree with him,' Richard Hayden said smiling. 'It's a bit tough on the kid when he's with you so constantly. Would you object if he called you something else?'

'Aunt Sheridan?' Sherry asked. 'That's a bit of a mouthful, too! Suppose he just calls me "Sherry"? I'm sure he won't take advantage of the informality.'

'No, I don't think he will,' Dick's father said seriously. 'You know, you've been wonderfully kind to him, Mrs Adams. He's deeply fond of you already. I – I should hate to think that – that you might have to go.'

Sherry put down her coffee cup and did not meet the man's gaze until the anxiety in her eyes was replaced by a vacancy of emotion she was by no means feeling.

'Go? Then you aren't fully satisfied that I–'

'Don't misunderstand me. I am more than satisfied,' her companion said quickly. 'But I think I owe it to you to warn you about something – something that simply had not crossed my mind when we made our arrangements in the first instance.'

'And that is?' Sherry prompted.

Richard Hayden pulled out his pipe and fingered the bowl.

'It sounds absurd, I know, but I'm afraid people in the village may be talking. You are young and attractive and – well, we are alone in the house quite a lot and you are – well, hardly the respectable kind of housekeeper – oh, blast it, I didn't mean that. I meant you aren't the usual type of housekeeper – dash it all, I'm making an awful hash of this!'

Sherry laughed, a gay laugh that took a load of Richard Hayden's mind.

'I quite see what you mean and I think it's too absurd. *I* don't mind what people say, if you don't. In fact, if they really wanted to gossip, they might as well pick on something that is true.'

('Now why did I say that?' she asked herself. 'I shall have to explain myself. Whatever made me bring up the subject of Bob.')

'I don't quite understand,' Richard Hayden said, looking at her questioningly.

Sherry's face was no longer happy but clouded with intense bitterness and unhappiness. He marvelled at the transparency of her emotions and at his own ability to read her facial expressions.

'Please don't say anything you would rather not,' he said hastily.

'No, I think I ought to tell you, it's only fair. Perhaps I should have told you before –

before I ever came here. But I thought it was all over and done with – so long ago. But the past is never really past, is it? There are always people who talk, who want to know something to their neighbour's discredit.'

'I'm quite certain you have never done anything that is to your discredit,' Richard heard himself saying – and meaning what he said.

'Nevertheless, they could gossip about me. You see, I wasn't really married at all to my husband – that is to say, he married me bigamously...'

Now that she had begun, she found she could not stop herself from pouring out the whole story. It had been bottled up inside her for so long and it was a relief to talk – to say it. Even with Susan, who had known the truth, she had been unwilling to talk about it. But to this man – this stranger – she could open her heart, because he was nothing to do with the past, and because above all else he was sympathetic and kind.

When she had finished, he did not speak for a moment, but handed her a cigarette which she took gratefully. When at last he voiced his thoughts, it was only to say:

'You don't – still love him?'

Sherry shook her head.

'No! I had loved him too much to be able to forgive him. If he had told me in the beginning, I'd have stood by him – waited for him – anything. But to marry me and let me bear his child, knowing all the time that she would have no right to his name – that was quite unforgivable.'

'I think you were very brave – to start out again on your own when there was no need,' Richard said thoughtfully. 'There are not so many women who would have had your courage.'

June – his wife? No, he thought ruefully. She had always been a hot-house plant, reared in luxury and unable to do without it. It was not her fault – for she was the only daughter of an extremely wealthy Australian sheep farmer and had been spoilt by rich, adoring parents since infancy. She would not have married me if I had been penniless, Richard thought suddenly and incongruously. It had never occurred to him before. June had been just June – the most attractive, piquant, charming and adored wife a man had ever had. Still, it was sobering to consider that he mightn't have had her at all – even for those blissful, happy years – if he had not been moderately well off and able to indulge her whims.

This going back to the past must be in the air, he thought wryly, and wondered at his ability to think of June purely considerately and without the passion of grief and loneliness that, until now, had surged over him at the merest thought of her. His young cousin, Tony, had written to him not long after June's death: *You'll get over it in time, old chap. Try not to be too gloomy. Get out and about a bit. Time's a great healer, they say, and I'm sure it's true, provided you don't nurse your grief.*

Was that what he had been doing – nursing his grief alone here in this house where he and June had lived? Was this what people meant when they said time was a healer – the ability to remember without grief and then, perhaps, to remember less and less often?

'Will you ever quite forget your husband?' he asked suddenly, needing her answer. 'You did love him once. Can you ever forget anyone who has once meant so much to you?'

Sherry felt the personal implications behind his question and thought a moment before she spoke. When at last she did so, it was to tell him what he himself believed.

'No, I don't think one ever forgets those one has loved. It is as if you have given them a part of yourself – and they hold it in their keeping for ever. You may want that little piece of you back, but it's theirs for always and always. I don't know if that is a good or a bad thing. But I'm sure it's true. One may not remember so often or so clearly, but I don't believe one can ever quite forget.'

'In some ways, our lives have been rather similar,' Richard said thoughtfully. 'We were both happy and lost our happiness.'

'I think one can be happy again,' Sherry replied. 'After all, I am not unhappy now. I love being here and I'm so grateful to you for being responsible for everything.'

'Then we are a mutual gratitude society,' said her companion with the smile that made him seem so many years younger than he normally looked. 'My only worry, I think, is that one of these days you'll marry again.'

'Never!' Sherry said violently. 'I shall never fall in love again.'

Richard Hayden looked at her searchingly.

'If you will forgive me for saying so, I think for once you are wrong. You are far too young and attractive to remain single for very long. And you would make far too good a wife for any sensible young man to overlook you very easily!'

'I may be domesticated,' Sherry said, refusing to joke about the subject, 'but that doesn't alter my feelings. I was married four years and I loved my husband with all my heart. I know I *couldn't* love anyone else in that way again.'

Although Richard Hayden could understand her sentiments – for, after all, there would never be another June in his life – he could not feel entirely convinced about this girl's future. She was still so young – so full of life. It was all wrong that she should have to face life alone and end it a lonely, perhaps embittered, spinster.

'I wonder why it is that I can talk of such things to this man!' Sherry was thinking. 'He's not only my employer but practically a stranger!' A sympathetic stranger, however, and one who was nice enough to bother about her. There had been no one but Susan to 'bother' for so long. Her parents had both died during the war and her only other relative, an aunt, had retired to a nursing home in Cornwall, bedridden and too old and ill to have any interest in Sherry or her child. Bob, his family and friends had been everything in her life and in renouncing the past, she had renounced practically everyone she had been friendly with. Only now was she beginning to realize how lonely her life had been – how empty and, but for Anne, meaningless. Now she had a job and not only Anne but young Dick and this house to keep her busy and happy, and the satisfying knowledge that she was making life easier, if not happier, for Dick's father.

'I've been meaning to tell you that if you have any friends you would like to visit you here, you are welcome to invite them,' Richard Hayden broke in on her thoughts with yet another proof of his consideration.

Sherry smiled.

'That's very kind of you, but there are only two people whom I care enough about to wish to see occasionally – my friend, Susan

Grieves, with whom I used to live, and her *fiancé*. If you really don't object, I'd love to ask them down for the day one Sunday.'

'Then please do so. If it suited them, why not next Sunday? It's young Dick's birthday, you know, and we could have a little party – that is, unless you would rather have your friends to yourself. I could always get Mary to mind the children for the afternoon.'

'Oh, no, Susan and Gerald love children,' Sherry protested quickly. 'And I know they'd enjoy a birthday party. Which reminds me, I meant to tell you that Dick has stated a wish for a pony. Has he told you?'

Richard nodded.

'I think he's a little bit young yet awhile. Perhaps next year. I thought I might get him a puppy of some kind. My old dog had to be put down several years ago and I haven't felt like replacing her. Still, it would be good for the children to grow up with an animal and I was making inquiries yesterday about a Boxer bitch. I rather like the breed. They aren't too big or too small and they are nice clean animals for indoors. What do you think?'

'That's a grand idea,' Sherry said enthusiastically. 'I read in a book that they are very good with children, too.'

'There are some breeders fairly near here – Wiley, their name is. They do a bit of showing and are walking off with quite a lot of prizes apparently, although they have a fairly new kennel. What do you say to running over there next Saturday with the children and letting Dick choose his puppy himself?'

'I'd love it, and I know the children would,' Sherry cried enthusiastically.

'That's sporting of you,' Richard said thoughtfully. 'Dogs do make a bit of mess in the house and – well, I thought maybe you wouldn't take to the idea.'

He was too loyal to mention that his wife, June, had disliked animals indoors and it had been her wish that old Bramble, his faithful friend and companion for fourteen years, should be put to sleep. Buried in his heart was a grudge against June which he had never openly admitted to himself for forcing him to part with Bramble. He had done so for her sake, but he had never forgiven her for asking him.

He turned his thoughts back to the girl beside him and as nearly always when he looked at her, the tautness of his muscles relaxed and he felt at peace. He wondered idly if she was aware how much it suited her to have that flush of excitement staining her cheeks and that bright sparkle in her eyes. But Sherry was as ignorant of the fact as she was of his thoughts, which would have surprised her a great deal indeed.

CHAPTER 3

Dick and Anne were walking ahead of the 'grown-ups' and chatting happily as they chased the puppy they had brought home yesterday. Today, Dick's birthday, Susan and Gerald had arrived early and with Richard and the children accompanying them, they had all set out for a walk before lunch.

It was a February day, but the sun shone warmly and it seemed to Sherry as if spring were really only just around the next corner. The earth smelt damp and leafy and the chestnut trees were glistening with sticky buds. She felt exhilarated and happy, and glad that Susan and Gerald were getting along so well with Dick and his father.

The two men were walking a little behind Susan and herself, talking 'business'. It was an ideal opportunity for her to chat to Susan whom she had not seen for over a month.

'How are things going – between you and Gerald?' she asked her friend. 'I dreamt of wedding bells the other night!'

The two girls laughed and Susan replied:

'That is supposed to mean the opposite of a wedding – a divorce, I imagine. But, in fact, you're right. Gerald and I are going to be married in March. We would have waited until June but someone told us we'd get a reduction of our income tax if we made the grade before the end of the financial year, so we're being very practical, as needs must, and having an Easter wedding. You'll come, of course, Sherry dear? I'd like you for Matron of Honour. And I'd just love to have Dick and Anne as bridesmaid and page. Do you think your nice Mr Hayden would agree? We'll invite him, too, of course!'

'I'm sure he wouldn't mind,' Sherry said. 'He's always most considerate and I have complete charge of Dick. He never interferes or says I must or must not do this or that.'

Susan looked at her friend with a question in her eyes, but Sherry turned to watch the two children. Susan wondered if it was a deliberate wish to avoid her look, which was meant to express her curiosity about the future. It was obvious to anyone that sooner or later Richard Hayden was going to ask Sherry to marry him. At any rate it was obvious to Susan, although Gerald, when she had whispered the idea to him, had told her she was jumping to conclusions. Perhaps it was a woman's intuition, Susan told herself, giggling a little at her thoughts, but one only had to put two and two together. Richard Hayden was clearly a perfectly contented man. There had been no sign of the grief-stricken, haggard widower Sherry had written to her about soon after her arrival. Then there was the way in which he watched Sherry all the time. Maybe he didn't know he was looking at her and Sherry certainly seemed unaware of it, but he did, all the same! As for Sherry – she was a changed person. She glowed! And if ever a woman was in her right *métier*, Sherry was in hers. It would be ridiculous if these two didn't marry – why, everything pointed to it. They would make an ideal couple – Richard just that much older than Sherry, each married before and needing the other now as much as they needed a mother and father for each of their children. Clearly, Richard Hayden liked young Anne and Sherry liked Dick. How long would it be before wedding bells were heard down here?

'Mummy, why is Honey called "Honey"?' Anne was asking her mother. 'Dickie doesn't know, even though he's seven.'

'Because she's the colour of honey – all golden and sweet!' Sherry answered and Anne raced forward on fat little legs to pass this information on to Dick. Within a minute, both of the children had fallen back and were asking:

'Then why'm I called "Dick" and Anne "Anne"?'

'Oh, the questions!' Sherry laughed. 'You know, Susan, Dick wanted me to tell them yesterday why you couldn't ring up heaven on the telephone when his daddy said you could ring up anywhere at all if you could afford it.'

'Rather a pathetic question,' Susan replied. 'I suppose he wanted to speak to his mummy.'

'Yes, but only to ask her where she'd put his fairy-cycle basket. Apparently, it hasn't been seen since she died and he's afraid she might have taken it with her!'

'Then he doesn't grieve for her?'

'Children get over these things very quickly,' Sherry replied. 'It shakes me a little to realize that Anne would, no doubt, just as quickly get over my death, if not sooner!'

'Only if she had someone like you to take the place of her mother,' was Susan's sensible rely. 'I'm sure you're responsible for Dick being such a normal, happy little boy.'

'That's what his father says,' Sherry agreed. 'But then you can't help loving him, can you? He's such a mischievous, charming, funny little boy.'

'But not so charming as his father,' Susan said, probing for Sherry's answer. But her friend did not blush or avoid the subject. She said quite simply:

'He *is* a nice person. I've been terribly lucky, Susan. I'm more than happy here and Richard Hayden has been very kind to me.'

'Then you've quite made up your mind to stay?'

‘For as long as I’m wanted,’ Sherry replied simply. ‘There’s only been one snag, which will make you laugh, Susan. It appears the village is gossiping.’

‘Gossiping? About you and Mr Hayden?’

Sherry nodded.

‘It’s absurd, of course, but I suppose they have to *make* scandal if they can’t find it.’

‘Well, not so absurd really. After all, you’re both very attractive and eligible people, living alone and unchaperoned.’

Sherry looked at her friend in amazement.

‘You don’t seriously think they have any reason to–’

‘Oh, of course not, silly, but that’s because I know you so well. If I didn’t know you, I might *wonder*–’

‘Well, you’d be wondering for nothing!’ Sherry broke in. ‘I think it’s too silly – just because I’m not middle-aged and plump and grey-haired, and Richard isn’t a doddering old man.’

‘For what other reason, then, than that you’re both young, and obviously ideally suited?’

Sherry laughed naturally and spontaneously.

‘You really are impossible, Susan! You’ve hardly known Richard five minutes and you say we are ideally suited – quite apart from the obvious fact that he’s still in love with his wife – or the memory of her – and I’m only his housekeeper.'

'For one thing, Sherry,' Susan warmed up to the subject, 'I may only have met Richard Hayden today, but you forget all the letters you have written to me, full to the brim with him. For another, he isn't showing any of the symptoms of a broken heart. If it *was* broken, then I'll personally guarantee that it's now mended. My dear, *he* may not know it, either, but he's obviously very attracted to you.'

The suggestion was so unexpected, and so ridiculous, that Sherry just laughed.

'That is what is known as wishful thinking!' she teased Susan. 'You've always wanted me to marry again, and this is the first chance you have of romanticizing.'

'But it isn't ridiculous, Sherry. You're not too blind to see, are you? He studies your face as if it were the chart of a treasure island! When you laugh, he's happy. When you look worried, he's worried. I bet if we turned round now, we'd find him looking at you.'

'Oh, how can you be so silly, Sue!' Sherry replied but not quite so forcefully as before.

'Will you take a bet on it?'

'This really is absurd!' Sherry answered, but not wishing Susan to think she was afraid to lose such a bet, however silly it might be, she added: 'If you really want to see how nonsensical this is, I'll look around.'

Susan's eyes sparkled mischievously.

'When I say "go", then – one, two, three – go–'

The two girls turned their heads together and coincidence or not, Richard Hayden was looking straight at them.

Susan, watching her friend's face, saw the colour come into it.

'It might just as well have been *you* he was looking at,' Sherry said defensively. She felt annoyed and a little angered at Susan's childishness. It was all very well to joke about these things, but it could be very embarrassing. Besides, she wasn't sure now that Susan *had* been joking.

'Blast you, Susan!' she said aloud, and with uncustomary violence. 'What do you want to go and mess things up for? We've been very good friends until now, and your silly suggestions will upset everything. Every time the man looks at me in a normal way to speak or pass me the bread and butter, I shall be remembering what you said and feeling a complete idiot.'

'I wouldn't feel an idiot because an attractive man like Richard Hayden was staring at me,' Susan said undaunted. 'You ought to be flattered. Most girls would be.'

'Well, I'm not!' Sherry answered tartly. 'I'm happy here, Sue, and I don't want anything to spoil my life. It would be the last straw if – if what you're thinking did come about. I'd have to go and I'd never find anywhere else so congenial.'

'Why would you have to go? Why couldn't marry him?' Susan asked boldly.

'Why? Because I don't love him and because – look, Susan, I'm not going on with this conversation. Here we are discussing what I would do if my employer asked me to marry him when I know for a fact that no idea is further from his mind. You've got an imagination like a – like – like an ox. It runs away with you and you almost had me running away too. Now, let's talk about something else.'

Susan was quite happy to let the matter drop. She had at least made Sherry *aware* of Richard Hayden as a man, and nothing happened during the day to make her change her mind. On the contrary, she felt her suspicions to be confirmed more than once. Richard Hayden had joined them for nursery tea, having tactfully left them alone while the children were having their afternoon rests. When he came into the cheerful, firelit room, his face seemed to brighten and he came towards them eagerly, his eyes on Sherry's laughing face. Dick and Anne were playing with Dick's new train set and he joined them for a while, and then stretched out on the curly black nursery rug at Sherry's feet, saying naturally and easily:

'It's been a grand birthday party. I'm

awfully glad your friends have come, Sherry.'

It was the first time he had called her by her Christian name but he was unaware of it, Susan could see. She knew it was the first time because of the sudden start Sherry gave and the colour that came into her cheeks.

The whole room seemed to become charged with a subdued excitement and electricity. Perhaps because of the children, who were almost too excited. Once, Anne and Dick came near to quarrelling and Anne turned to Sherry saying:

'It's my turn, Mummy, isn't it?'

And Dick shouted:

'No, mine. It's my birthday, so I'm first – aren't I, Mummy?'

A natural enough occurrence in the heat of the moment, but Sherry noticed it and, above all, Richard Hayden noticed it. His eyes went from his son's scarlet little face to the girl his son had called 'Mummy', and met Sherry's gaze. For one long second, they stared at one another and the moment was broken by the children's voices. Richard Hayden looked away and said gruffly:

'We'll toss for it. Heads or tails?'

Soon after this incident, it was time for Susan and Gerald to catch their train back to London. Richard Hayden said he would take them by car to the station as it would be cold waiting for the village bus, and suggested that next time they come for the whole week-end.

'The house has about three spare rooms,' he said, 'and it's been such fun having you.'

'We'd love to come,' Susan and Gerald said warmly.

'Perhaps Dick could go to the station with you, as a last treat?' Sherry suggested. 'I'll pop Anne into bed.'

'Why can't I go? Let me go, too. I want to go, too!' Anne cried, not far from tears.

It was Dick who answered her.'

'You're only little,' he said. 'You can go when *you're* seven. But I tell you what – we'll leave Honey behind and she can watch you have your bath.'

Mollified, Anne allowed herself to be led away and the rest of the party went out to the station. On the way back, Richard and his son were alone in the car, and Dick chattered happily to his father about his presents and his plans for next day. But Richard wasn't listening. His mind was on the strange, rather terrifying moment of awakening that had come to him only a few hours ago. Dick had called Sherry 'Mummy', and it was as if those words had been a revelation to him. *He knew then that he wanted Sheridan Adams to become his wife.*

No other fact but this was clear to him yet. His mind teemed with questions. How could he be so sure about a vital question of this nature when he had only known Sherry a month – when they were not even on terms of using one another's Christian names? How could he, Richard Hayden, who had believed himself doomed to a future of loneliness and regrets when his adored, pampered wife had died, be considering replacing her so soon and so contentedly? And what, above everything else, would Sheridan Adams think if he were to tell her what was in his mind?

He recalled only too clearly her conversation the other night. Then she had told him that marriage was a thing of the past as far as she was concerned. That she could never fall in love again. Prophetically, perhaps, he had assured her that she would, that it would be depriving some man of too much to continue her spinsterhood for ever. At that moment, he had never consciously imagined himself to be 'the man', but could his sub-conscious mind have prompted his words?

Richard Hayden felt exhilarated and, at the same time, almost stunned by his feelings. He was quiet and controlled by nature, but now his thoughts seemed quite uncontrolled.

How would he feel if Sherry refused to become his wife? Could he ever dare ask her? The answer to the last question was already known to him. In his present state of mind, he would dare anything! Had he any right to ask her to marry him? What had to offer her besides his name and security? Could he offer her love and devotion such as must be her due? All women wanted to be loved and yet he could not be sure that Sherry came under the heading of 'all women'. She had been bitterly hurt by her last experience and had turned her back on that side of life. Besides, was he offering her love? His feelings for her, now that he considered them for the first time, were not those of the young Richard Hayden who had begged and pleaded with the tantalizing glamorous June to make up her mind and set him free of suspense. He had adored her, watched over her, slaved for her and run to her bidding. It had not occurred to him before that he had been her slave. These were not the feelings he had for Sherry. How could a man be sure of his emotions when they were so different from his only previous experience of love? The only thing he could be certain of was that he *wanted to marry her.* He knew it would be right – the two of them together – right that she should take the place of Dick's mother to his small son – right that she should always be here, to welcome him home, to be his companion and to share his life. Was this another kind of love? An older, more settled and sensible kind?

'Daddy, you nearly went into the hedge!'

Dick's voice brought him back with a jolt and he realized that he had been driving completely automatically. He pulled himself together and slowed the car down, to his son's disappointment.

'The slower we go the later you'll be in bed, old chap,' his father comforted him and, while he smiled at Dick's satisfaction, he could not prevent himself thinking: 'And therefore longer before I shall be alone with Sherry.'

Yet when at last they *were* alone together, Richard Hayden found himself strangely tongue-tied. It seemed as if Sherry were more remote than she had ever been before. He was ignorant of the fact that she was, for the first time since she had arrived here, acutely uncomfortable in his presence. Susan's remarks, her suggestions and her all-too-obvious hopes that Richard Hayden was attracted to her, had made her conscious for the first time that he was a man – a youngish, attractive and eligible man. Someone she might have fallen in love with if she had not ever loved Bob and renounced that all too bitter-sweet emotion for ever.

It was unfair of Susan to upset the easy relationship that had existed between her and her employer. Just because they were both widowed and had small children and –

oh, how silly it was to worry what Susan or anyone else thought! How silly to make such a song and dance in her mind about the embarrassing moment when Dick had called her 'Mummy' and she had looked up to find Richard's blue eyes fastened on her.

Now, sitting alone with him over coffee, she, too, felt herself to be tongue-tied and she could not bring herself to look at him. She could not help wondering if he noticed any difference in her. He, too, remained silent and it was not the silence of companionship such as they had often experienced in past weeks.

'I – I liked your friends,' Richard broke the silence, in an effort to gain her attention. 'I do hope they will come again soon.'

'They liked you, too,' Sherry said. 'It was very kind of you to let me have them here – and to be such a good host, too. There was no need – that is to say, there aren't many employers who would give their housekeeper's friends a whisky before lunch, then sit at the same table with them, and–' she broke off, confused and all too well aware that her words sounded *gauche* and her tone effusive, almost defiant.

'I don't quite understand,' Richard said, quietly. 'Would you have preferred it if I had left you alone with them?'

A quick flush spread over Sherry's otherwise pale face.

'Oh, please forgive me. I didn't mean to sound as I did. I really *am* grateful to you. It's been a lovely day – I'm just tired, I think.'

'Do you – really think of me as an employer?' Richard asked, after a moment's silence. 'I had hoped that our relationship was a friendly one. At any rate, that is how I have thought of it. I never think of you as my housekeeper.'

'That's only because I'm not like your preconceived idea of a housekeeper!' Sherry said, with a faint smile.

'No, it isn't that. You see, I've been thinking about you quite a bit and – and about the past – and the future...' he hesitated, watching Sherry's face for some lead as to her thoughts, but her hands were busy with something she was knitting for little Anne and her eyes were lowered to her work. 'And about your position here. You were not very concerned about the gossips, but I think you should have been, for your sake – and for Anne's. What of *her* future, Sherry?'

The quick colour rushed to her face at the sound of her Christian name, which came so easily and naturally to his lips. Could she as easily call him Richard? Would he notice if she did? Where was this one-sided conversation leading them? She was afraid, and yet powerless to break or to stop Richard

Hayden from speaking. She knew she must hear what it was he was trying to tell her.

But as she waited for him to continue, no words came from him, and she felt compelled to look up and meet his gaze. It was a kindly, sympathetic, half-apologetic look, and so puzzled, that Sherry felt suddenly sorry for him. Whatever he had to say, it was proving difficult to get out.

'Is it something to do with my staying on here?' she asked, trying to help him, and forgetting herself in her desire to do so. 'You've perhaps reconsidered the position? After all, there is your reputation and Dick's to consider.'

'What I am trying to say affects all of us – all four of us,' Richard heard himself saying with sudden conviction. 'I know this may sound quite crazy to you, that you may want to slap my face or leave tomorrow, but I must say it. I'm not usually as impulsive person, but I just can't keep this bottled up inside me. Sherry – I'm trying to ask you to marry me.'

Again that bright colour rushed to Sherry's face, and receded leaving her deathly white. She had never really, for one instant, believed Richard Hayden was *in love* with her, attracted to her, perhaps, as Susan had suggested; but that he should want to marry her – it was too fantastic.

'I can see the idea hadn't exactly occurred

to *you*,' Richard said, with a whimsical smile. 'But I'd be so happy if you could think about it now. To be truthful, it only struck me this afternoon – when my son called you "Mummy". I think he would like to have you as his mother – and I should very much like to be "Daddy" to young Anne. I can't offer you a great deal – but I could give your daughter a name – and a ready-made father and brother – a home – and a future. I could give *you* security and a very real devotion. I know you don't want love – and I quite understand your feelings.'

'It's all so sudden – so utterly unexpected,' Sherry murmured confused, and not a little upset. After all, what could she say? She didn't love Richard Hayden, although she had already grown fond of him, and she had a great respect for him. But *marriage*...

'I wanted to explain that when I asked you to be my wife, I meant in one way only – that is to say, I imagined that we would continue to live much as we are doing – separate rooms and– Oh, why is it always so difficult to talk of these things. What I'm trying to say is that I wouldn't ask you to sleep with me, my dear. I know you wouldn't want that part of married life. It's just the legal side of it, and for the children.'

'Marriage in name only?' the words were whispered, but he heard them and nodded his head.

'If that would be acceptable to you.'

Was this what she wanted? Did she want to be married at all? Was this fair to the man who might be her husband? He was giving her everything – a home, a name, a future, security; above all, a name for her child. What could she give him in return? Would it work out? Surely, in time, he would want more from her than that? He was human and no doubt had a man's passions and desires. Why should he wish to tie himself down for life?

'I can't quite understand why you should want this at all,' she said. 'You are offering me everything, and yet expecting nothing in return.'

Richard Hayden smiled at her, and in that moment she came nearer than she had thought it possible to loving again.

'My dear, you underrate yourself. Simply to know that I had such a charming person waiting for me when I came home – to have your companionship – to know that my home was always comfortable and contented because you ran it, to know that Dick was lacking nothing of a mother's care and love. You do love my son, don't you?'

'Yes, yes, I love Dick.'

'Then you will consider it? Believe me, it would make me the happiest man alive if you said "yes". And I would never let you regret it.'

For a long moment, Sherry sat in silence, trying to marshal her thoughts. It was at first consideration so utterly impossible, and yet, why shouldn't it work out? In fact, her position would be very little different from what it was now. Richard was asking her merely to change the name of housekeeper to that of wife. She would relinquish her own sitting-room and share his – which she was doing now, in any case. She would act as hostess to his friends, as he had today acted host to hers. She would become Dick's stepmother as he would become Anne's stepfather. She had everything to gain – nothing except her freedom to lose – and what did that matter? She knew she would never fall in love, had known for years that she was not the type of nature that would love twice. She could grow fond of Richard, and he of her and they could be good friends. Wasn't this enough for a successful marriage? It wasn't even as if he loved her. He, too, had renounced love when his wife died. Why shouldn't they pick up the bits of their broken lives and mend them together?

'I don't know – I don't know what to say!' Sherry whispered at last.

'Then at least you aren't turning me down flat!' Richard said, grinning in relief. 'There's no need to hurry over your decision. You see, I'm fairly confident that the more you think about it, the more sensible the idea will seem. Only one thing could make it unreasonable, and that would be if – if you loved someone else.'

'Never, never, never!' Sherry cried, violently.

Richard Hayden did not pursue the subject, but changed the conversation, saying: 'Then please give me a chance to prove that my idea will work. We won't discuss it again, unless you choose to do so, and when you've reached a decision, please tell me. This hasn't exactly been a romantic proposal, has it?'

Sherry smiled for the first time.

'Perhaps that is why I haven't said "no" – even if I can't say "yes". I think if you had gone on both knees and begged me in Hollywood film fashion to be yours, I should have packed and left tomorrow!'

Richard smiled, but his voice was serious when he said:

'You're very frightened of love, aren't you, Sherry? I think you must have been very, very unhappy and the bitterness remains deep in your heart.'

'Nothing remains!' Sherry said quickly, too quickly. 'My heart is empty. There's no room for love.'

'Then I must take good care not to fall in love with you myself, or I should soon have my heart broken!'

Sherry reached out a hand impulsively, and laid it over his. 'No woman would enjoy breaking your heart, Richard. You are far too nice a person. I wonder if I can ever show you how much I appreciate all that you are – and all you've done for me?'

Richard covered her hand with his own, and held it lightly there for a moment as he said, with his slow smile:

'That's easily done, my dear. You have only to do me the honour of accepting my unromantic proposal.'

'I'd like to – I hope I can say "yes"!' Sherry said obtusely. 'Just give me a little time to get used to the idea.'

'Then let's start getting used to it right away,' Richard said. 'Let's discuss which prep. school we'll send young Dick to and what we'll do about Anne when she's grown up and breaking hearts!'

'That's jumping a few years!' Sherry said laughing. But she was thinking quite seriously, 'Richard is right. Those are the things which make married life – real married life – not the dancing and parties and holidays abroad, the flowers and rings and having a good time. It's quiet discussions in the evening – just two people, talking about their children's future, perhaps arguing sometimes, but always there to back the other up. It could be nice – so nice – and with Richard, it could be fun, too. He has a great sense of humour and he's kind – above all, he's kind. He'd take care of me and of Anne.'

She had never quite realized until then just how much she wanted someone to take care of her – to take some of the responsibility of parenthood off her shoulders – to have someone to turn to.

'I need him,' she thought, 'and he needs me. And the children needs us both.'

In that moment, she decided her answer, but it was a week before she finally told him that she would be greatly honoured to become his wife.

CHAPTER 4

'She's not your mummy – she's my mummy, so there!'

'No, she isn't – she's mine, too, now. She's just as much my mummy as my daddy's yours.'

'He isn't, he's mine!'

'Anne! Stop that shouting and be quiet at once. Both of you. I will not have this quarrelling!'

Sherry looked from one to the other in distress. It was barely two weeks since she and Richard had been married and here were the children, of all people, arguing over the consequences! Then her face softened and she knelt down on the floor with an arm around each of them. It must be a little confusing for them, after all, poor little scraps.

'Once and for all, you two, I want you to understand that Daddy is Anne's daddy, too – ever since the day we went to London and were married. And I'm Dick's mummy now. Both of us belong to both of you.'

Dick looked mollified, but still a little puzzled.

'Mary said you were only my step-mother.

What is a step-mother?'

Sherry took a deep breath. Without going into the question of births, deaths and marriages, how was she going to explain?

'Well, you real mummy and daddy are the very first ones you ever have – the ones Father God sends you to when you are born. If one or other of those mothers or fathers die, then sometimes you have another one. The second one is always a step – one step further on. Do you see?'

'One step further on where?' Dick asked.

Fortunately, Sherry was able to distract his thoughts when Anne said with typical childish sequence of ideas:

'Let's *play* grandmother's steps. Mummy can be grandmother and Dick and I will try to touch you!'

They played for half an hour and then grew tired of the game and settled down to Ludo, a favourite pastime, but one Anne was never good at. She was always too kind-hearted to 'block' Dick who invariably won. But it kept them quiet and gave Sherry time to get on with her sewing or mending. She had decided to send Anne to the local nursery school in the summer term and she had started to make her some suitable dresses.

The children's voices making a pleasant background to her thoughts, Sherry reviewed the past two weeks of her life. So much had happened of such importance, and yet here she sat as if it were the day she had arrived!

They had had a quiet registry office wedding because neither had wished for any 'publicity' and neither had a great number of friends they wished to have present. Susan and Gerald had been there, of course, and one of Richard's friends from his office. The children had been left behind with Mary because they had decided the less upheaval that attended their wedding the better for the children's point of view. They were too young to understand its implications and would have been tired out and over-excited with the trip to town.

'We shall have to have a honeymoon when they've both gone to boarding school!' Richard had joked afterwards. But Sherry knew that the real reason they had decided to go straight home was because a honeymoon would have been ridiculous under the circumstances. They were for young people desperately and passionately in love, who could not bear to be parted from one another and wanted to enjoy their love alone. What could she and Richard have done with themselves all day – during the evenings? How could any honeymoon couple book in at a hotel and ask for two rooms?

It had its humorous side, Sherry thought,

and was glad that Richard had passed the question off so lightly. He had, however, insisted that, at the first opportunity, they arrange for Mary to come in and spend the night with the children, so that they could go to town for an evening to dine and dance – to celebrate.

'I have no evening dress,' Sherry had said, but Richard had told her she had the next few weeks to go and buy one or have one made, and her wished her to make use of the bank account he had opened for her to buy anything else she wanted.

Her first inclination had been to refuse, but she remembered in time that as Richard's wife it was his prerogative to make her as many gifts as he chose and his method of doing so had been so tactfully and thoughtfully arranged that she would not belittle the gesture by refusing it. It gave her a feeling of independence to know that she still had a little of her own money saved which she could draw on if she wished, and meanwhile, there were many things she *did* need for herself that she had had to do without.

Richard had spoken of her entertaining occasionally for him, and she could hardly present herself as his wife in the clothes she had had and all but worn out these past two years!

Since their wedding, Richard had stopped

giving her her weekly salary without discussing the subject, beyond telling her that he was having a regular allowance put to her account for her use and that if it was inadequate, she was to let him know. She was also to tell him what sum of money she needed for household expenses and for the children, which he would give her monthly and in advance.

He had, in fact, been over-generous, and she realized for the first time, when she had a brief interview with her new bank manager, that her husband was a moderately wealthy man. His generosity had not been confined to her bank account. His wedding gift to her had been a pigskin jewel-case containing a very beautiful diamond pendant with drop ear-rings to match, a tiny gold fob watch with a diamond and ruby ring.

'They belonged to my god-mother,' he said. 'She died last year, a very wealthy woman, and left me these which she wished me to sell if I wanted to. I thought they were too beautiful to part with, so I put them in the bank and forgot about them. They are very old, you know, and quite unique.'

They were very, very beautiful and Sherry treasured them as greatly as she treasured the fact that he should have so honoured her by wishing her to have them. She could not forget that they were still practically strangers – and yet when she was with him, it was hard to believe that they had not been married for years. Richard was in every way the perfect husband, without ever once touching her physically. He had only kissed her once – immediately after the wedding ceremony when it was obviously expected of the groom that he should kiss his bride.

When it came for 'good nights' he always held her hand for a moment or two in his and asked: 'Happy?' It had become a ritual before she went away from him to her own room.

Was she happy? Yes, yes, yes! Sherry thought. No one could be kinder or more considerate than Richard. He was the perfect husband. Once or twice he had brought home flowers, and he never failed to show his appreciation if she had done anything for him – or to notice if she had hung new curtains, planned a specially nice meal. She could not remember being so *contented* in her life before – except during the few weeks after Anne was born. There had been then the same rather dreamy placidity and sense of well being.

And what of Richard? she asked herself. Was he as satisfied with his part of the bargain? She thought that he was, for he was nearly always smiling these days, and the drawn, unhappy look had gone completely from his face. He looked about ten years younger than when she had first met him. If only she could rid herself of the fear that this was a very one-sided bargain between them. It seemed to her as if all the benefits were hers. And Richard was a very human person. Surely he felt as other men felt and longed sometimes for a more tangible and physical proof of her affection for him?

The thought nagged at the back of her mind and she wondered, not unnaturally, about her own reactions to this peculiar marriage. Richard was an attractive man and it was a very long while since any man had kissed her – made love to her. She would not have objected if Richard kissed her good night! Perhaps he was waiting for her to make the first move? In fact, thought Sherry with a rueful smile at herself, it is possible she might have kissed him before now if she hadn't been afraid that Richard would read another meaning into her action. She could show her affection for him – but she couldn't love him and, without love, she couldn't be a real wife to him.

Richard, however, was not waiting for Sherry to make the first move. He had known long ago, from the evening he had asked her to marry him, that he was desperately and violently attracted to her. He had curbed his emotions, knowing that Sherry was quite unresponsive. But, with an unusual understanding, he had felt a new intimacy in their relationship. Her smile had seemed warmer and she had made no move to withdraw her hand from his. He began to hope that this was the beginning – the first sign that she was growing to love him as he knew with all his heart he loved her.

He would have been too loyal to admit that he had realized at last that his marriage to his first wife had been in many ways a farce. It had not been a 'sharing' in any way. He had adored June, but she had taken every advantage of his adoration and used him to obtain her own way in everything. He knew, without consciously admitting it, that she had been wilful and selfish, and that while he loved her – for her charm and beauty and for the times when she was sweet and yielding, there was no true union between them, no companionship or even friendship, no respect. The depth of his feeling for Sherry, growing every day, surprised and stirred him. He was a little frightened by it too. Suppose Sherry should never grow to care for him. It began to mean more than anything in the world to him that she should love him – that their marriage could be made complete.

But he was willing to wait. He knew better than to try to force love where it did not exist. He was old enough and wise enough to use patience and tolerance, and in his heart he *knew* that Sherry belonged to him

– must belong to him – not only in name, but in heart and mind.

His hopes bounded skywards the evening they were finally able to arrange their 'celebration'. They had been married nearly a month when at last Sherry told him that she had arranged for Mary to come in for the night and they could go to London any evening he chose.

'In fact, there's no need for you to come home, if we make it a week-day,' she had said. 'I'll catch the six-thirty after the children are in bed and meet you up there. The only snag is finding somewhere to change as I can't very well travel in evening dress.'

In the end, he had caught his usual train home and then driven her back to town by car. This was to be a very special evening, and he wanted everything to run on smooth wheels. He was glad that he had remembered flowers when Sherry came downstairs in her new evening frock. It was the latest shade of coronation red, bare across one creamy white shoulder, fitting her long, slender figure tightly to the hips and then flaring to her ankles. Spanish style. She wore the diamond pendant and ear-rings and looked as *soignée* as might have done a mannequin from one of the leading fashion houses.

He realized then that he had only seen her

in jumpers and skirts – except on their wedding day when she had worn a simple, tailored coat and skirt. He realized, too, how very beautiful she was and how proud he would be to be able to introduce her to any of his friends as his wife.

Sherry, too, felt the excitement of this party night mounting in her. The simple, but expensive, dress made her feel self-confident and radiant. She *knew* she would be one of the best-dressed women wherever Richard should have planned to take her, and that not many other women would have such unusual and valuable jewellery. She was proud, too, of Richard. She had never seen him in a dinner-jacket, and he looked distinguished and very handsome as he came forward to give her the spray of camelias he had chosen.

'Don't wear them if they will spoil the effect,' he said. 'It doesn't look to a mere male as if you need any more adornment, my dear.'

He drove well and Sherry enjoyed the trip into London. Sensibly, Richard parked the car in an all-night garage, and took a taxi to the Caprice where he had booked a table.

It was a long time since either of them had wined, dined or danced in a fashionable restaurant. Sherry had almost forgotten such a life ever existed, far less that she had once done this kind of thing regularly. And

Richard danced beautifully, unlike Bob who had been apt to jive or play the fool. It seemed part of the magic of the evening that she could remember dancing with Bob without a qualm.

At midnight, Richard asked her if she wanted to go home or should they go down to one of the Soho restaurants for a late supper. Sherry, a little tired, but unwilling to relinquish the evening too soon, chose to have supper.

It was past one o'clock when they were finally on the road out of town. Sherry felt sleepy and very happy and, quite naturally, she leant her head against Richard's shoulder. Once they had left the traffic of London streets behind them, Richard felt for her hand and she drew closer against him. He knew then that he could kiss her if he wished to and knew too, that he had never wanted anything else so much in his life as that kiss.

He stopped the car on the hills overlooking their home. Quite simply and naturally, Sherry turned to him as he put his arms round her and lifted her face to his.

But Richard had under-estimated his passion for this girl who had become his wife. He had thought he could kiss her lightly, gently and without betraying himself, but the sweetness of her lips against his, the softness of her slim young body in his arms, proved too much for him. The gentle kiss became a deep, hard pressure of his mouth against hers.

But the intoxicating moment when he felt her response was so brief-lived that, afterwards, he wondered if he had imagined it. He knew only too well that he had not imagined her two small hands pushing against him, her voice low and husky, saying:

'No, Richard, no, no. Please, please, let me go!'

With a little groan, he released her – thrust her away from him almost roughly as he fought to still the racing of his blood. With hands that trembled, he found his cigarette case and lit a cigarette. Her voice, barely audible, forced him to forget for a moment the battle that was raging within him.

'Please, may I have one?'

With a murmured apology, he lit a cigarette for her and for a moment they smoked nervously, heavily, in silence.

'I've frightened her, repulsed her – will she ever forgive me?' the man thought desperately. 'How can she know how desperately I want her? That it is because I love her that I need *her* love, physical and spiritual?'

But, whereas she was frightened, Sherry had not been repulsed. She was only human and Richard was far from unattractive to her. The intimacy of their evening together, dancing with their bodies moving rhythmically against one another, had made her want Richard's kisses as much as he wanted to give them. She had been a married woman, known what it meant to have physical needs and the thrill and perfection of a close and intimate union. She had been starved of all that her ardent feminine nature demanded for over four years. But it wasn't until tonight that she had realized how great was her need for love. She had believed herself beyond all that – believed that when her love for Bob died, her heart and body were dead for always. And she was frightened to find herself so poignantly and tensely alive in all her senses. She was frightened of her physical self – and deeply frightened because she was experienced enough to have guessed, when Richard started to kiss her, *that he was in love with her.*

'What can I do?' she thought, as she smoked furiously in an effort to steady her nerves. 'I'm Richard's wife and although we both agreed that our marriage was to be nothing more than a "friendly" one, how could either of us have imagined for one moment that we could go on like that? We are only human – both of us. Richard is a man and I am a woman, and we are alone – unhampered by any kind of restrictions. We are legally entitled to do as we wish and yet what we both wanted in that moment wouldn't have been right. It would have been morally wrong.'

Wrong, Sherry told herself bitterly, because she did not love her husband. Wrong, because while she was deeply fond of Richard – and found him attractive – she knew that she could only enjoy physical intimacy with a man she loved. But she could not expect him to have these sentiments and even if he did, they were not relevant since she was now practically convinced that he loved her. It was an appalling muddle!

Impulsively, she turned to Richard and said:

'Please forgive me, Richard! You must hate me at this moment!'

Her words were so unexpected, that they took him off guard, His voice was low and almost angry as he said:

'Hate you? I love you, Sherry.'

The words lay between them, each knowing that they had to be spoken and yet wishing they had never been said. The silence became unbearable and with an effort Richard spoke again, his voice more normal and with a lightness he was far from feeling:

'Now it is time for you to forgive me, Sherry. I've broken our bargain, haven't I. When we agreed to – to marry, we never imagined this, did we? I'm afraid I've behaved rather badly.'

Sherry's eyes filled with sudden and unexpected tears.

'Oh, no, no, you mustn't say that – ever. It isn't true. You've been wonderfully good to me. It isn't your fault that you – that this has happened. I think I knew, anyway. And tonight – well, it was just as much my fault. I *wanted* you to kiss me.'

He gave her a quick, searching look and then turned away from her, his eyes bitter even while they were understanding.

'I understand, my dear. After all, we are both still young, aren't we? And there are biological explanations that make our behaviour perfectly normal.'

Something of his unhappiness and frustration touched her with such pain that the tears, held in check until now, flowed suddenly and silently down her cheeks.

'Why do I have to hurt him?' she thought. 'Why shouldn't I pretend? There's no point both of us being miserable! I could belong to him if I loved him. Why not forget about love and make the best of a life without it?'

Turning to her, Richard saw her tears and cursed himself for an idiot. He had ruined their evening – maybe ruined everything for them. Angrily, he threw his cigarette away and put his arms around her with tenderness.

'Don't cry, Sherry, please. You make me

feel such an awful swine. I've made you unhappy, and that was the last thing in the world I wanted to do.'

She stayed in his arms, comforted by his tenderness and knowing that, for the moment, passion was dead between them. If only this could go on for always – this calm, uncomplicated relationship. Resting in his arms, she could feel safe and unworried and content. Her feeling for him was more than friendship – it was a very real affection.

'Oh, Richard, you're much too kind to me. I *am* fond of you – deeply fond. Do you – do you think – it might work? I mean, I'm willing to try – if you are.'

He understood what she was offering and the effort it cost her to tell him she was willing to be a real wife to him – for his sake. Even while temptation rose swiftly to accept her offer, he knew that it wasn't after all what he wanted. Sherry was unlike many other women. He judged correctly that she was at heart completely innocent and moral. She could not entertain the idea of an affair for the physical satisfaction she would get out of it. For her it would be all – or nothing; and for it to be all, she must love with her heart as well as her body.

Recognizing this in her, the man respected her and knew then that she deserved his love as no other woman could ever do. And he would not belittle it by taking what she was offering. Now, more than ever, he wanted her love. And he felt convinced that this would be no way to win it. She might end up by hating him for violating her ideals. If he could only be a little patient, she might yet grow to love him. She was afraid of love still – because of that young rotter of a 'husband' of hers. But in time he could show her that she need not be afraid – that he would never let her faith in *him* be misplaced. And when she trusted him, and herself, she might love him. Such a goal was so well worth waiting for.

'You – haven't – answered me,' Sherry's voice, infinitely young and touching in its uncertainty, broke in on his thoughts.

'I was thinking, my darling child,' he told her with a wry smile. 'And maybe it will be best for us both if I tell you what is in my mind. There must always be truth and honesty and complete understanding between us. If we can manage that, then we shall always be fond of each other. Shall I tell you now what my answer is?'

Sherry nodded her head and listened while he spoke of all that was in his heart. When he had finished, she was crying again – not because she was unhappy, but because she was bitter with this queer life that brought the right things at the wrong moment. She had loved and trusted and respected Bob who was unworthy of any part of all she gave him. If it had only been Richard she had known *first,* Richard who was fine and good and so very much to be respected. She might have loved him then – if there had been no Bob to deaden her heart for always. Now Richard had come into her life – and it was too late.

'I wish I could say – say that I loved you. Or that I knew I would do one day,' she whispered. 'But I don't know. I don't know! And it would be such a waste of *your* life if–'

Richard put his hand gently against her lips.

'There is to be no "if," he said firmly. 'I refuse to allow you to destroy all hope. And my life will not be wasted, Sherry, if in any way at all I can make you happy.'

'If I ever love anyone, it will be you!' Sherry cried with all her heart. But they were both to remember those words in so short a while ahead, when an ironical fate decided to prolong their unhappiness and complicate their lives still more.

CHAPTER 5

Dick saw him first. It was a lovely, fresh sunny April afternoon and Sherry was out playing in the garden with the two children and Honey when Dick shouted:

'There's someone coming up the drive. I think it's Daddy!'

They all turned towards the man who was walking towards them, and for a moment Sherry thought Dick was right and that it *was* Richard. But, apart from the fact that Richard would be in town working, and that he would have driven the car back from the station if he'd taken the afternoon off, there was something else that made her certain it was not he. This man had a quick, springy pace. Richard's walk was slow and steady, his long legs taking large, even strides.

'I don't think it is Daddy,' she said. 'I wonder–'

'But he looks like Daddy,' Dick said with a small boy's persistence. 'I'm going to see.'

Before Sherry could stop him, he had raced off to meet the visitor; Anne, with a 'Me, too,' chasing after him.

From a distance, Sherry stood perfectly still watching the children and the man merge into a group. She could hear Dick shouting, but couldn't make out what he said. Then Anne was lifted on to the man's shoulders and they came towards her.

Remembering this moment, Sherry wondered if one always had a presentiment – a queer extra knowledge forewarning important events in one's life. Yet vitally important things *did* happen without one having this queer emotion she was experiencing just now as the three figures, one tall and the children short and squat, came towards her. Her feet had taken an involuntary step backwards and she knew a desire to turn and go into the safety of the house.

'Why did I think of safety?' she asked herself, and then they were within speaking distance, and Dick was calling to her.

'It's Uncle Tony, Mummy. All the way from Africa. Isn't it inciting?'

Sherry tried frantically to recall 'Uncle Tony' but could remember no one among the few relatives Richard still had living. Then she looked up and her heart jolted as she found herself gazing into a face so like Richard's and yet so different that it was more than disturbing. The eyes were the same identical blue and yet they were bright, gay sparkling eyes, with an amused provocative expression that brought a sudden shyness to her. The face was the same shape as Richard's but the nose neither so long nor straight. This man looked as if he was a rugger player or a boxer and had had his nose broken a few times.

'Well, who's going to do the introductions?' he was asking, his face broken up in a wide grin now, and as unlike Richard's as it had once seemed identical.

'I will, I will,' Dick shouted. 'This is Uncle Tony, Mummy, and this is Mummy.'

He held out a hand and Sherry took it, but did not leave it long in his grasp. He put Anne down and drew out a packet of Camel cigarettes, offering her one.

'Only got these American ones,' he said.

Sherry shook her head in refusal.

'Dick's introductions seem a little inadequate,' he went on, laughter at the back of his voice. 'I'm Richard's first cousin. I gather he hasn't mentioned me – at any rate, by name. I've just come back from Africa on six months leave. Thought I'd look old Richard up before I go and beat up good old London. He's about the only relative I've got left. Now do please answer me the intriguing question of who *you* are?'

'She's Mummy – my new mummy,' Dick broke in.

'She's not new!' Anne said indignantly.

Sherry told them to run off and play by themselves for a few minutes which they did when they saw the firm expression on her lips. When Mummy had *that* look, she meant what she said.

'I'm Richard's second wife!' she told the young man. 'I suppose you heard that – that June died?'

'As a matter of fact, I didn't know. Neither Richard nor I have ever kept up a correspondence. As a matter of fact, our relationship is a pretty queer one, I suppose. I come back to this country once in about four years and we usually see a lot of each other. Then I go off again and we don't exchange another word for another four years. So I'm very out of touch with current events. Please tell me more, my new cousin-in-law.'

'There isn't very much to tell,' Sherry said. 'June died of pneumonia a little over a year ago. Richard and I were married three months back.'

'Three months – is that all? Then whose child is–'

'Anne's my little girl,' Sherry broke in. 'I was a widow.'

Cousin Tony blew a cloud of smoke into the air and gave a quick, almost sarcastic, laugh.

'How romantic! Widow meets widower and two broken hearts are mended, and a family made!'

Sherry found herself resenting his words

and knew a sudden antipathy towards this man. But it was gone almost immediately when he said:

'Well, I hope I haven't barged in at the wrong time. I should have announced myself, but the fact of the matter is I only arrived by air this morning and I thought I'd give the old boy a surprise. If it's a nuisance, I can always push off again.'

'Goodness, no! Richard will be delighted to see you, I'm sure,' Sherry said quickly. 'Come indoors and let me get you something. Lunch should be ready soon, but I expect you'd like a drink first.'

Again that quick laugh and he touched her briefly on the shoulder – an unconscious gesture, but Sherry felt as if his hands burned through her light wool frock and into her flesh.

'Just the job! You know, it really is rather odd coming back like this and finding everything so changed. Last time I was here, Dick was only an infant in long clothes or what have you. What *do* babies wear these days?'

Sherry laughed for the first time as she matched her step to his.

'Just clothes – but not long ones. They're old fashioned.'

'Then you see how out of date I am! You know, I'm not sorry to find *you* here. Fact is, I didn't much care for the pretty June.

Selfish little bitch!'

His words stunned her and shocked her at the same time. What a way to talk of the woman she had imagined to be so sweet and feminine and lovable.

'Led Richard a hell of a dance,' Cousin Tony went on. 'Not my type at all. But she got away with it with him. He doted on her, poor chap.'

He looked down at Sherry's wide gaze and gave an apologetic laugh.

'Sorry! That was hardly tactful, was it? I'm too unused to civilized ways. You'll have to forgive me. But obviously he's got over all that. Dare say he got wise to her. The take-everything-and-give-nothing sort, she was. Still, she did give him Dick, who seems a nice enough kid.'

Sherry was glad to be on home ground.

'Oh, he's a wonderful child,' she said. 'I'm very nearly as fond of him as I am of Anne – in fact, every bit as fond, only it doesn't seem right not to love your own child just a bit more, does it? Of course, Dick *is* my child now.'

'You're a funny kid!' her companion said unexpectedly. 'Serious! June was frivolous. Oh, Lord, there I go making comparisons again. Perhaps you'll pardon them on the strength of the fact that the comparisons are all in your favour?'

Not knowing how to reply, Sherry

remained silent and wished that Richard would come home and take the strain of conversation with this disturbing relative of his. There was a strong family resemblance between them and yet they were totally unalike. Richard was quiet, thoughtful, more often than not serious and the opposite of impulsive. Apparently, Cousin Tony was without any kind of self-consciousness and said whatever came into his head.

'We were having nursery lunch, but I'll tell Mary to lay ours in the dining-room,' she said, hoping he would refuse. But he nodded his head.

'I remember Mary. Braw young country lass! So she's the same, if everything else in unfamiliar.'

'You won't find the house changed at all,' Sherry said quickly.

'June did have good taste. That was one of her few qualities,' Richard's cousin remarked. 'Now do please tell me more about yourself. What do you do while the man of the house earns the daily bread? Other than minding the kids and cutting flowers and sorting laundry?'

'That is about the extent of my activities!' Sherry said smiling. 'Does it sound very dull to you? It isn't to me. I'm very domesticated.'

'The perfect wife.'

Sherry's face coloured at his words, and

she was annoyed to find his eyes on her – to know that he had noticed her rising colour.

'Nobody is ever perfect!' she countered.

'I refuse to have my illusions shattered. I am convinced that you *are* the perfect wife.'

He was teasing her and yet she could not joke about it. She was glad that they had reached the house and she could busy herself getting him a drink.

'You'll have one, too?' he asked her as she took the tray into the sitting-room. It was unusual for Sherry to drink anything before evening, but for once she felt in need of it. She let him pour her a glass of sherry and asked him to tell her about Africa so that she could adjust herself to his presence.

'I've grown unused to meeting people and being sociable,' she told herself, conscious of her nervousness and trying to find its cause. 'It's ages since I spoke to any man except Richard. How odd, when my life used to be so full of people. Bob was always bringing friends home and it never worried me. Now Cousin Tony – what am I to call him – I can't go on with Cousin Tony – it sounds mid-Victorian – he'll think I'm gauche and silly. Heaven knows what I look like. I can't even remember if I've made up my face since I got up this morning.'

'You haven't heard a word I've been saying, and I would be mortified if I weren't so interested in knowing *what* you were thinking about so seriously. Your face is most revealing, you know. You looked in a state of complete agony!'

'Oh, really!' Sherry protested, but she had to laugh – he was so near the truth.

'Let me guess! You were wondering if three pork chops would go round four people.'

She laughed outright this time.

'It's shepherd's pie – which will certainly do four people!' she told him. 'I hope you don't mind it? If I'd known you were coming–'

'You'd have baked a cake! We even heard that tune in darkest Africa!'

They laughed together and Sherry knew suddenly that she *did* like Cousin Tony after all – and that it would be fun to have him staying here for a while. Ever since the night they had been dancing, her relationship with Richard had been strained. It seemed almost as if they could no longer be natural with one another, and that they had been best able to be themselves when she was in tears and Richard's arms were around her. Since then, they had both been acting a part – each trying to make the other think that night had never happened – each making a conscious effort to resume the old companionship but finding only constraint between them. Perhaps they could be more natural with a third person with them.

'If only I could be a real wife to Richard,' Sherry thought for the hundredth time. 'If only I could love him.' But love did not come at one's bidding and the more one thought about the very word, the more ambiguous and evasive it became. What *did* it mean – to love? She had loved Bob in a wild carefree ecstatic way when life had been one long laugh; a gay, irresponsible almost childlike feeling, when one was happy simply because one felt happy! They had lived from day to day, without cares, without thought for the past or the future. And where had that got her? Discovery of Bob's duplicity had put a speedy end to her love for him and she could not help but wonder, when she read the classics and famous tragedies, how it was that her love had died when things went wrong where other women's endured, in spite of betrayal. Was what she had felt for Bob not love at all? Was this fondness for Richard, this wishing to make him happy, a different form of love? Yet she could not feel involved herself. However much she could admire Richard, respect him and – yes, even be attracted by him, they did not make a whole. Her feelings for him came singly and not in an irresistible urge.

'We shall have to be natural now,' she thought grimly. Otherwise this cousin of Richard's was going to think it very odd.

After all, she and Richard were only a few months married – newly-weds. They could not behave as if the other had scarlet fever!

Richard was forgotten by both of them during the rest of the day. Tony Hayden was an amusing, vivacious and humorous companion, and it was impossible not to be silly and young and gay with him. The children thought him wonderful and went into shrieks of laughter. Sherry knew it meant they were both a little over-excited and would be difficult when bedtime came.

Tony was helping her bath Anne, with Dick as a noisy onlooker, when they heard Richard's voice calling:

'Is there nobody at home?'

Sherry realized then, in a sudden moment of shame, that this was the first evening there had been no one to welcome Richard as he came through the door (Dick usually waited for the sound of the car) and the first time she herself had forgotten to see that his drink was waiting for him and the fire lit. In fact, she had forgotten it was time for him to come home.

'Run and tell Daddy I'm putting Anne to bed and take Uncle Tony with you,' she told Dick quickly, almost guiltily. Tony gave her a quick look, but she was too upset to notice it. Then he turned and went downstairs with the boy.

It was Richard who came up with Dick a

half-hour later.

'Time this young scamp was in bed,' he said, smiling at Sherry. 'Tony and I can't get a word in edgeways.'

'I'm afraid he's rather over-excited,' Sherry said apologetically.

'Well, we don't have odd uncles from Africa turning up every day,' Richard remarked. 'Sure it's okay with you for Tony to stay, Sherry? I mean food – and that sort of thing?'

'Of course – as long as he likes,' Sherry said, not meeting Richard's eyes.

'Better not tell him that, or he'll be here his whole leave,' was Richard's reply. 'Still, it's nice to see him. I don't think I ever mentioned him, did I?'

'No! It seemed odd – a first cousin, but Tony explained you were both bad letter-writers.'

If he noticed the easy she said 'Tony', he did not remark on it.

'Well, come down as soon as you can,' he said. 'And you behave yourself, young man. Don't play up and keep Mummy from joining us.'

'I think it's a swizz!' Dick said. 'Grown-ups have all the fun. When'll I be old enough to have dinner and stay up late?'

Sherry coped with his questions for the next half-hour and then hurried along to her room to change. She was halfway into one of her new spring frocks before she realized that she did not often change at night although she usually 'tidied up' before she went down to dinner. She slipped her arms through the sleeves and sat down at her dressing-table, staring at the flushed face of her reflection. Her hands went to her cheeks and she thought with surprise. 'I'm over-excited, too. What *is* the matter with me?'

Of course, she told herself, it was nothing to do with the young man downstairs – at least, only indirectly. Richard would want her to look her best – to make a good impression and she had looked so untidy and dishevelled all day romping round with the children. Tony would think his cousin had married a country bumpkin.

Reassured, she made up her face carefully and brushed her hair until it shone. Then hurried downstairs.

Both men stood up as she came into the room. Richard came towards her with a glass of sherry in his hand and his eyes were showing his appreciation – for she looked very lovely, with her heightened colour and the new dress bringing out the half-tones of her grey-green eyes.

But it was not Richard's admiration Sherry noticed. It was Tony's. He leant against the mantelpiece, a pipe in one hand, glass in the other, and where Richard was silent, he said easily:

'How charming you look, Cousin Sherry. Richard, I really must come out of the backwoods and congratulate you. Your wife is not only charming but very pretty.'

'I'm very lucky!' Richard said, turning away from Sherry to pour himself another whisky. 'How about you, Tony? No wedding bells?'

Tony laughed.

'You know me, old boy – the confirmed bachelor. Still, if your wife were not your wife, I might have been persuaded to renounce my freedom!'

It was a compliment that was said jokingly and yet it left a strange silence in the room. Sherry to her horror, knew that she was blushing. Richard had not smiled and the smile that had been on Tony's face faded out and he looked embarrassed. Then Mary opened the door and told them dinner was ready, and the moment was broken. They went into the dining-room talking naturally.

But Richard was far from feeling natural. He was for the first time in his life consumed with the fires of jealousy. Oh, not because there was any reason for it, but because he was afraid one day there might be reason. Suppose Sherry *did* fall in love with a chap like Tony? He had imagined himself waiting through the years for her to love him, never thinking that she might love someone else. It was a sobering thought.

Now that it had entered his mind, he knew he would be jealous of any personable young man whom Sherry might find attractive, amusing. Not that she would ever be unfaithful to him – if one can be unfaithful to a husband who isn't a husband. But it was the state of her heart that concerned him. She could not help falling in love with some fellow any more than she could help not loving him.

He checked his trend of thought sharply. Sherry had not after all fallen in love with anybody! And she was his wife. Besides, she was not the type to give her heart lightly or easily. He would have plenty of warning. Time enough then to be jealous!

Nevertheless, he could not help but notice that Sherry was unusually gay tonight. She had not laughed so wholly or so often since he had known her. Of course, Tony was an amusing fellow; had lots of amusing anecdotes and plenty of personal experiences of life in Africa that he could relate in an entertaining way. He always had been a stimulating kind of chap, a good conversationalist, and he wasn't in the least shy with women. Tony had been a bit of a lad, Richard knew. He fell in love just about as often as he fell out of love, and women adored him. Surprising how many names cropped up in the short months of Tony's leaves. Beside Tony, one could not help feeling a bit of a bore, dull, pompous. It was the life he led, no doubt – the lives they both led that made them so opposite.

He turned to say something to Sherry but she was listening to some story Tony was telling her. Richard knew then that he was sorry he had asked Tony to stay 'for as long as he wanted'. In the past he had always been so pleased to see him – even in the days when June was alive. Now he knew that he resented the third person; he wanted Sherry to himself!

'What are your plans for this leave, Tony?' he said after a lull in the conversation.

'Nothing much, old boy. I shall have to go up to town for a few days, of course. Get some clothes. And I've got to visit a sister of one of our chaps out there. Promised I would. Thought I'd pop up next week-end if that's okay with you?'

Richard tried not to show his relief. At least he would have Sherry to himself again at the week-end. And if Tony had a 'date' she would be certain to take his mind as well as his attention from Sherry.

'How ridiculous I'm being,' he pulled himself up sharply. 'I'm behaving as if I suspected an affair between these two and nothing is more improbable. Trouble with me is that I'm getting far too introspective – brooding too much. No wonder if Sherry finds me dull company these days. If only I hadn't been a darned fool as to give myself away that night. Things were perfectly all right until she knew I was in love with her. since then, we've both been behaving like a couple of cats on hot bricks. I must try and be more normal – put her at ease with me again.'

But it was Tony and not Richard who was putting Sherry at ease this evening. His conversation, amusing and light-hearted, lifted her out of herself and her laughter came so easily and spontaneously that Richard marvelled at the change in her – marvelled and feared. He had never known Sherry so happy, nor so pretty or vivacious. It was like discovering a new person and another side to her, which he found as attractive and surprising as the woman he already knew; the sweet, thoughtful and serious Sherry, who had been his close companion and the perfect mother to his son and to her own little girl. How wonderful life could be if one were free to love and if one were loved by this woman! How greatly he *did* love her and what torture it was to have to hide his emotions. He wanted so desperately to shower her with gifts and attentions, and to be able to hold her in his arms and know that only he could give her true happiness and perfection from life.

It was with renewed feelings of remorse that Sherry turned to Richard, realizing that he had dropped out of the conversation some little time ago.

'Don't you agree, Richard?' she asked him, referring to the discussion she and Tony had been having.

'I'm afraid I wasn't paying much attention,' he said awkwardly. 'A bit tired – a heavy day at the office–'

'You look a big fagged out,' Tony said considerately. 'As a matter of fact, it's past ten and I've had a long day, too. Shall we turn in?'

Richard rose to his feet, grateful for the excuse to end this evening – even though it meant parting company with Sherry for the night. Somehow he did feel tired – too tired to stand any more thinking and worrying and trying to appear as if nothing were on his mind.

'I'm afraid I've clean forgotten to show you your room,' Sherry said to Tony. 'Your luggage arrived by taxi this afternoon and I had Mary make up the bed in the Tudor room. Is that all right?'

'There's no need to give me all that space,' Tony said laughing. 'June always used to dump me upstairs next to the nursery. I'm not used to the sprung beds and down pillows of your best spare room.'

There was a moment's embarrassed silence which Tony thought was due to his perhaps unfortunate reference to Richard's first wife. In fact, it was nothing of the sort. Both Richard and Sherry were wondering how they were going to explain that she was using the room next to the nursery, on the floor above her husband's room. It had been agreed between them that she would keep the bedroom she had had when she was the housekeeper, as she had grown used to it and there seemed no point in moving. Richard had had one of the divan beds from the Tudor room moved upstairs and the large double spare room next to Richard's had remained empty.

'Tony is bound to notice since he's staying here,' Richard thought. He said almost aggressively:

'Sherry has the room you usually have, Tony. So you'll have to have the best spare room for a change.'

'Oh, good show!' Tony remarked lightly, but they could see the surprise in his face.

'Oh, damn, damn, damn,' Sherry thought with unexpected viciousness 'Why did this have to happen to spoil the evening? It's been such fun – now Richard will be upset.'

'I wanted to be near the children,' she said. 'Anne sometimes has nightmares.'

It was a reasonable excuse but it sounded unnatural to all of them; to Richard and herself because they knew it was untrue; to Tony because he was unusually perceptive, and he saw their discomfort and guessed they hadn't wanted it known they weren't sharing a bedroom or even adjoining rooms. After all, they were newly-weds – practically a honeymoon couple. What, he wondered, was going on?

'Why should I care what he thinks!' Sherry asked herself. But she did care. Somehow she wanted to prove to Tony that she was Richard's wife – whatever he might be thinking. She turned and slipped a hand through Richard's arm – something she had never done before – and said:

'You're not too tired to come up and have a last cigarette, darling?'

Richard, too surprised to think of a reply, merely nodded his head.

'Then I'll go up,' Sherry continued. 'Perhaps you'll see Tony has everything he wants?'

In her own room, she sat on her bed and wondered if she were stark staring crazy. What would happen now? Would Richard come? Would he realize she was just putting up a show for Tony's benefit? Should she go to bed or stay up in case he did come? What a fool she had been to place them both in such an awkward situation!

'Oh, well!' she told herself with a rueful smile. 'It's done now, and it's up to Richard. Poor dear! I wonder what he's thinking.'

In fact, Richard was thinking exactly as she was. He had quite understood when she had first mentioned Anne's non-existent nightmares that she had been talking for Tony's benefit – a rather touching way of protecting him, Richard. She had no doubt guessed, with her perceptive mind, that he had wanted to keep the peculiarity of their relationship from his cousin's knowledge. But what should he do now? Did she mean him to go to her room? He'd look a big enough fool if he turned up and she had not expected him. On the other hand, she really might want a word alone with him and be surprised if he didn't go.

In the end, he decided to knock on her door first and wait. It was almost a surprise to him when he heard her voice telling him to come in.

CHAPTER 6

Sherry was sitting by the electric fire in one of the two large armchairs when she heard his knock and told him to come in. She was fully dressed and stood up quickly as the door opened.

'Oh, Richard, I wasn't sure if you would come,' she said almost laughing now that the tension was eased. 'Now you *are* here, come and sit down and have that cigarette.'

His face relaxed as he, too, smiled. He went over and sat down on the edge of the bed, handing her a cigarette and lighting one for himself.

'You must think me absolutely mad,' Sherry said apologetically.

'On the contrary, Sherry. I was very touched by your efforts to make things appear as normal as possible in front of one of my relatives. Still, I admit you had me puzzled for a moment or two. I didn't know if you meant me to come up here or not!'

'I wasn't sure either!' Sherry answered, and they both laughed.

For a moment they smoked in silence and then Richard said:

'Do you like Tony? He's an amusing fellow!'

'Yes – I think I do like him. He's so full of life and fun. You and I take things rather too seriously, don't we?'

The coupling of their names pleased him but worried him, too.

'Perhaps I'm a bad influence on you, Sherry. On the whole, I am rather a serious person – always have been. I couldn't help wondering if you weren't more yourself tonight – your real self, I mean – gay and light-hearted.'

'Oh, I don't think so. I don't really know,' Sherry said nervously. 'I used to be like that, I think – when I was married to Bob. But I changed. People do change, don't they?'

Richard smoked a moment in silence, then said thoughtfully:

'I'm not sure that they do, Sherry. Fundamentally, I mean. Circumstances might change them for a little while, but underneath I don't think the basic character is altered. I mean, if you've got a sense of humour, then sooner or later it's going to appear; or a bad temper – or any other trait.'

'Yes, but sudden shock, for instance, very often seems to change people for good,' Sherry lost herself in the argument. 'Or great unhappiness – that kind of thing. You hear of people who never got over something. I think if any experience is big enough, it changes people a little bit.'

'Yet people can undergo the experiences

of child-birth and not change at all,' Richard returned, thinking how little having Dick had changed June.

Another short silence fell between them, but it was a silence without strain, and Sherry said suddenly:

'We've not had a conversation like this for ages, have we?'

'No! I'm glad we're back to our old footing. If Tony is to be thanked for it, then I thank him heartily.'

The mention of Tony's name brought a tiny frown to Sherry's forehead. Somehow the very thought of Richard's cousin was disturbing. He seemed to be having too much influence over their lives right at the moment, making her behave so oddly and bringing about this visit of Richard to her bedroom and the return of their old, easy friendly discussions on life in general.

'Do you think he'll stay long?' she asked Richard suddenly.

'You never know with Tony. He comes and goes; he's a restless kind of chap; rather like his father – my father's brother. Uncle Giles was always chucking up his job and trying something new. I think he was nearly seventy when he emigrated to South Africa and started in business there, the same business Tony now runs. Tony and I were at school together and I think those school years were about the only settled period of

Tony's life. Of course, he was younger than I so we weren't together much, but he spent some of his holidays with me and we got along well together as kids. Tony would dare anything. I think he's still like that – restless and reckless.'

'Do you think he'll ever settle down?' Sherry heard herself asking, the question almost forced from her against her will. There was so much she wanted to know about this perturbing young man.

'Who can say? I doubt it – unless he really falls in love. He thinks he's been in love a dozen times at least – but I don't think any woman has really captured my elusive cousin. When that happens, if it happens, then I think he might settle. But she'd have to be an exceptional woman.'

'Why exceptional?'

'Oh, because he's known too many of them, I suppose. He's spoilt! I think on the whole most women would bore him. He likes variety. But you simply cannot lay down rules for people like Tony. He's so utterly unpredictable.'

'Yes, that's the right word,' Sherry thought. One was never sure what he would say or do next and it was fascinating – exciting – to wait and find out. She had learnt this much for herself in a single day. Only a day, and yet it seemed a hundred years ago since she had seen him coming up the drive and thought he was Richard– Richard! Why was it she was always forgetting his presence tonight?

'You said you were tired, Richard,' she reminded him. 'Don't let me keep you up if you want to get to bed.'

'Tired!' Richard thought. 'I've never been more awake. And even if I were on my last legs, I wouldn't be too tired to stay here with her.'

But he stood up, not wishing to outstay his welcome. He went across to her and gently took her hands in his.

'Happy?' he asked.

It was the ritual of their earlier days together which had been dropped since the night of the dance. Both knew that this was Richard's way of saying: 'Let's get back to that old footing, Sherry.' More than willingly, she smiled and nodded her head.

But after Richard was gone, she knew that she was not happy, even while she could be glad that they were 'friends' again. There was too much to worry her. Richard was not happy, either. *He* had not joined in the laughter and idle chatter this evening. His face had been sad and thoughtful, and she was afraid that it was her fault.

'I ought not to have married him,' she told herself. 'I had no right to do so. If I had only suspected that he might fall in love with me! But I thought he felt as I did – that love was finished and done with for ever.'

Now their bargain was entirely one-sided. It was not really her fault and yet she could not but feel guilty, guilty because the man she was married to was unhappy, on her account.

'Why can't I love him – why can't I?' she asked herself. 'He's wonderful to me, and he matters so much to me. I can't bear it when I see him miserable and yet I'm the one person who *could* put it right, and yet can't. Will my heart ever come to life again? I used to think it was broken by Bob's duplicity; but hearts don't break. They die. Or else they sleep. Won't anything wake my heart to Richard's love?'

Wearily, she undressed and went along the corridor to run her bath. The house was strangely silent, and it seemed as if both the men on the floor below were already asleep. How lonely it was! And how wide-awake she was! Perhaps a hot, steamy bath would make her sleep or less restless.

But for once the hot water only served to freshen her. She climbed into bed, even more wide awake than before. She put out her hand for her library book and knew that it wasn't there. She had left it in the sitting-room.

For a few minutes, she tried to compose herself for sleep, but she knew she wouldn't sleep yet. She must fetch her book since reading always tired her eyes and, however exciting the story, acted as a soporific.

She pulled on her dressing-gown and slipped down the two flights of stairs. In the hall she paused, seeing the sitting-room light was still on, throwing a golden glimmer through the half-open door.

'Someone forgot to turn it out when they came up,' she thought, and pushed the door open.

A man was standing with his back towards her, his hands spread out to the fire. She might have imagined it was Richard had it not been for the dressing-gown he had put on in place of his jacket. He turned round as he heard her little gasp of surprise.

'Oh, hullo! Funny you should appear. I was thinking about you.'

'Tony! I came down for my library book. It's by the window, I think.'

How appallingly fast her heart was beating. Why should she feel like this – guiltily, startled, nervous, shy – all at the one time.

She moved towards the window-seat, but Tony was there before her, and their hands touched across the leather back of the book. Instantly, they both let go and the book slipped to the floor. They stood in silence, looking at one another. Sherry's face was chalk-white.

How long the moment lasted while they looked into each other's eyes, neither of them knew. Then Tony took a step towards her and his arms were around her, and his lips against hers.

For one wild, heady moment, Sherry felt her body responding to that kiss, felt her knees tremble and her heart somersault; then her mind regained control of her emotions. She pulled away from him and he released his hold of her immediately.

Sherry stood perfectly still, staring at Tony. She wondered how he could be so perfectly at ease, his hands now in his dressing-gown pockets, a faint enigmatic smile on his face.

'I suppose I ought to apologize,' he said, after a moment. 'But I can't be sorry over what *had* to happen.'

'I don't understand,' she whispered.

Tony gave a quick, half-nervous laugh.

'Don't you? I think you do. I think we did the impossible, and fell in love at first sight.'

His words were lightly spoken, but she couldn't believe he would joke about such a subject.

'It isn't true!' she said swiftly. 'You shouldn't–'

'Be honest,' he broke in before she could continue. 'Surely that is what we should be, Sherry; honest with each other. Maybe I'm being presumptious about your feelings for me. But I do know I'm in love with *you* and it's a devilish awkward position to find myself in.'

It isn't true! Sherry reiterated in her mind. He can't fall in love with me. I can't possibly be in love with him. It doesn't happen all of a sudden, in a day. Yet it *had* happened in exactly that way to her once before – with Bob. She had known immediately, and she knew now. She had fallen in love with Richard's cousin.

'Richard!' the name broke from her lips aloud. Tony heard and took a deep breath.

'Come and sit down for a moment,' he said. 'You look ghastly. Let's talk this over calmly.'

Sherry allowed him to lead her to the fire where she sat down thankfully on the wing chair. Tony seated himself on a stool a little away from her. She watched him as if hoping to gather some of his coolness and detachment, his control. But she could only see the way his hair curled a little over his forehead, like Dick's; the way his eyelashes, absurdly long for a man, curled down over those brilliant blue eyes. Her heart turned over suddenly and began to race once more. It was true – terribly true. She did love him. She wanted to be near him, with him always. She wanted him to kiss her; to hold her; to make love to her. She wanted...

'Of course, you're not in love with Richard.'

His words cut across her mind and she gave an involuntary shudder.

'I – I'm terribly fond of him. I – I'm his wife, Tony. I've got to remember that. We must both remember that.'

'That's the part I don't understand,' Tony said, looking full into her eyes. 'You've been married only three months but you behave as if you were quite indifferent to each other.'

'You're wrong!' Sherry cried. 'You don't understand. That's just a pose – a sort of cover for our real emotions.'

'And just what are those emotions?' Tony went on calmly. 'I simply can't make you out – either of you. Why did you marry Richard if you didn't love him? Just because he's in love with you?'

Sherry covered her face with her hands and tried to think coherently. She ought not to be discussing her marriage with a stranger; it was disloyal to Richard, quite crazy, and yet because of what was between them, she must tell Tony, make him understand.

When she had finished her story, Tony turned away from her and lit a cigarette. Sherry waited for him to speak.

'You were crazy – both of you!' he said, briefly. 'It wasn't fair of Richard to take advantage of your state of mind. He must have known you'd get over that "deadness" in time. If he'd known anything about women at all, he'd have realized you weren't the type to nurse a broken heart for ever.'

'You mustn't blame him,' Sherry said. 'It was just as much my responsibility. I told him I'd never get over the past. And I could have refused to marry him. But I wanted the things he was offering me – companionship, security, a home, affection, a father for Anne. And if I could swear to him I knew I couldn't love anyone ever again, why shouldn't he believe me?'

'If course he believed you. He wanted to believe you then. But I think he's as crazy as you are, Sherry, arranging a marriage just because it was so convenient.'

'It wasn't only that,' Sherry cried. 'We were both very fond of one another. We've always been good friends, enjoyed each other's company – at least, until – until I discovered that Richard was in love with me. Since then, it hasn't been so simple.'

'Surely you might have guessed he'd fall in love with you. An attractive, beautiful girl like yourself! What are you going to do now, Sherry?'

She looked at him in momentary surprise.

'Do? What can I do? I must try to be a good wife to Richard and repay some of his love and kindness to me. What else is there for me to do?'

'You could get a divorce – marry me!'

His words brought a rush of colour to her cheeks.

'Richard is your cousin – you can't mean

that!' she said quickly.

He stood up and came towards her but she backed away from him, and his hands dropped to his sides.

'You're being old fashioned, my darling, sweet, little innocent. It's absurd to ruin three people's lives when nothing is to be gained from it. In this case, not even Richard is going to be happy. He must know you don't love him. He'll know even more surely once he sees how things are between us.'

'There's nothing between us,' she cried, but denied her statement with her next words. 'He won't know. I shan't let him guess. You must go away, make some excuse–'

'And make everything even more obvious? Look, here Sherry, I'm serious. I've never asked any girl to marry me before – never wanted to get married. But I've known all day that if you were free, I'd marry you tomorrow if you'd have me. You've felt it, too, haven't you? Now I find you aren't really Richard's wife at all. You don't belong to him – except in law. Your marriage to him could be annulled. He'd get over it.'

'No, no! Don't talk like that. You don't understand!' Sherry cried. 'Richard doesn't fall in love easily. I think it would break up his life for good. Besides, you've forgotten the children. They are the ones whom this marriage has really made happy. They adore one another, and I love Dick as much as Richard loves Anne. We're a family, Tony, for all I've never shared my husband's bed. If only for their sake, I couldn't leave Richard, even if I wanted to.'

'If reasoning won't, perhaps this will change your mind,' Tony said and, before she could stop him, he had pulled her to her feet and taken her in his arms. She fought wildly to free herself, but only for a moment. Within that brief time, she felt his lips once more on hers, felt her body responding to the fierce demands of his hands as they caressed her body through the soft silk of her dressing-gown. Then she gave way to the blinding sweetness that could no longer be denied and returned his kisses with all the answering fire within her.

It was Tony who found his head first. He broke away from her with a stifled groan.

'I've never made love to another man's wife yet, and Richard is my cousin. But when you're free, Sherry, my dearest, darling heart, you shall belong to me. Then I will show you what love can mean.'

Sherry pressed her trembling hands against her burning cheeks and knew that she was lost – lost completely in this mad infatuation for her husband's cousin. The desires of her body, so long subdued and almost forgotten, had reawakened with appalling intensity. She realized that had Tony not been decent enough to remember Richard, she might have forgotten him – forgotten everything but her need for this man to take her as he wanted to do. She was ashamed and yet so stimulated by her emotion that she could not feel the shame for the glory. Shame would come afterwards, she knew – was already on its way.

'Now tell me you don't love me,' Tony was saying breathlessly. 'Tell me you can forget me easily if I go away tomorrow?'

'Don't! Don't!' Sherry whispered. 'That's cruel, Tony.'

'Then you *do* care. You will ask Richard to release you and then marry me? I'll take you back to Africa with me. You can start a new life and forget these last few months, forget you ever married Richard.'

'No, no, no!' Sherry cried, her heart torn with longing to agree to his demands. 'You mustn't ask me, Tony. You don't understand. It wouldn't be fair to Richard – or to the children. I made a bargain and I must keep my side of it. Richard doesn't ask much of me. What he has asked – that I should look after him and his house and his child – I must go on doing, for as long as he wants me, whatever the cost to myself.'

'Then his happiness means more than yours or mine?'

Sherry's voice was quiet now and she

spoke to Tony rather as she might have spoken to one of the children who was hurt and puzzled.

'Happiness doesn't come into it, Tony. It's a question of conscience. Richard has been wonderfully good to me – kind, generous and self-sacrificing. I've given him little enough in return. It would be beyond me, now that I know he loves me, to go to him an ask him to set me free – to marry you. I couldn't do it.'

'I could!' Tony cried in a hurt, angry voice. 'You were crazy to marry him under such conditions and you're even crazier to continue with it. It isn't yet too late to call it a day. You don't belong to Richard. If you stay with him, you might give way one day and then you will really have been his wife.'

'I shall never do that!' Sherry cried. But there was no conviction in her voice. How could there be when she could not trust her own feelings any longer. She had known a normal healthy desire when Richard had kissed her in the car, known that she was capable of weakening. And now she, who had believed herself to be completely in control of herself, finished with love, immune to sex, had been swept off her feet by Tony's love-making to a pitch where she would have given herself to him, blindly and uncaringly. How could she then be sure that her truant emotions would not betray her again? She didn't love Richard, but Tony had reawakened all that was feminine in her. She had rediscovered her body's needs, and they might not be so easily subdued again.

'What kind of a wife will you be to Richard?' Tony followed up her remark. His voice held a note of bitterness. 'A wife in name only. It's utterly nonsensical, Sherry. You *must* see that.'

'Everything seems nonsensical at the moment,' Sherry whispered. 'That I should feel like this about you – in a day – you, a complete stranger! Perhaps tomorrow I shall wake up and find this is all a dream – a nightmare.'

'That won't happen, Sherry, because when you wake up tomorrow I shall be here. I shan't leave until I have your word that you will ask Richard to set you free. Until then, I shall stay and talk you into reason.'

Sherry looked at him horrified.

'You can't stay now, you mustn't. It isn't fair, Tony. You must go away, give me time to think. No, I don't need time. My mind is made up. You can't change it. You can only make my life with Richard impossible by staying. And he'll be bound to guess, even if you don't tell him.'

'I would tell him this moment, if I thought it would make up your mind for you,' Tony said truthfully. 'But I think I know enough about you, Sherry, to realize that your kind heart would reject me for ever if I were the one to hurt Richard. *I* shan't give myself away. But are you sure you won't?'

'I'm not sure! That's why you must go.' Sherry cried desperately. 'Oh, Tony, if you *do* love me, have pity on me. How can I behave normally when you are around? The children will guess, if Richard doesn't. They are terribly intuitive – like animals.'

Tony did not reply for a moment or two. For all he had spoken with such firm conviction, he was not inwardly so sure of himself. As Richard had known, there had been quite a number of women in his bachelor life, but they had always been unmarried women. He had a certain code of morals which did not allow him to break up another chap's home. He had flirted and fallen in and out of love with a lot of beautiful, amusing and very varied women who were perfectly free to love him or not as they chose.

This was the first time he had come up against his own code of morals. He had not – chiefly because he avoided them – come into close contact with any married women, and those he had known had not attracted him. But it had been only a matter of hours before he realized he was head over heels in love with Sherry, that he wanted her desperately – so much so that, for the first time in his life, he had proposed marriage.

He could not help wondering if it was some sixth sense that had told him of her 'unmarried' state. She had never belonged to Richard physically, and was not in love with him. He knew that for a fact now, but he felt there must have been something in her behaviour that let him know this inwardly from the first moment he set eyes on her. He had never intended to let things come to a head so soon. Nothing could have been further from his mind when he came down to the sitting-room to find his pipe, than a late-night rendezvous with his cousin's wife.

Sherry had been very much on his mind and, because of her, he could not sleep and had decided to have one last smoke. When she, too, came downstairs and they had come face to face so unexpectedly, his guard was down and, acting entirely on impulse, he had kissed her. The very instant he felt her draw away from him, he had let her go, half expecting her to slap his face and tell him she loved her husband and to get out of the house. But only half expecting it, for he had known the instant his lips touched hers that she was responsive to his kiss, that she was attracted to him. It followed on that she was not in love with her husband. Girls like Sherry did not take love lightly. And his suspicions during the evening when he had seen her with her husband, noticed their peculiar way of talking and behaving together, that all was not right between them, were more than confirmed.

Hope had risen in him and the ensuing conversation had been entirely impulsive and without premeditation. It was as if they were both acting parts that had been preconceived for the time, place and setting.

That she was as much attracted to him as he was to her, he was now fairly convinced. Surprise had been succeeded by a desperate hope that he might win her over to his way of thinking. His sudden wish to marry her was incensed by her reluctance to fall into his arms without thought for the consequences. That he was being unfair to Richard, not only his cousin but his host and friend, did not occur to him for he judged other men by his own standards and he, personally, would never wish to hold on to any woman who did not want him. He could not understand Sherry's behaviour. To try and pretend that there was nothing between them, that she could pick up the life of yesterday as if today had never been, seemed ludicrous to him.

To Sherry, who intended to do this, it seemed not so ludicrous as impossible. How could one put the clock back? How could one wipe out twenty-four such hours and resume life as if they had never existed? Perhaps with Tony gone, she could convince herself that this had never happened. But if he stayed, then it was going to be the most terrible task to wipe him off the face of her heart.

'Oh, I don't love him. I can't love him,' she told herself in a desperate desire to undo these last hours. 'He's a stranger to me, someone I don't know and wasn't even sure this morning if I liked. It's just that I find him attractive – nothing more. I must believe that. *He* must believe it.'

'Tony, listen to me,' she said, her voice low and urgent. 'I don't even know if I would marry you were I free to do so. It's madness to go on talking the way we have been doing. We don't know anything about each other. We're probably totally unsuited to one another. And you – well, you've never wanted to get married before, have you? How *can* you be so sure you want to marry me?'

'I don't know,' Tony answered truthfully. 'I'm only certain that if you were free, I'd take you off to Gretna Green tonight. I mean that. I'm not just saying it because you aren't free.'

'But you might be – you can't know how you would feel then,' Sherry argued. 'And nor do I know how I would behave. We are attracted to each other and that's all we can be sure of. Let's leave it at that, Tony. We must leave it at that. You've got to help me, please!'

The man gave a hollow laugh.

'My dear child, how can you ask me to help you when you are fighting for the opposite of what I want. You wish to convince yourself that I'm not in love with you; that you aren't in love with me. I can't help you. You must make up your own mind. I'll try not to influence you, but I won't go away.'

'It'll be different in the morning,' Sherry cried, more to herself than to him. 'When we wake up, everything will seem normal again. I shall wonder how this ever happened.'

Tony stood up as she rose to her feet. He did not try to touch her and perversely, she was disappointed.

'Then, I'll wish you sweet dreams, darling,' he said, and stood back to allow her to walk slowly past him out of the room.

She did not turn her head, but in her heart she saw him standing there and knew that this was not good night but good-bye. In the morning, the girl he thought he loved would be no more to him than Richard's wife. In the morning, the Tony of tonight would be Cousin Tony again – a stranger, someone she had been pleased to see but hoped soon never to see again.

'It's good-bye, my darling,' she whispered, tears of exhaustion and emotion flowing slowly down her cheeks as she climbed the stairs. Then drained of all but despair, she fell wearily into bed, and hid her face in the pillow.

CHAPTER 7

Surprisingly enough, Sherry slept soundly that night, without dreaming. It had been some time after she left Tony that she had at last found release from her thoughts in the deep sleep of exhaustion. But within a few moments of waking, all her worries returned to taunt her. Useless to say 'It couldn't happen' or 'I only imagined it.' Last night she had let Tony kiss her – worse than that, she was in love with him, and nothing would alter it. There remained only the question of how to keep this knowledge from Richard.

The children, calling from their rooms, claimed her attention until breakfast time. But as she took them to the dining-room, her heart started its painful hurried beat, as she realized Tony might already be down.

But Richard was alone in the dining-room and gave her his quick smile as she came in with the children.

'Bit late this morning,' he remarked cheerfully. 'Children been playing up?'

'No, I overslept,' Sherry said.

'I wish I hadn't to go to town today! It's a beautiful morning. We might have gone off somewhere in the car – taken a picnic. It's really warm.'

The idea appealed instantly to the children who clamoured round Richard's chair trying to persuade him not to go to London. It appealed, too, to Sherry. It would help her to get away from this house – from Tony – to be with Richard and the children doing something they all enjoyed, to be happy together.

'Couldn't you *possibly* take a day off?' she asked him.

Her voice was so full of appeal, that Richard gave her a quick, happy look.

'You know there's nothing I'd enjoy more,' he told her. 'Unfortunately, I've fixed a lunch with one of the directors and I daren't put him off at the last moment. But it's nice to know you wanted me so much.'

Sherry gave the children their cereal and slowly buttered a piece of toast for herself. How easy it was to make Richard happy, though he had in fact mistaken her anxiety to be away from Tony for anxiety to be with him.

'Why don't you get Tony to take you?' Richard was saying. 'I'm sure he would love to and I could leave the car at the station for him to pick up later in the morning.'

'Oh, yes, let's go. Do let's go, Mummy!' Dick shouted through a mouthful of cornflakes.

'Please, please!' Anne begged in her turn.

With an effort, Sherry quietened them down, and said:

'If Uncle Tony would like to go, then we will. But I do wish *you* could have taken us, Richard.'

It was true. She wished with all her heart that Tony would never put in an appearance this morning; that Richard would drive her and the children somewhere where she had nothing whatever to remind her of Tony – of last night.

'I'm afraid,' she thought. 'Afraid of myself, and of him.'

'You look a bit pale this morning, Sherry,' Richard said solicitously. 'Feeling all right?'

Sherry felt the colour come into her cheeks.

'I'm just tired,' she lied. 'I didn't sleep too well – I read rather late.'

'So it was you I heard going down to the drawing-room. I guessed it was either you or Tony going for a book. Well, I must be off or I shall miss my train. If Tony won't take you today, we'll all go tomorrow instead. Thank goodness for the week-end. Tony will be going up to London, I suppose, so we'll be on our own again.'

'*If* he goes!' Sherry thought wildly. 'He must go. He's got to understand that I can't go on like this. He must go – *and not come back!*'

The children went to wave good-bye to

Richard and returned with Tony following them. Sherry looked up and met his eyes nervously.

'Better late than never. I overslept!' he said easily. 'Lovely morning. Like summer.'

'We're going for a picnic, you and Anne and me and Mummy,' Dick shouted, dancing round Tony who stood by Sherry's chair, looking down at her.

'For all the whole day!' Anne told him, banging her spoon on the table in her excitement.

'Oh? Jolly good idea. Did you think of it, Sherry?' Tony asked pointedly.

'Oh, no. Daddy suggested it,' Dick answered for her. 'He would have taken us himself, but he has to go and have lunch with some silly old d'rector. So you're to take us instead.'

'Only if you'd like to,' Sherry said, quickly. 'Richard will take us tomorrow if not – when you go to town.'

Tony sat down and helped himself to coffee.

'Oh, yes, London. I'd forgotten. Well, no need to worry about tomorrow today, is there. I'd love to go picnicking with you – nothing I'd like more.'

Sherry knew he was watching her, waiting for her to meet his eyes, but she refused to do so. There would be no more looks or words between them that would betray her heart to him. He must be made to understand that whatever had been alive last night was dead this morning – gone for always. But Tony had no intention of letting things be.

'Did you sleep well?' he questioned her. 'No dreams – or nightmares!'

'Like a log!' Sherry forced the words to come naturally, lightly. 'Now perhaps you'd keep an eye on the children while I go and tell Mary to pack up a picnic lunch.'

'You're to go and get Daddy's car from the station,' Dick told him eagerly. 'I'll come with you, Uncle Tony. We'll go on the bus. We can sit next to the driver. It isn't a double decker like London buses. Do you have buses in Africa?'

Sherry left them with relief and escaped to the kitchen. She had only been up an hour and yet already she felt as tired as she had done the night before. The nervous strain was exhausting. She wondered how she was going to get through today. Obviously, Tony had no intention of taking her at her word. He believed that all was fair in love and war and he was not going to let her go easily. How could she make him see that she meant every word she had said? *She was Richard's wife* – and she owed him far too much to leave him; she loved the children far too much to take her happiness at the expense of theirs. Surely Tony must understand that there was no possible future for their love.

But Tony did not want to understand. He, too, had woken with full memory of all that had been said last night. In the cold light of early morning, he was more certain than ever that he loved Sherry; that he wanted to marry her. He could not believe that she would hold out for very long against the dictates of her heart. For she did love him. He knew the signs too well, had noticed with satisfaction, how she avoided his gaze; refused to recognize the implications behind his words at breakfast; feared his physical presence. Even a fool would know that she was afraid because she did not trust herself.

Well, he had all day to convince her of the seriousness of his intentions – and a glorious day it was going to be! The sun shone warm and brilliantly for so early a spring day and only the faintest of breezes stirred the trees. It was England in April – poets choice of the seasons, and for Tony, used to the hot, humid, extreme temperatures of Africa, it was perfection, the perfect welcome home.

What a home-coming it was turning out to be! How little he had realized when he left Africa only three days ago, that within a few hours of touching down at London Airport, he was to fall in love, not just temporarily, for the convenient length of his leave, but seriously. It was a darned shame that the girl had turned out to be Richard's wife.

As a matter of fact, Tony had imagined that he might have a brief affair with the sister of the chap he worked with, whom he had promised to visit. But that wouldn't come to anything now, however much he liked the look of her from her brother's photographs. He'd have to go and see her, of course, but he'd give her lunch and Jim's news and then get back here as soon as he could. Perhaps a day without him would convince Sherry that she would miss him pretty badly if he left for good.

Following up the kind of fun he intended they should have today, the contrast of tomorrow would be marked, and in his favour.

Tony could not feel any remorse for his cousin. He and Richard had been long-standing friends as well as cousins, but only in a vague and masculine way. Tony liked Richard, respected him, but that simply didn't affect the question of Sherry. Tony knew now that Sherry didn't give a row of pins for her husband – at least, she might be fond of him and feel indebted to him, but she didn't love him. So he, Tony, could not feel that he would be taking anything from Richard that he already had.

It was impossible for Tony to conceive that Richard might prefer even Sherry's friendship to no Sherry at all. He could only judge by his own standards and he knew that in Richard's shoes, he could not be content with anything less than love from *his* wife. How Richard could live side by side with her and yet have no physical contact with her was utterly beyond Tony's comprehension.

But he had no chance to discuss their affair with Sherry until late afternoon. Until then, the children were constantly with them and Sherry seemed bent on ignoring him and giving the two little scamps all her attention. They needed it, of course. As soon as they set off in the car, they were up to mischief. Tony stopped the car in some woods and found a clearing where they spread out macs and rugs to sit on, and had an early meal. As if she were afraid to be alone with him, Tony, Sherry kept the children within ear-shot all the time. She fooled neither herself nor Tony who was pleasantly aware that she was doing her utmost to avoid a tête-à-tête with him. Lunch over, she made the children rest for a while on the rugs, and it was nearly three o'clock before she at last gave way to their repeated requests to be off on their own.

'We want to explore. Why can't we?' Dick kept asking until even Sherry's list of excuses had run dry.

'Well, don't go too far,' she warned them.

'Blow your whistle, Dick, and if you don't hear our voices, you're to come straight back. And look after Anne. You're not to leave her alone for a moment. Do you understand?'

Tony gave her a quizzical look as the children disappeared.

'I really *am* worried about them, Tony,' Sherry said defensively. 'Anne's only a baby and they might get lost.'

'That's nonsense. They won't go far. And the woods aren't thick. We'd find them in a few minutes wherever they got to. Now relax, Sherry, and talk to me for a change. Remember me? Tony? The guy that loves you?'

Sherry bit her lip. She knew she could no longer avoid the issue. She leant back against the picnic basket and lit a cigarette.

'Had you forgotten your promise not to influence me?' she asked him.

Tony smiled down at her.

'Then you admit that I do have some influence over you? Otherwise it wouldn't matter what I said.' His voice became suddenly serious. 'Sherry, *darling,* why go on trying to fight the inevitable? You do love me – I know you do. You wouldn't look so desperately unhappy if you didn't care. You can't honestly mean to send me away.'

'I do mean to, Tony. You should have gone today, and you *must* go tomorrow. If you do care for me at all, *then I beg you to go away and leave me in peace.* Haven't you any sympathy for other people? Don't you consider for a moment how unfair this is to Richard?'

Tony reached for her hand, but she pulled away from him.

'Don't touch me. You've got to play fair, Tony.'

'Fair!' he repeated. 'How can I be fair, Sherry, when the very word means something different to each of us. I don't think it's fair for you to go on living the life you do with Richard. It's unfair to you and unfair to him. Neither of you can be happy.'

'We *were* happy – until you came,' Sherry cried.

'Were you? I doubt if Richard was.'

The thrust went home. No one knew better than Sherry how miserable and unsettled Richard had been of late. No one had thought more about the one-sidedness of their bargain. Richard wanted her, as any man wants the woman he loves, and she could give him nothing, nothing at all. It wasn't fair to him, but how much more unfair it would be if she were to leave him to marry Tony.

Tony noticed the tortured expression on her face and his self-control vanished. With a swift motion, he was by her side and put his arms around her. She struggled against him, but he held her tightly until presently he felt her relaxing against him, and then he kissed her upturned mouth.

'Darling, darling, *darling* Sherry. I love you,' he said huskily.

But she was acquiescent in his arms only for a brief instant. Then, with one last effort, she pushed him away from her and cried brokenly:

'Don't, Tony! Please, please don't make love to me. I won't leave Richard. Do you understand that? I won't leave him. *I can't.* You're only torturing us both by trying to change my mind. Besides, the children might come back and–'

'See us? Perhaps that would make you see sense,' Tony said harshly, hurt by her stubborn denial of him, wanting to hurt her back. 'They'd soon tell Richard and then the fat would be in the fire. I'm sure he wouldn't ask you to stay against your will.'

Understanding his perplexity, Sherry spoke more gently.

'Don't you see it is *because* he wouldn't try to keep me that I can't go. All the time it has been Richard considering me and I have done nothing – nothing in return.'

'And what do you intend to do?' Tony asked scornfully. 'You won't be a real wife to him, Sherry, as long as you deny him your body. Until you give yourself to him he isn't going to have any peace. And until you do, I shan't believe that your marriage will ever come to anything. Nothing else would convince me that you really meant to make a go of it. So, since you assure me it is out of the question, I won't give up hoping you'll come to me – if not now, then sometime soon.'

'Then you are going away?' Sherry asked with a mixture of hope and despair.

Tony turned away from her with a rough gesture of indecision.

'How do you expect me to know what to do? I'm certain of nothing now. You've turned my life upside down. I love you, Sherry. I want to marry you and I truly believe you want to marry me. But how do I know that you won't forget all about me if I go away? You've told me outright that it is what you'll try to do. I don't *want* you to forget me. I shall never forget you.'

'And I wouldn't forget you, ever!' The words came from her in an involuntary cry. 'But that's all we'll ever be to each other, Tony – a memory of what might have been.'

Tony gave a bitter laugh.

'That sounds very romantic and dramatic, but it isn't much to live on, is it? I don't want to make you unhappy, Sherry, but I don't think you'll be happy if I do go. Suppose things come to head with you and Richard and I'm miles away in Africa? No, I've got to stay and fight for you Sherry, since you won't fight for yourself.'

Sherry felt the tears starting to her eyes, but she refused to give way to them. Somehow, she must convince Tony that whatever she might feel for him, she could never marry him, never ask Richard for her freedom. Time had healed the wound in her heart that Bob, her other love, had inflicted. Time might heal this – for both of them.

'Tony, if I were really Richard's wife, you wouldn't have tried to take me away from him, would you?'

'Perhaps not! How can one say what one would do in different circumstances. If you were really Richard's wife as you put it, you would probably be in love with him and I should have known it was hopeless from the start.'

'But don't you see that I *am* Richard's wife? Whether I love him or not – belong to him or not – can't alter the facts. I'm his wife, Tony, by law, and I promised to stick by him. That was only four months ago and I meant it then. I still mean it. He's given me a home and security, and, above all, he's made Anne his own child. I couldn't return that kindness in the way you want me to do. Surely you see that?'

'Duty!' Tony's voice was scathing. 'I could not love thee dear so much, loved I not honour more! Somewhat old fashioned, aren't you?'

'Oh, Tony, don't talk like that. You don't mean it. You're only trying to hurt me because I'm hurting you. It *is* duty, in a way – and honour. We can't go through life taking everything and giving nothing – at least I can't. We met a few months too late, my dearest Tony, and nothing can put that right now.'

'Richard could put it right. He could release you from your obligations!'

'But he loves me, Tony. He told me so. I couldn't hurt him.'

'Yet you can hurt me?'

'Only because my first duty is to him, whatever my heart tells me,' Sherry whispered. 'Can't you understand, Tony?'

But he couldn't or wouldn't understand. For him, it boiled down to a very simple factor – either she intended to become Richard's wife and live a normal married existence with him, or else she left Richard and married him, Tony. He told her so.

'There can't be any half measures,' he said. 'You can't expect me to believe that you're chucking me up for the kind of life you've told me you live with Richard. You can't go on for ever as his "housekeeper" who happens to have acquired some marriage lines. As I see it, it's all a question of this: are you going to be *his* wife or *my* wife?'

'But I am his wife – I am!' Sherry argued, knowing that in a way it wasn't true. She was nothing to either of the two men who loved her, useless to both.

'Well, this discussion isn't getting us anywhere. I suggest we find the kids and go home,' Tony said truculently. 'I shall go to town tomorrow, Sherry, and stay a couple of nights. We can talk this over when I come back. Perhaps by then you'll have had time to think things over a bit and see daylight. You can give me your decision then. And try not to look so unhappy – or I swear I'll forget honour and conscience and everything else and make you forget it, too!'

'Oh, Tony, Tony,' she whispered. 'If only we could. If only we could.'

He took a step towards her but, at that moment, Dick came running through the trees towards them crying:

'Look, Mummy, we found a frog!'

'A 'normous one,' Anne screamed. 'Can we take it home?'

They were far too excited to find anything unusual in the attitude or expression of the grown-ups and both Sherry and Tony had time to get themselves under control. Both were suddenly desperately unhappy and lonely. It was as if the children had come between them, not only physically but mentally.

'If it weren't for them, she might leave Richard,' Tony was thinking. And Sherry thought:

'Even if it weren't for Richard, I couldn't break up their lives. They adore each other, and I love Dick, too. I couldn't leave him any more easily than I could leave my own daughter. My life is here with them, not in some wild remote place in Africa with Tony.'

But with an arm around each of the children as they walked back to the car, it was of Tony that she thought, aware in every nerve of her body of his nearness – and dearness. She had hurt him, but only to avoid hurt to three other people. If only he could understand!

They were silent during the drive home, lost in their own thoughts and glad that the children kept up a steady chatter leaving them free of the necessity to make conversation. The sun had lost its warmth and a greyness had come into the air to remind them that summer was not yet here, after all. It fitted Sherry's mood of despair and tiredness.

She was quite unprepared for the decision that Tony's thoughts had led him to. When he announced that he would push off to town that evening, she gave a little cry of dismay.

'Now? Tonight? But why, Tony? Why not tomorrow morning?'

'How perverse are women!' Tony said lightly. 'A little while ago you were wishing me far away from here. Now you sound as if you don't want me to go.'

'Tony, don't!' Sherry said in an undertone lest the children overheard. *'Of course* you must go. I was just surprised that you should decide so suddenly.'

'Well, there's no point my staying at the moment, is there?' Tony returned, his heart lifting as he saw her unhappiness. 'It will only mean another awkward evening with the three of us trying to cover up our real emotions. I'll be back Monday.'

'But what will Richard think – you going off so suddenly?'

Tony gave a bitter laugh.

'Oh, he's fairly used to my unsettled moods. He won't think anything odd about it. After all, what's to keep me here?'

She knew he was only taunting her, but she could not prevent his words from hurting her. It was true, after all. What was there to keep him? She herself had begged him to go, longed for him to go, and now she could not bear the thought of his absence. Life would be appallingly empty without him.

'I can drive myself in and leave the car at the station for Richard. It works out very well,' Tony said as they drove up to the house. 'I'll just go and pack a few things and then I'll push off. Will you come and say good-bye to me, Sherry?'

Good-bye! Yes, it would be good-bye. This must be the real end to everything between them. She would find some way while he was gone to prove to him that he must not come back, that her decision from which she would never falter was for always.

'I'll get the children their supper and come back,' she told him.

The minutes later, she was locked in Tony's arms in the shadow of the great fir tree that overhung the garage. Her arms were clasped tightly round his neck and her lips were pressed to his, as if she could not bear to let him go. He was both surprised and worried by the desperation of her passionate farewell.

'I'll be back on Monday, my darling,' he whispered against her hair. 'It won't be long.'

'It's for always – always!' Sherry cried, the tears pouring down her cheeks. 'This is good-bye for always, Tony. We shall never be together again – like this.'

'We will,' Tony tried to reassure her. 'I shan't let you go easily, my silly, stupid, darling girl. Now let me kiss you again, to remember you by.'

'He doesn't believe this is the last time!' Sherry thought as she clung to him desperately. 'Oh, Tony! Tony! Why did you come into my life too late?'

She could not bear the torture of this silent farewell to him any longer. He seemed so confident now that it would all come right for them – as confident that she would leave Richard as she was that she could never leave her husband. The knowledge that was hers now would be his later, and the pain that accompanied it. For her mind was made up – before Tony returned, she would have given to Richard everything but the one thing she could not help denying him – her love. And even that, he would not know.

CHAPTER 8

At first it was not so difficult to carry out her plan. Richard came home in one of his most endearing moods. He was gay, attentive, even talkative. It seemed as if he had gained a new hope from the short talk they had had – could it be only twenty-four hours ago? – in her room.

As a matter of fact, this was exactly what had happened. The difficult few weeks after their evening's dancing had become no more than an unpleasant memory. They were back on their old friendly footing and Richard felt that he had gained rather than lost by their event. Certainly, he had drawn hope from the way Sherry had looked so crestfallen that he, Richard, could not join them on the picnic. His heart had jumped at the realization that it was himself and not Tony she desired for company. When he arrived home, she seemed almost eager to be alone with him and, of her own accord, came to sit beside him on the sofa while she poured their coffee.

'Had a good day?' he asked her.

'I wish *you* could have been with us,' was her pleasing reply.

'Well, we'll have a day just like it whenever you want,' he said, lighting his pipe contentedly. 'Wonder what old Tony's doing now! Just like him to rush off to town at a moment's notice.'

'Oh, don't let's talk about Tony!' Sherry cried involuntarily.

Richard looked at her quizzically.

'Don't you like him, Sherry? I thought you two were getting along pretty well.'

Sherry paused before answering. She would not lie to him.

'I prefer it when you and I are alone – like this,' she told him at last. At least this was true. She had always enjoyed her evenings alone with Richard, but with Tony as a third, the effort of pretending he meant nothing to her had been a strain. She could be relaxed now and without that wearying tension of her nerves. How exhausting a hopeless love could be! she thought. This must be what Richard suffered – on her account.

A rush of tenderness for him swept through her and, acting on impulse, she put her hand out to him. His face flushed slightly with pleasure as he grasped her fingers and held them.

'My dear,' he said gently. 'I'm so lucky to have you, Sherry, and so grateful to you.'

'Don't say that, please!' Sherry whispered. 'I don't deserve it. I've not been much of a wife to you.'

Richard looked surprised, partly at her vehemence and partly at her words.

'But Sherry, darling,' – the endearment slipped out unnoticed by him, but touching beneath Sherry's armour making her wish to cry – 'that isn't the least true. You're everything a man could want in his wife. Shall I list your wifely assets?' He was teasing her gently and she answered his smile.

'Spare me that,' she told him. 'It's I who don't deserve *you* for a husband. I wish I could believe–' she broke off, unable to continue. But he guessed her meaning.

'That it would all come right between us?' he finished for her. 'It will, Sherry, it will, if we both want it to. After all, isn't that the way of most marriages? They may start a little differently from ours, but I'm convinced that a perfect unity between two people isn't achieved in the early days. People grow together – as we will.'

'But I want us to be together now!' The cry was wrung from her. 'I want everything to be right for us *now.*'

Richard turned to look at her, his face alight with hope.

'Sherry! What are you trying to tell me? Could it be that you – you are beginning to – to care?'

Still she could not lie to him, but her words were only too true as she said desperately:

'I want to care, Richard. Make me care.

Make me love you!'

A more experienced man that Richard might have realized what was behind those cries from her heart, but he was a simple, kindly person and he did not fully understand women. It had been more than difficult for him to understand his first wife, the charming, dainty, selfish, little June. It was not until he had met Sherry that he began to see through June, to realize just how selfish and self-centred she had been. How else did one judge people unless by contrast? There had been no other women in his life, no love affairs such as there had been in Tony's life, and Richard's essentially male mind did not instinctively see through the intricacies of feminine emotions.

As he put his arms around Sherry and drew her to him, his own passionate reaction to her words was subdued by an overwhelming tenderness for her. His happiness was so intense that he was unusually sensitive to her emotional needs and had realized instinctively that where passion and haste would have repelled her, gentleness and understanding would draw her closer to him. Naturally, he knew nothing of the reason for her feelings. He could not know that while she longed for the comfort of his arms and her own released tears, she could not want from him the ardour of Tony's love-making.

He held her close for a little while until,

turning her face to his, he saw her tears.

'Oh, my dearest! Don't cry! Please. I've made you unhappy.'

'No, no. Don't think that. It's just– Oh, just that I'm being over-emotional and silly,' Sherry told him, smiling a little through her tears.

'I'd rather anything in the world than that you should be unhappy.'

'Would you? Would you?' The thought sped through her mind. 'Would you rather I went away with Tony – your cousin? Oh, Richard, don't be so good – so unselfish. I don't deserve it!'

She clung to him then in an agony of mind which he mistook for something else. She felt his arms tighten around her and knew an instant's frantic desire to break free from him. But she controlled the mounting hysteria and remained where she was, pressed tightly against him. She could feel his heart beating against her, his lips against her hair. Gradually, her eyes closed, and it was no longer Richard who held her in his arms – it was Tony.

'I mustn't! I mustn't!' she thought, but she seemed no longer in control of her thoughts, no longer responsible for her actions. With a little cry of anguish, her arms went round his neck, and she drew his head down to her.

'I love you! I love you so much!' Tony's voice – no, Richard's voice. How madly her heart was beating. If only she could think for a moment; but Richard, no longer able to keep calm, was kissing her with all the pent-up ardour of his feelings. It was too late now to draw back. In a mad moment she had committed herself, given way to her longings for Tony, and deceived Richard into believing she wanted *him*.

'You belong to me – to me,' he was saying. 'Darling, darling–'

'Perhaps it is best this way,' Sherry thought. 'This way Tony will believe me. He'll hate me for doing this, he'll go away. Oh, Tony, Tony – what am I doing?'

'You do love me a little Sherry? Tell me you do.'

His voice was husky and filled with longing which she knew she could not deny him now. Her own heart was beating in time with his and her body was responding to the gentle, sure touch of his hands. What did anything matter? She was Richard's wife. She would forget Tony, forget everything else but this moment.

If Richard had paused for a while – suggested they go upstairs to her room – he would have lost her. Sanity would have returned and she would have realized that this was no answer to her problems. Nor was it the kind of behaviour she could have countenanced in her right mind. Later she was to remember this moment with deep shame; that she could have given way to her passion for one man in the arms of another. But now, her mind was utterly confused, her thoughts whirling and body afire with the same longing that consumed the man who held her in his arms. Richard and Tony had become one and she was lost.

After a short while, she realized that Richard was smoothing the hair back from her forehead and talking to her gently, as he might have calmed an over-excited child.

'You're so sweet, my darling, so very sweet. I love you so much – too much. I never knew before what it meant to love anyone as I love you. We shall be so happy together, my dearest darling – you and Dick and Anne and I. People will look at us and wonder how we can be so happy. You *are* happy, aren't you, darling?'

'Dear God!' Sherry thought. 'What have I done? How can I undo this new ghastly tangle I have made of our lives? Richard, will you ever forgive me?'

But she could not speak aloud. Her tortured thoughts must remain her own as she pressed her burning cheeks against his shoulder so that he could not see the agony of her face.

How she despised herself! What greater wrong could any woman do a man than to let him make love to her pretending he was someone else? And yet it had not been of

Tony she had thought all the time. In the end, it had ceased to matter; thought had ceased to function and only her body lived and breathed and drew comfort from the gift of Richard's love. Their union had been a perfect one, as physically perfect as it had been spiritually void.

'You belong to me!' Richard was saying proudly. 'You're so very beautiful, Sherry – my wife, my wife.'

'No, no, no!' Sherry thought wildly. 'You don't understand. Oh, Richard, how can I make you understand. I love Tony, Tony, Tony! I have been unfaithful to both of you. I hate myself bitterly!'

Tears poured down her cheeks, tears of shame and incomprehension. She did not know herself, did not understand this person she had become. How could she have allowed Richard to take her in the way he had just done, when she did not love him? How could she have enjoyed it and known the feeling that it was *right* between them, right and yet horribly, horribly wrong?

'Tears again? Sherry, you must tell me. What's wrong, my darling? Is it anything I've said? Are you sorry?'

'No, don't take any notice of me, Richard. I'm over-emotional and over-tired. This is all so – so unexpected. I feel as if it isn't really me here at all. Let me go now, Richard, *dear* Richard. I want a little time to

– to re-orient myself. You do understand?'

He didn't understand, but he wanted her to have whatever it was she wanted. If it was solitude, then he could bear to part from her for her sake, much as he wanted to hold her to him again. He had hoped that he might hold her in his arms through the night; wake to find her head against his shoulders, proof that this magical evening had really transpired.

He couldn't understand her wish to be alone, so opposite from his own desires, but he could grant that wish gracefully because she had already made him so happy – because he loved her so desperately that only *her* happiness counted. He would not hurry her. His patience had already been rewarded, and in her own time she would come to him again. She reminded him of a highly strung, shy fawn who needed gentleness and love to give her confidence.

Controlling his emotions, he kissed her lightly and helped her to her feet.

'You run along to bed, darling. I'll come and kiss you good night in a few minutes, then leave you to sleep.' He looked into her face and felt a moment's concern. The beautiful colour that had so recently stained her cheeks had now disappeared leaving her chalk-white. There were deep shadows beneath eyes that were still full of tears. She looked ill with fatigue, and he wondered anxiously if she were not in too good health.

'You need me to take care of you, sweetheart,' he said tenderly.

In the privacy of her own room, Sherry stood with her back against the door and pressed her hands to her throbbing temples. What a ghastly mess she was making of her life – her life and Richard's. She despised herself for her deception and for the fact that she had let her emotions betray her into an irretrievable position. *Richard now believed she loved him* – if not wholly, then at least sufficient to wish to live with him as man and wife were meant to live together. What possible explanation could she give for refusing to do so in the future? Tonight she could plead fatigue, and it was true that she felt too exhausted even to think coherently. But what of tomorrow and the next night and the next? Richard would not understand and, without telling him the truth about this last hour, what reason could she give him for denying him everything he wanted from her?

If he were only less kind – less considerate! If his love-making had been selfish or brutal or thoughtless, she might have hated him. But he had been as perfect a lover as he was husband.

'Why, why, why did I have to meet Tony?' she thought desperately. 'If it weren't for him, I might have loved Richard. Oh, what can I do? How can I live this dreadful lie? How can I tell Richard the truth? How can I face Tony on Monday? How can I face myself?'

Desperate to a point where she felt hysterical, Sherry forced herself to undress and climb into bed. She remembered then that Richard would shortly be coming to her room to say good night to her, and she was afraid – afraid of what he might say and do; of what *she* might say in her utter confusion. Hating herself for her cowardice, she closed her eyes and feigned sleep. When Richard knocked on the door, she did not answer, though her heart was beating so wildly she felt he must hear it. But though the door opened, he did not come into the room – merely stood for a moment looking at her inert form – then went away closing the door quietly behind him.

Sherry lay wide-eyed and wakeful long into the night. Her thoughts chased each other round in hopeless circles – thoughts of Tony, of the children, of Richard, of the intimacy that had been between them. She asked herself again and again how she could have done such a thing. She could understand how some women, desperately in love, could be unfaithful to their husbands. It was understandable even if she personally violently disapproved of anyone breaking the vows they had made. But to be unfaithful with one's husband, which is what she knew herself to have been, that was incomprehensible. It even sounded mad, put into words.

What would Richard think of her, if he knew? He would hate her as much as she hated herself! It might be easier to bear her shame if he did. His love was much harder to bear, for it made her feel unbearably guilty. As for Tony, what would he think of her? Would he understand? How could he understand her when she failed to understand herself? She might have found excuses – that she wanted to prove to him that she meant to stay with Richard; that she felt it to be her duty; but, in the last resort, she knew that it had been the weakness of her own body that had betrayed her. She had wanted Richard as much as he had wanted her.

'I'm only human,' she defended her actions against herself. 'It's been so long since any man has made love to me.'

Bob had awakened her to the knowledge of herself and while he, too, had dulled for a time all her natural feminine emotions, they had only been dormant – not dead. The unnaturalness of her life with Richard, followed by Tony's impassioned kisses, had stirred her out of her emotional hibernation. If only it could have been Tony, then there would have been no shame, no regrets, for her heart lay with him.

'No regrets?' she questioned her own

thoughts wearily. There would have been thousands of them – regrets for having hurt Richard and divorcing him *would* hurt him; regrets for breaking up the children's home just when they had settled down to their new life so well; regrets for her own inability to keep a bargain when she made one.

So it boiled down to the fact that she couldn't be happy either way. With Tony lay the certain unhappiness of an uneasy conscience. With Richard lay the constant knowledge of deception and the pretence at a love she could not feel for him.

'If I could put the clock back!'

Even as the thought struck her mind, she realized how many countless times other people must have had the same wish. Only forty-eight hours ago she had never seen Tony, never known he existed. In that brief while, her life had been made unbearable and she had been caught in a whirlwind of emotion that had got beyond her control. And none of it could be undone. She could not fall out of love with Tony and she could only wish that she had never allowed Richard to touch her. Both were facts now, facts which nothing would undo.

'Perhaps Tony will hate me when he knows,' she told herself. For he must know. He would sense a difference in Richard, a guilt in herself, just as easily as he had sensed that she had not belonged to Richard and that she did not love him. If Tony hated her, he would go away for good and she could try to forget him. She had resolved to take some decisive action to force him to leave. Now it was done and with all her heart she wished it otherwise.

There was only one last consolation for her, that, for a short, brief space of time, she had made Richard completely happy. She would, and did, cling to this thought until at last, shortly before the dawn of another day, she fell into an uneasy sleep.

But Richard was not happy – not any longer. Lying awake in the darkness of his room, he was trying to account for this sudden, unreasonable mood of depression that had settled over him. He had known an hour of complete happiness, of perfection and peace. Now it was gone and in its place was a deep concern.

It was not simply because Sherry had been asleep when he had gone to her room; not even that she had wished to spend the rest of the night alone. June had always had her own bedroom and he supposed that many married couples had separate rooms, preferring to sleep by themselves when their love-making was over. He had not questioned the fact when he was married to June and he did not question it now; but he did long to have Sherry with him, or to be with her. There was so much he wanted to tell her of his love and longing, his plans for their future. He wanted, too, to lie beside her with their bodies unhampered by clothes and as near as nature meant them to be; to feel reassured by her physical presence.

He wondered why he felt this need for reassurance and, remembering every detail of what had passed between them, knew that she had never once said she loved him – only that she *wanted* to love him. At first it had seemed sufficient that she had wanted him to love her, permitted him to make love to her; that she had been as responsive as he had ever dreamed she might be. It had been a perfect and satisfying union and yet he could not prevent that feeling now that something had gone wrong.

Could it be that Sherry had not really wanted to do what they had done? Could there have been some motive that he had overlooked? An unselfish desire to please him? A wish to put things right? A sense of duty?

He turned away from such thoughts with a shudder. They *could* not be true for Sherry had been as ardent and passionate as he. There had been no reluctance in her, no fighting against him. She had seemed as eager as he for all that had passed between them. And Sherry was no light-hearted young girl who would do a thing like that just for the fun of it. She knew he loved her, knew that he would never expect her to come to him unless she wanted it as much as he. If only he could be sure that, for a little while at least, she had loved him – truly loved him, as he loved her.

He thought about her past and was comforted by the memory of what had gone before. That husband of hers had destroyed her faith in men. It was only natural that she should be reticent about the very word love, that she should be cautious and wary of giving her heart a second time. He must be patient, understanding, gain her confidence. He would not rush her, force her before she was ready to accept what was between them. Tomorrow he would let her see that nothing was changed between them, that he was perfectly willing to go back to their old friendly relationship if she wished it. He would make no crude suggestions that she should change her room – move nearer to him. Everything should come from her – of her own accord and in her own time. Above all, he would not frighten her with his own love, his own longing and desires.

'Oh, Sherry, my darling child,' he thought with great tenderness. 'We do belong together, and one day you will know that as surely as I do. It will be worth waiting for, even if the waiting means loneliness for a little while longer. One day you will come to me and you will know, as surely as I know, that we were meant to be man and wife!'

It was a comforting thought, and soon after it, he fell asleep.

CHAPTER 9

Tony Hayden sat back in his chair, outwardly watching the dancers and inwardly cursing himself for a fool. It was absurd to be taking this affair with Sherry so seriously. After all, he hadn't known her two days ago, so he should be able to forget her just as easily as he had fallen in love with her.

But the trouble was Sherry wouldn't be forgotten so easily. It wasn't for lack of trying, Tony decided, as he lit another cigarette. Here he was dining, wining and dancing with a girl who, by most men's standards of beauty, would be judged twice as pretty as Sherry, had most of what it takes in the way of 'oomph', and was as gay and amusing a companion as ever he'd hoped to have for a date.

Jim's sister, Minx ('My real name's Minetta, but everyone calls me Minx') was his type, Tony reflected. She lived up to her pet name and was full of fun. She was quite a little thing – five feet or so, with raven dark hair cut short in a boyish fringe, which she had explained was the 'urchin cut' – whatever that meant. At any rate, it suited her tiny face, with its upturned nose, mischievous smile and little, pointed chin. She had been flirting outrageously with him ever since he had phoned her from Paddington Station when his train got in.

'So you're the Tony Jim writes about so often. I suppose you know he's determined to find a husband for me? I felt I should warn you in case you aren't the marrying type.'

'Are you?' Tony countered, with a grin she couldn't see.

'No! And I think we shall hit it off after all,' came her voice with its gay, impish laughter following her words. 'I don't usually care for Jim's prospective catches.'

'Are you free tonight, by any chance? I've just arrived in London and don't know a soul. I hoped very much you might be free to dine somewhere.'

'Why, I'd love to. I was going to a flick with a girl friend, but we've an understanding; that is to say, we can always put each other off if anything better turns up.'

'Thanks for the compliment. I'll try to better the flick.'

She was his type – he had known it from those first words. In fact, he'd guessed it when Jim had shown him her photograph and told him about her. He knew it for sure when they finally met and he found her not only as pretty as he'd expected but loads of fun and game for anything. Just the companion he needed to put Sherry out of his mind.

'I'm a responsibility to my poor brother,' she told him, twinkling those dark eyes of hers and blowing out a cloud of smoke so that it curled round his head and drifted away behind them. 'Jim has had to support me ever since Mother and Father died, so he's crazy to find me a nice, suitable husband. When he wrote to me about you, I thought you were probably a staid, wealthy, very eligible young man.'

'Perhaps I am!' Tony told her laughing.

'Eligible, maybe! Wealthy, maybe; but staid – never!'

'I gather you don't exactly want to settle down?'

She laughed.

'Not me! I have far too much fun as a spinster. Perhaps the day will come, but it hasn't yet. Personally, I doubt it. I'm not the settling down sort.'

'You never know!' Tony said seriously, thinking: 'I thought as she did, yet I'd marry a girl I've known only two days tomorrow, if she were free. Oh, blast and damn Sherry Hayden! I'll forget her and have a good time instead.'

In a way, he *was* having a good time, but memories of Sherry kept interrupting his pleasure. Disturbing and unreasonable memories. Dancing with Minx, his cheek against her hair, he said:

'That's a nice perfume, Minx. What is it?'

'Something called Blue Grass. You wouldn't know it!'

But he did. It was the same perfume Sherry used.

'When did you arrive in England, Tony? Not today, surely?'

'No. Last Friday. I've been staying in the country with my cousin.'

'Male of female?' Her eyes teased him. But he couldn't laugh with her.

'My cousin Richard – and his wife.'

They danced several times and then sat down to the kind of dinner Tony had thought about often in Africa. This was a night-club of Minx's choosing – and he heartily approved. The food was good, the music just the right blend of rhythm and romance. The lights not too bright an the tables not too close together – the ideal setting, in fact, for an evening's flirtation with a pretty girl. And Minx was asking for it. She teased him constantly and flirted so openly that he could not help but be amused by her as well as enchanted by her. There were no obvious subtleties about Minx. She was out for a good time, and she meant to have it.

'This is fun, Tony. Will we do it more often?'

'I hope so!' he said, and found himself

wondering if he would come here with her again. It depended so much on Sherry and whether she would nerve herself to leave Richard.

'Tell me more about yourself, Tony. What do you and Jim do in Africa – other than work, I mean. No girl friends?'

'Very few white women where we are,' Tony told her. 'Which should be a warning to you, young lady. When we get back to civilization, we're liable to go berserk.'

'I can take care of myself,' Minx said smiling, and he realized it was true. He wondered how old she was – twenty-five or six. Younger than Jim, he knew. The mixture of impishness and sophistication was very attractive.

'Let's dance again!' he said.

She pressed close against him, and he felt himself responding to her proximity, to the soft lights and the music. He wondered how the evening would end, and then stopped wondering while they danced. Minx was as light as a feather, yet he was always conscious of her slim young body moving beneath his hands. He kissed the top of her head and she snuggled closer against him.

'This *is* fun!' she said. 'You're nice – but nice.'

They held hands when they were back in their chairs. There was no one to see or to care. Tony felt mellow, happy, excited. Then

Minx said:

'Tell me about your cousin. Is he like you?' And he remembered Sherry again.

'I'd rather talk about you,' he said quickly. 'What do you do all your life?'

'Just fritter it away. I do a bit of photographic modelling sometimes – hats, that kind of thing – just to earn some pocket money. Otherwise I have a good time.'

'Who with?' But he wasn't really jealous – just curious.

'Oh, dozens of people. Americans, sometimes French – and an occasional Englishman. The girl friend I share a flat with is in the American Embassy, so we date up a lot there.'

'No one in particular?'

'Not yet! But there could be.' She looked up at him provocatively through her long, dark lashes. Tony held her hand a little tighter.

'Could be,' he said. But it was a statement rather than a confirmation. It all depended on Sherry. Why couldn't he get her out of his mind and enjoy this evening?

'No one special for you?' she asked him.

He couldn't think of an evasive reply quick enough. Minx pouted.

'The girl with my perfume?' she said astutely.

He looked surprised.

'How d'you know?'

'Feminine intuition. Tell me about her.'

'Certainly not. I don't take out a girl and talk about another one. It isn't done in the best circles.'

'But I'm not the best circles,' Minx said smiling. 'Do tell Tony. I really want to know.'

'As a matter of fact, it's a hell of a mess up,' Tony said after a moment. 'Fact is – well, she's married.'

Minx raised her eyebrows.

'That does complicate matters. Does she – feel the same about you?'

'I think so! But she won't make up her mind to leave her husband.'

'I thought you said there weren't any white women in Africa?'

'She's my cousin's wife!' Tony said, and then: 'I didn't mean to tell that to a damn soul. Why I should confide in you, goodness knows!'

'Because I'm a sympathetic listener,' Minx told him. 'And because I'm playing the part of your sister.'

'Never that!' Tony replied, meaning it, and they both smiled.

'Well, tell me the rest. I'm intrigued,' Minx said persuasively. 'Maybe I can be Dorothy Dix and offer some sound advice.'

He told her, and waited to hear what she would say in reply.

'It's difficult to know what to say,' she said at length. 'I've never fallen "all of a heap" myself, so I can't altogether understand it. I've read about it in books, of course, but it hasn't seemed to happen that way with me – at least, not yet.' She looked strangely thoughtful, her forehead puckered in a frown. 'Maybe it does happen – sometimes. Are you quite sure, Tony? About your side of it, I mean?'

'I'd marry her tomorrow if I could,' he said shortly. 'I suppose I ought to feel a bit of a cad about Richard, and all that, but damn it all, she doesn't really belong to him. It's such a crazy set-up. A wife and not a wife. He loves her, I think, but he can't want her if she's in love with someone else. Then the kids complicate things. She might leave him if it weren't for them. I don't know. I felt I had to get away from it for a bit – give us both time to think it over. She didn't like my going when it came to the point, but she's – well, different from most girls – sort of stuck with this idea of *owing* Richard something. Now let's talk of something else. This must be boring you.'

'It isn't, but you want to forget and that's more than okay with me. Let's dance again, shall we?'

'You're a good sport, Minx. Lots of girls would have passed up the evening after the last ten minutes' conversation.'

'Nonsense! I like to know the opposition,' was Minx's reply, then she rose to her feet and he followed her back on to the dance floor. She behaved exactly as if he had never mentioned Sherry, dancing just as close as before, answering the pressure of his fingers, smiling up at him through those dark lashes every now and again. She made it possible for him to forget Sherry again and he was grateful.

'What time is it?' Minx asked when the dance ended.

'Twelve-thirty. Tired?'

'Never that! But I thought we might go back to my flat and have a drink. I've got a nice bottle of Scotch saved for just such an occasion – American loot.'

Tony gave her a quick look. Was there anything behind her suggestion that they go for a nightcap to her flat? She had made the offer so easily, casually. It was one of her chief attractions that she could be natural where other girls would have been coy or suggestive. He couldn't altogether make her out and he was intrigued.

'Will the girl-friend be there?' he asked her.

She gave him her mischievous smile.

'What do you think? She's away for the week-end, so we shall be *toute seule*. Does the idea appeal to your majesty?'

Tony grinned.

'What do you think?'

But in the taxi, she made him think again.

'I don't often ask people back to the flat at this time of night – at least, not people in the singular. We have parties sometimes. A friend has to be pretty special to be the only one.'

'I'm flattered!' Tony said, not quite understanding until she said:

'As Jim's friend, I know I can trust you, Tony.' Her voice was quite serious.

'Then you ought not to, but you can just this once,' he replied. 'I'll behave.'

She laughed lightly and told the taxi-driver where to stop.

Her flat was a fairly large three-roomed affair in a modern block. It was nicely furnished in a very feminine way. Tony noticed an excessive number of black cats – ornaments, stuffed toys, calendars.

'For luck!' Minx said, handing him a drink. 'I'm superstitious. Someone found out and now all my friends shower me with black cats. I like them.'

'You *are* a strange kid,' Tony said, wondering about her. She had removed the fur coat and had slipped something soft and fluffy over her bare shoulders.

'A stole,' Minx said, laughing. 'Obviously not in vogue in Africa, judging by your expression.'

'Anything you wore would soon be the vogue in Africa,' Tony replied. 'May I kiss you?'

She came over to him and he took her in his arms. Her mouth was soft and warm and her kiss very experienced. He wondered where this was leading him when she broke away from him laughing.

'That's enough to begin with, Tony; I'm a good girl.'

'Far be it from me to contradict you,' Tony replied. 'But I wish you weren't.'

'Only because of your girl-friend.'

Tony frowned.

'That beats me, Minx. What did you mean?'

'Simply what I said. If it weren't for her, you'd be pleased I wasn't too willing too soon. As it is, you want to work off your emotions on me.'

'What a beastly thing to say!' Tony said angrily. But he knew in a way it was true. 'You know an awful lot about men for a good girl, don't you?'

'That was unkind, but I understand,' Minx said quietly. 'If it helps any to know it, it did hurt. And while we're on the subject, I said I *am* a good girl – not that I was.'

'I'm sorry, Minx. Please forgive me.'

She smiled – but without the vivacity he had grown used to.

'I'll forgive – and forget. But I'd like to finish telling you, Tony, so there won't be any more misunderstandings. I had an affair – a real one – with an American. He was married. I knew it all along, but I just didn't care. In the end, he went back to the States. But before he went, I'd learned my way around. So now you know.'

'I'm sorry, Minx,' Tony said helplessly. 'What a rotten lot of people there are in the world.'

'He wasn't rotten,' Minx said. 'He was nice. He wanted to be faithful to his wife – but I wouldn't let him be. I was in love with him. I knew I'd be hurt just as he knew it – but I wanted it that way all the same. I'm not sorry.'

'Do you still love him?'

Minx gave a sigh.

'Love? I don't know. I thought my heart was broken, but I got over it – or used to it. I'm never quite sure which. I'm happy enough, if that's what you mean. No good crying over the inevitable, is there?'

'Not if it *is* inevitable. It's easier for you in a way. You knew where you stood. I don't.'

'Well, from all you tell me, you stand a fairly even chance of getting what you want,' Minx said, pouring out another couple of drinks.

Tony shook his head.

'I thought so earlier this evening. Now I'm not so sure. What would you do, Minx, if you were her?'

'Marry you, I expect,' Minx said, but he could see she was teasing him again. 'No, seriously speaking, I'm not sure. You've only told me your view of the set-up. There may be extenuating circumstances, or whatever they are called. Besides, I've never had a child that needed a name, so I don't know how grateful I'd be to the man that took it on. And lastly, I've never valued security as such so I can't understand your Sherry being so grateful, as you put it, to your cousin for giving it to her. And last, but not least, I'd want to know far more about you before I flung my cap over the windmill for you.'

She brushed him lightly on the shoulder with her hand, laughing at him. Tony caught the hand and held it.

'Would you, Minx? I don't think you're that sort of a girl. I think it's all or nothing with you.'

She drew her hand away, her eyes smiling.

'Maybe. But I'm a fool. Your girl-friend probably isn't. And she has a child to think of, too. Kids change women. At least, the women I know have changed once they had babies; sort of settled down in their minds and more practical.'

'You're not much of a help, Minx.'

She came back across the room to him and looked straight into his eyes. What she saw there seemed to make up her mind. She put down her glass carefully on the table and without any awkwardness, slipped on to his lap and wound her arms round his neck.

'Perhaps I can help this way!' she said in a whisper. 'Kiss me, Tony. Kiss me – and forget!'

He might not have given way to her if she hadn't told him about the other affair in her life. He was no moralist, but his code of behaviour did not include seducing innocent young girls. But Minx was no innocent young thing and she knew what she was doing. His arms went around her, drawing her down to him – and for a time, he did forget. But later, when Minx lay quiet and motionless in his arms, he remembered again and knew that he was sorry for what had just happened – sorry because of Sherry; a little ashamed because Minx was such a nice girl and regretful because he might have fallen in love with her if–

'It's no good, is it?' Minx's voice broke his reverie.

He ran a hand lightly over her dark curls.

'You're so sweet, darling,' he said, meaning it. But she would not let him be evasive.

'What will you do now, Tony? Go back and try again?'

'I don't know, darling. Don't let's talk about *her.*'

She stirred restlessly in his arms.

'But I want to talk about her, Tony. It matters to me – now.'

'Why should it? It's my worry.'

He could not see her face, so he did not see the expression in her eyes.

'All the same, I'd like to share it with you. Let me really be a sister to you, Tony.'

He laughed then, the movement of his body shaking hers so that she laughed, too.

'Well, I know it sounds silly after – after this. But I do want to help, Tony. Suppose I come down with you and make her wildly jealous. That might make up her mind for her.'

'I wish it would!' Tony said. 'I feel so damned unsettled. It's never happened to me this way before.'

She sat up and ran a finger along his lips.

'No! All the other girls fell into your lap. This is the first one you've had to fight for.'

'You're a divining but gorgeous little witch. Anyway, it isn't true.'

'But it is!' she laughed. 'And I'm not a witch. I just understand you because we are so alike.'

'Alike!' Tony gasped, tugging her hair. 'A little five-foot-one-inch black cat–'

'And a big, six-foot-one-inch tiger. We are alike, Tony. We always want what we can't have. What we can get easily, we don't want for long. I'm like that and you are, too. If Sherry had fallen into your arms without a murmur, you wouldn't be interested. Nor would I be interested in you if you'd fallen head over heels in love with me tonight.'

He kissed her lips and said:

'I wish I were in love with you, Minx.'

'So do I!' she said, but he did not know if she were talking seriously for her face was turned away from him again.

'You're sweet! You're the nicest sister a guy ever had.'

'Silly! Be serious now. Why not take me down with you? I'll behave – really I will. And she will be jealous. Any woman would be if competition turned up. And if I can't rival her in your affections, I can rival her in one thing – I'm not married. Do let me come, Tony.'

'But why, Minx? It won't be any fun for you. Honestly, the more I learn of women, the less I understand them.'

'That's why they're such fun!' Minx told him. 'Answer me, Tony, may I come?'

'I suppose if you really want to – but I simply can't see what you'll get out of it.'

'I might get the broken pieces to pick up,' Minx said, teasing him again. He silenced her laugh with a kiss. 'You'll need someone to mend your broken heart if she turns you down,' she went on, as if he had not interrupted her. 'Well, that's the kind of girl I am – a mender of broken hearts and a picker-upper of pieces!'

'You're sweet and I love you!'

'No, you don't, but I like to hear you say it all the same. Say it again.'

'I love you, love you, love you, and it's very late and high time I went home,' Tony said, lifting her off his lap and swinging his legs to the ground.

'Where's home – since, in your case, it can't be where the heart is?'

Tony lit a cigarette and grinned at her.

'Come to think of it, nowhere. I shall go to one of the station hotels.'

'Why not stay here?'

'That's impossible. What about your reputation? Besides, you're a good girl.'

She came over and he took her in his arms and kissed her without passion.

'You wouldn't like me if I was a good girl,' she contradicted her earlier statement. 'You like me just as I am.'

'By God, that's true!' Tony said. 'And I like you enough not to let the hall porter bring up the paper and find me here in the morning. So I'm going. I'll ring you when I get in wherever it is, and tell you I'm not walking the streets.'

Half an hour later, he called her number from his hotel. She sounded sleepy but happy.

'When are we going to the country?' she asked him.

'Not until Monday – who said "we", anyway?'

'I did! Then what will we do tomorrow – I mean, today?'

'Whatever you say, Minx. And, darling–'

'Yes?'

'Thank you.'

'You've such nice manners, darling. If I wasn't your sister I'd be so much in love with you.'

'Good night, Minx. I'll phone you in a little while.'

'Good night, Tiger!' she said, and rang off.

He lay awake for a little while, thinking about her and not understanding her. She had made him understand in the taxi that she was asking him back to her flat because she could trust him to behave. But she had been the one who made the running and it hadn't turned out in the least as he'd expected. He couldn't make her out. She wasn't the type of girl a man expected to behave that way simply because they had been flirting during the evening. And he knew from his own experience that she wasn't hard-bitten or indifferent to moral standards. Experienced she might be on her own admission, but, at the same time, there was something fresh and unspoilt about her that Tony had not come across before. In the past, the women had all been of a certain type, hard-drinking, out for a good time and very modern in their attitude to life and sex. It had suited Tony very well to have an occasional mild love affair with one or other of these women. There would be no strings attached; not talk of love; it was simply accepted on both sides that they were having a good time for as long as Tony's leave lasted. Minx was not like that. He felt it, rather than knew it.

But Minx was not Sherry, much as he had enjoyed his evening with her and much as he liked her. Sherry was something quite apart in his life. He had never fallen for her type before and it was a new experience for him to respect the girl of the moment – as new as the wish to make the moment permanent. He was surprised at his own certainty that he wanted to marry her – he, who had sworn never to marry and was not the settling-down type of bachelor girls expected to propose.

'I wish I didn't love her!' he thought incongruously. It was his last coherent thought before sleep claimed him, as a clock somewhere in the vicinity struck six and the rest of the world was waking up.

CHAPTER 10

Sherry lay on her bed watching the afternoon sun pouring through the half-open curtains on to her eider-down. She felt lazy and rested after two hours solid sleep. Richard was out somewhere with the children.

'You look all in, Sherry. I'll take them off your hands while you lie down for an hour or two.'

She had argued half-heartedly against this suggestion, but in the end had allowed herself to be persuaded. She was wretchedly tired and knew she needed the rest. It meant, too, that she could avoid any awkward discussions with Richard, or at least postpone them a little while longer.

Somewhere in the distance, she heard the sound of a car and wondered a little as it came closer. Their country lane was usually quiet – especially on a Sunday afternoon. At last, she was forced to realize that it was coming up the drive. Her mind leaped to the only obvious conclusion – it must be Tony, although she had not expected him until tomorrow.

She sprang out of bed and hurried into a

pair of slacks and her new pale blue twin set.

'Don't let it be Tony!' she voiced a silent prayer as she ran a comb through her hair and powdered her nose with anxious haste. 'I'm not ready to see him again – not yet.'

But she knew her prayer was unanswered before she had closed her bedroom door behind her.

'Anybody at home?' It was Tony's voice.

She started slowly downstairs and then paused on the second step as she heard another voice – a woman's voice, saying:

'Perhaps they're all out, Tony.'

'They won't be far. It's nearly tea-time. Come on, Minx. We'll go into the drawing-room. Let me take your coat.'

Their voices disappeared with them into the drawing-room, and Sherry put a hand to her cheeks. They were burning hot.

Tony here – with some woman. Who was she? Why had he brought her down with him without telling them? Had he phoned Richard while she was resting? A thousand questions poured through her mind, but she refused to voice the uppermost one – what was this woman to Tony? She had sounded young – was it some girl-friend? What did she mean to him?

'I can't just stand here,' she thought. 'I'll have to go down and meet them.'

Her feet dragged her slowly to the drawing-room and her hands opened the door. Laughter broke off suddenly as she went in.

'Sherry, we thought you must be out! The house was as quiet as the grave.'

Her eyes went to Tony's face – and her heart turned over. If the strange girl weren't in the room, she would have flung herself into his arms. She looked at the girl, taking in every detail of her tiny, perfect little figure, her dainty, pretty little face and dark, inquiring curious eyes. She noted the beautifully cut country tweed dress and felt herself to be shabby, clumsy and unfeminine in her slacks. This girl was like a Dresden figurine.

'This is Minx – Minx Rogers – Jim's sister. Sherry Hayden.'

Minx held out her hand.

'It's nice to meet you, Mrs Hayden. Tony has talked of little else but you ever since I met him. I've been longing to see you in person.'

Sherry felt the colour rush back into her cheeks. So Tony had been telling this girl about *them.* He had no right to discuss her with a stranger. Why had he brought this girl here?

'I hope you don't mind us turning up like this, Sherry? Sunday in London is pretty ghastly so I asked Minx to come down here for a couple of nights.'

She found her voice with difficulty.

'Of course – it's perfectly all right. We shall be a foursome – perhaps we can play some bridge.'

'Oh, Lord!' she thought. 'Why can't I find something intelligent to say? Why am I so confused – so upset?'

'Please don't go to any trouble on my behalf, Mrs Hayden. Tony told me you haven't any domestic help on Sundays. Let me help in any way I can, won't you? I'm quite a good cook and I can make up my own bed.'

'Thank you. I shall be able to manage. I'll go and get you some tea. I expect you need it after the train journey.'

'I'll get it!' Tony said, grinning. 'You two girls can sit down and get to know each other.'

'Let me make it,' Minx said, firmly. 'That is, if you don't mind another woman poking about your kitchen, Mrs Hayden? You and Tony must have lots to talk about.'

'I wouldn't dream–' Sherry began when Tony interrupted her.

'Nonsense! Let Minx feel at home. Besides, I presume the rest of the family will be back soon, and I do want to talk to you, Sherry.'

Sherry started to protest again, but the matter was taken out of her hands.

'Kitchen is second door on the right, Minx,' Tony said, and, before Sherry could prevent it, she and Tony were alone.

Immediately the door closed behind Minx, Tony went across to Sherry and tried to take her in his arms, but she slipped past him and walked across to the window where she stared out on to the sunlit lawn with unseeing eyes.

'Sherry, darling. You're not angry – because I brought Minx down here? She's a nice kid and I thought she'd liven the place up a bit. A threesome is always a bit trying and she wanted to meet you. I told her all about us. She wants to help.'

'Why?'

Tony looked surprised.

'Well, I don't know. Don't ask me why women choose to do these things.'

Sherry swung round to face him.

'You shouldn't have told her about us,' she said. 'A stranger!'

Tony walked away and lit a cigarette.

'She's not a stranger, Sherry. I know I only met her yesterday, but she's the sort of girl one gets to know very quickly.'

'I see!'

His face flushed slightly at her tone.

'No, Sherry, you don't see. I felt pretty low last night, and I looked up Jim's sister because I promised I would. Minx was doing nothing special so we went dancing. She was very sympathetic and understanding. She wants to help us.'

'How can she help us? How can anyone help us?' the cry was wrung from her heart. 'Oh, Tony, can't you understand that it's all over? When you said good-bye yesterday, it was for good. I hoped you'd be decent enough not to come back – *ever.*'

He flung his cigarette away and went across to her. This time he would not let her escape him. He held her tightly at arm's length and looked down at her distraught face.

'Are you telling me you're not in love with me any longer?'

'I didn't say that – only that everything is over between us, Tony. Nothing can come of it. It's finished. It's just the same as if I didn't love you.'

'It isn't the same at all,' Tony cried. 'Nothing is over until you stop loving me. I mean to fight for you, Sherry, all the way. I tried to forget you, last night, but I couldn't. You're in my blood and I've got to have you.'

She turned her face away as he tried to kiss her, but he was stronger than she and forced her head round until she was looking into his eyes.

'Tony, don't – don't, please, kiss me. Let me go. You don't understand. Everything is different – changed – since yesterday.'

'What's different? What has changed? If you think because Minx–'

'It has nothing to do with her. It's – it's

quite irrevocable, Tony. While you were dancing last night with *her*, Richard and I – we– Oh, God in heaven, I wish I were dead. I wish I were dead!'

Tony was staring at her, his face white and taut as he guessed her meaning.

'But, why – Sherry? *Why did you have to do that?* You knew I was coming back. I told you I'd be back by Monday. I don't understand. What made you do it?'

Sherry broke free from his arms and went wearily to the settee where she sat down as if her legs could not support her.

'I don't know! Last night I thought I knew. I meant to show you once and for all that I – I belong to Richard. It was to prove to you and to myself that I – that I was his wife. It sounds crazy now, doesn't it? I hate myself, Tony. You must hate me, too.'

'Hate you? You crazy little fool! What did you hope to prove to me by that kind of gesture? What did you prove to yourself?'

'Nothing – nothing at all. Only how weak and stupid and unfair I am – what a ghastly mess I've made of everything – and most of all, how much *you* mean to me, Tony.'

She hadn't meant to say those words but they slipped out unbidden. In an instant, Tony was on his knees beside her.

'Darling, don't look so unhappy. It doesn't matter so much. I do understand. In a way, I tried to do the same thing – to forget you.

It didn't work out for me either. *I love you Sherry.*'

But she wasn't listening to those last words – only to her heart which was caught in a wild uprush of jealousy. Tony had tried to forget her – last night – with that girl. He had taken from some other woman what she had denied him – had held *Minx* in his arms. How could he? How could he? Yet she had done the same. Of all people, she, least of all, could condemn him. But it hurt – it hurt terribly.

'Sherry, say you will marry me? Tell me you'll come away with me, tonight? At least tomorrow?'

For one wild moment, her heart weakened and she knew the longing to give way – to throw herself into his arms and tell him she would go with him now – anywhere – away from this house and…

'You forget, Tony. Nothing else is altered. Richard – and the children.'

He stood up abruptly, his face cold and unhappy.

'This bloody sense of duty to others you keep shoving down my throat!' he cried, and then: 'I'm sorry, darling. I didn't mean to swear at you. It's all such a terrible muddle. We love each other. That makes sense and that's about all that does. After that, full stop. Surely there's some way out?'

'There's no way – no way,' Sherry cried

desperately. 'Now, more than ever, it's hopeless, Tony – because of last night. Richard is – he's terribly happy. He believes I love him – believes it's all coming right at last. I let him think so. I couldn't explain the real reason for what I did. We've got to end all this – say good-bye.'

He would have argued, pleaded with her but, at that moment, Minx came in with the tea-trolley. She appeared not to notice the strained atmosphere or their silence and chattered while they tried to think of everyday things.

'I expect I've got the wrong tea-pot and used far too much tea. I cut a plate of bread and butter, too, as I thought the others might be hungry when they got in. No sign of them yet? I'm longing to meet Tony's cousin – and the children. I hear they're sweet.'

At that moment, the door burst open and Dick came rushing in, his face hot and excited. He looked round at them and flung himself on Sherry.

'Mummy, we saw the taxi on the way back to the station and I guessed Uncle Tony had come back. I guessed right, didn't I? Who's this lady? Is she Uncle Tony's wife?'

Minx laughed easily.

'No, just one of his girl-friends. So you're Dick?'

'Yes, an' Daddy and Anne are just coming.

Anne can't run as fast as me so Daddy has to go slowly or her legs get tired. We walked ever such a long way, and Mummy, we saw a hedgehog. It was walking across the road, but when we touched it, it curled up in a ball. We put it in the hedge, case a car ran it over, and squashed it. Anne wanted to bring it home, but Daddy said it would prick Honey's nose with its prickles. Why do hedgehogs have prickles?'

Richard came in with Anne, her face glowing and flushed from her walk. She, too, ran straight to Sherry so that she had an arm around each of the children.

'I'm ever so hungry, Mummy. Are you having tea, now? Can we have ours down here, too?'

'If Daddy doesn't mind,' Sherry said. 'I'll go and get the rest of it. Richard, let me introduce a friend of Tony's – Miss Rogers. Miss Rogers – this is my husband.'

'Your wife has kindly said I can stay a few nights,' Minx said, holding out her hand to Richard. 'Tony rather rudely invited me without asking your permission first. I hope you're not annoyed.'

Richard smiled. On the contrary, he was delighted. If this girl were here to keep Tony company, he would have Sherry more to himself.

'I'll help you get the children's tea,' he said, following Sherry to the kitchen. 'We had a grand walk. I wish you'd come with us. Did you sleep well or did Tony and girl-friend disturb you?'

'They only arrived a short while ago. I slept beautifully.'

'Rather a pretty girl – Tony's latest. What's she like?'

Sherry busied herself with the tea-tray.

'She seems very nice. I gather she and Tony hit the high spots last night.'

'So I imagine! Tony doesn't believe in wasting any time.'

'What do you mean, Richard?'

Jealousy was surging in her again however hard she might try to quell it.

'Only that he's a bit of a lad, as the saying goes. You're not annoyed with him for bringing her here without asking? Just like him. It's not really bad manners with him, you know. He just doesn't think.'

'That's all right. I don't mind.'

But she did mind. She minded dreadfully. It was difficult enough to put Tony out of her mind – out of her life without having to throw him into the arms of another woman. Perversely, though she knew she could not have him herself, she was human enough not to want to see him go off with Minx Rogers. From the way Richard was talking, it wouldn't be long before Tony found ample consolation.

'Perhaps he'll marry her?'

Richard laughed.

'I doubt that. He's just not the marrying sort. It'll probably go the way of his other *affaires de cœur* and end when his leave expires.'

'When will that be?'

'Oh, in a couple of months, I suppose. Three, I think he gets as a rule.'

Three months – then he would be gone – out of her life for ever. Or, at least, for several years. The thought was unbearable – life had become unbearable. And Richard suspected nothing. He looked happy and contented and pleased with life. She could almost hate him in her own unhappiness.

'You know, Sherry, Anne is the sweetest child. She was asking me if I believe in fairies! I told her I wasn't sure, so she said she'd got one that lived under her pillow and its name was Jane, but I couldn't see it because I was a grown-up. Did you ever hear such a story!'

'Oh, she has a very vivid imagination,' Sherry said. 'She and Dick make up all sorts of fantastic things and half the time, they believe they are true – even though they know they aren't, if you understand what I mean.'

'It's grand the way those two get on so well. They just adore each other. At least, Anne adores Dick and he's very patient and protective towards her. It's been a great success, hasn't it, Sherry?'

'Yes!' she said, thinking: 'If no one else, at least the children are happy. That's one of the reasons I can't leave you, Richard. One of the barriers between me and happiness.'

'There, that seems to be everything. I'll take the tray.'

She went back with him to the drawing-room.

Free for a little while to watch and listen, Minx looked round the room and tried to categorize her thoughts. Sherry, for instance. She wasn't as pretty as she, Minx, had imagined but she could see what Tony admired about her. The opposite of herself, Sherry was tall, graceful and essentially 'sweet'. There was no subterfuge, no complications about her looks; they showed in every line her goodness and strength of character. Minx could admire and respect a girl of Sherry's worth even while she knew that she did not wish to emulate it. She preferred to be gay and light-hearted and skim over the surface of things – happy-go-lucky, in fact.

Why do people always attract their opposites, she wondered, knowing that Tony was like herself and as different from Sherry as chalk from cheese. She and Tony were two of a kind. And so, in some ways, was Sherry and her husband.

Minx studied the older of the two men

and found him attractive. He was definitely like Tony physically – a strong family likeness which no doubt became less apparent when one knew them both well. Richard's face was thinner – more lined – more mature.

'It's a finer face than Tony's,' she thought, but it could not alter her feelings. Tony Hayden attracted her as no man had done – since the days of her American. At first, she'd resolved not to get involved with Tony. She had no intention of getting her heart broken twice and she knew instinctively that Tony wasn't the marrying type, even if she wanted it that way, and even if there had been no Sherry. But as last evening had worn on, she had realized her emotions were for the second time in her life, getting the better of her common sense. She knew she had to see Tony again, knew that there was only one sure way of keeping him interested. Time was against her, but she still had some weapons and knew how to use them.

When she had asked Tony to bring her down here, she had really wanted to come to see the extent of her competition, not from idle curiosity but so that she could see more clearly where she stood. She had been fully prepared to back out of things gracefully. At first, seeing the expression on Tony's face as he looked at Sherry, she had imagined that the moment for her to fade tactfully away had arrived. But now she wasn't so sure. She began to see that Tony was going to have quite a fight to get his own way this time. For Sherry had Richard and the children lined up beside her.

'They are a family,' Minx thought with a sense of surprise. 'One would imagine they had been married for years and that they were both parents to both the kids. They seem to belong – to be united. It is as if Tony and I are only onlookers.'

Minx looked again at Sherry.

'Does she really love Tony?' she wondered. 'Could she make him happy? I ought to be jealous of her, but I'm not – just sorry for her. She looks desperately unhappy. The tension only leaves her face when she looks at one or other of the children. Wonder how I'd feel in her shoes!'

'You're very quiet, Minx!' Tony's voice interrupted her thought. She grinned up at him.

'Just sleepy and replete from such an enormous tea!'

'What's 'plete?' Anne asked.

'Full up!' Richard told her smiling.

'F.T.B.,' Dick said, with his mouth full. 'Full to jolly old bursting. Can I have another cake, Daddy?'

'She won't leave them – she can't!' Minx thought, suddenly certain of it. 'Other women might, but Sherry won't. Does Tony realize it now?'

But Tony seemed to have shelved the problem momentarily. He was helping Anne set out the Ludo board.

'Come on, Minx!' he said. 'It's Anne and I against Dick and you.'

'Bags I be red!' Dick said. 'And Anne's blue. So you and the small lady will have to toss for green and yellow.'

They all laughed at Dick's description of Minx.

'I'm not really so little!' she said.

'You're not *much* taller than me. Daddy's tallest of everybody and Anne's littlest. I shall be as tall as Daddy when I'm growed up.'

The game started and Richard and Sherry sat back to watch them, Richard smoking his pipe, Sherry with her hands clasped together in her lap.

She was looking at Tony, wondering about him as he played with the children, as he grinned occasionally at Minx; as he threw himself heart and soul into the game as if he were Dick's age.

'I do love him,' she thought. 'I could be happy with him. If Dick were his child – but that isn't fair to Richard. He and Dick and Richard are all rather alike. Dick could have been Tony's son. How pretty Minx is! Will Tony fall in love with her? Oh, Tony, what will happen to us both? You'll go away with her and I shall be left here to live out my life, wishing that it could have been otherwise. I shan't be able to bear it. Tony, Tony – take me with you. If only you could – if only – but it's useless, useless. I married Richard, believing this could never happen to me ever again. If one could turn the clock back – if…'

She was lost in the deep well of her unhappiness, too lost to notice Richard's eyes on her, too far away to hear the quick intake of his breath as he followed the direction of her gaze. His teeth clenched down on his pipe and his knuckles whitened.

'I'm imagining things – it can't be true! Not after last night. She's watching the children.'

But she wasn't. He knew it in his heart and for a moment he felt a wild desire to get up from his chair, smash his fist into Tony's face and throw him out of the house. He hated him bitterly. Jealousy became a knife of torture that was cutting his heart in two. Sherry loved him – she loved Tony, his cousin. That was why she had behaved so strangely, why she had flung herself so desperately into his arms last night.

'Oh, dear God!' he thought. 'How blind I have been – how self-opinionated to think she was beginning to care for *me*. How could she have given herself to me under those conditions – how *could* she?'

He tried to hate her, but he knew it was only an armour against his love – against the pain of truth. His own lack of perception astounded him. Now that he had guessed the truth it seemed so obvious. Her expression was so sad – so hopeless that in an instant, his heart was full of pity for her.

'My poor darling,' he thought. 'What can come of it?'

It was not until that moment that he began to wonder if Tony returned her love. He had been too pre-occupied with his own reactions to Sherry's feelings, he had not stopped to consider Tony's. Did he love her? If he did, why had he brought this dark girl here? To camouflage the truth? No, surely not that. Tony had always been above-board – or, at the least, he was nearly always obvious. How far had all this gone? Was Tony aware that Sherry loved him?

Richard passed a hand across his forehead as if trying to clear his thoughts. In that instant, Sherry turned away from Tony and when Richard looked up, her face had lost its former expression.

'Tired?' she asked him.

'A little!' The words were automatic. Until he knew more of all this, he must not let Sherry realize he had guessed her secret. What a knock-out blow this was – after all his vain hopes and plans. He had stupidly believed that everything was at last working out for them both.

'We must start thinking about holidays soon – somewhere by the sea for the children.'

It was a test remark; it had slipped out in spite of his better feelings.

'Holidays? Oh, summer holidays – yes! I suppose we must.'

So it hadn't occurred to her before. Perhaps she had other plans in mind? Perhaps she was going to leave him? Go back to Africa with Tony? No, it couldn't happen. He could bear anything but her loss. At least, almost anything. He wondered how long he would be able to endure her unhappiness now that he knew of its existence.

'We'll have to have it out,' he thought. 'But not yet. I'd rather she came and told me of her own accord. *If it's true.* Perhaps I was wrong. I've assumed too much from a mere expression on her face.'

Because he wanted so desperately to disbelieve his suspicions, Richard found a hundred reasons why they could have been unfounded. But in spite of himself and his resolve to forget about it, he found himself watching Sherry, watching Tony, looking for further signs that would give them away – and hating himself for spying on them. As the evening wore on, only Minx, the stranger amongst them, seemed to notice his silent, thoughtful air and said in her light, direct way:

'Are you always as quiet as this, Richard, or is it that you just can't get a word in edgeways? I'm often being told I talk too much. I'm afraid it makes for trouble sometimes – saying whatever comes into your head. I must learn to be more reticent.'

'No, don't,' Richard said with a sharpness which caused them all to stare at him. 'It's always better to speak out. Then people know how they stand with you. If it's a fault, then it's a good one. Don't change.'

Sherry thought, 'What's Richard getting at? Is that a dig at me? How unlike him.'

Tony thought, 'He's behaving rather oddly tonight. Wonder what's up!'

Only Minx guessed the truth when she said to herself, 'Now the fat's in the fire. Richard suspects his darling Sherry is in love with Tony and he means to find out!'

'Shall we play another rubber?' she asked in her light, clear voice. 'Tony and I have had all the luck so far.' She smiled mischievously and said, 'Cheer up, Richard. Now's your chance to win it all back.'

No one spoke as Tony deftly dealt another hand.

CHAPTER 11

To Sherry's uneasiness was added new uncertainty when at last Richard announced it was time they turned in; Tony said he wasn't tired and Minx offered to stay up for a little while 'for a chat'. It was not so much jealousy Sherry felt – for the look in Tony's eyes told her that he would have preferred *her* company to that of Minx – as the fact that she was not free to make her own choice. Her place must be beside Richard.

With a quiet good night, she left them standing there, and wondered if she only imagined they saw through her attempt to behave naturally.

In her own bedroom, she gave way to overtaxed emotions and, flinging herself on the bed, cried as if her heart would break.

'It is breaking, *it is!*' she told herself childishly. It was comforting to lie there, sobbing – feeling the misery pour out of her in the flood of tears.

She did not hear Richard come in; did not know he was there in her room until she felt his weight on the bed beside her and felt his hand on her hair.

'Sherry, darling, don't cry! I can bear anything but your tears!'

In her present state of mind, she believed that there might be a second meaning in his words and she swung round to look at him.

'Richard! What did you mean!' The words were wrung from her.

'Exactly what I said, Sherry. Anything would be preferable to your unhappiness. You are very unhappy, aren't you?'

'He has guessed – somehow he knows!' she thought, panic-stricken. She stared at him through her tears.

His next words confirmed her fears.

'It's Tony, isn't it?'

She bit her lip, struggling against the desire to cry again. There was so much gentleness and understanding in Richard's voice – no contempt – no hatred which she deserved.

'You must hate me – now you know,' she whispered. 'I'm so ashamed, Richard – so terribly ashamed.'

He looked down at her distraught face and knew that his love was big enough to bear anything – anything for her sake.

'Won't you tell me, Sherry, all about it?'

'There's nothing to tell, Richard,' she said miserably in a broken little voice. 'At least – not much. It just happened – that's all. I didn't believe it *could* happen to me again. I thought that kind of love was part of my past. I never realized it could come again.'

'And Tony?'

Sherry looked at him helplessly.

'He's in love with me, too. That's what makes it so much harder to bear. He wants to marry me, Richard. I can't make him understand that I'm not free.'

For a long moment, Richard said nothing. Then:

'You could be, if you wanted it that way, Sherry. I wouldn't hold you to a bargain that I see now ought never to have been made.'

'But, Richard, we made it, rightly or wrongly. I wouldn't back out of it, now.'

For a moment, her loyalty eased the pain in his heart.

'Sherry, our bargain did not place either of us under any obligation to love the other.'

'But we married, Richard. Nothing can change that fact.'

'Except divorce.'

'Richard, you're not suggesting–'

'I'm not suggesting anything, my dear,' he broke in. 'I just want to be sure that you understand the position clearly. You are quite free to marry Tony – if that's what you want to do.'

She buried her face in her hands, her mind in a turmoil. That Richard should be taking this so calmly, so unemotionally. It was past her understanding.

As if he read her thoughts, he said gently:

'I love you, Sherry. You know that. But there could be no happiness for me if I thought you were giving up your happiness for *my* sake. At the time of our marriage, we believed we only wanted companionship. The fact that I found myself in love with you wasn't your fault – any more than is the fact that you have fallen in love with Tony. Unfortunately, we chose with our hearts and not with our minds the objects of our affections!'

His voice held a bitterness Sherry was quick to detect.

'Richard, how can you be so understanding – so kind? If only you were hard and–'

'So that you could hate me?'

'Richard, I didn't mean that.'

'But you did, my dear. You would feel so much easier in your conscience about leaving me then. But I can't change myself – even to help you. I can only assure you that consideration for me should not come into your decision as to whether you are going to marry Tony or not.'

'Richard, believe me, until this moment, I never even considered it a possibility. I told Tony it was out of the question from the very first. I meant it. I had no intention of going away with him. Surely you know that?'

'Yes! I do believe you. It's one of the things

I admire about you, Sherry, your strong sense of loyalty. But it mustn't stand between you and your happiness. I want you to feel absolutely free in your mind when you do decide.'

Sherry took a deep, shuddering breath.

'I can't think clearly. This has all gone beyond me. I imagined it was hopeless. Now you've given me hope – and my mind is in a whirl. I'm frightened, Richard – frightened.'

'Love is always rather frightening,' Richard said gently. 'It makes you think that you haven't really known yourself at all – not the real you. It's surprising how much power as well as weakness there is in being in love.'

'It is weakness, not strength. It makes one so selfish. I hate myself so much, Richard. I can't understand why you don't hate me, too.'

'Because, my darling child, none of this is your fault. You would never have willed it to happen. I know you well enough for that. Whatever happens, Sherry, I shall be grateful to you for these few months.'

'Richard, I couldn't go – I just couldn't. Apart from everything else, there are the children – I couldn't leave them.'

Somehow, Richard had momentarily forgotten the children. He had been viewing the whole thing from three points of view: Sherry's, Tony's, his own.

'You know I wouldn't try to keep Anne from you, Sherry.'

'But I couldn't part her from Dick!' Sherry cried. 'They adore each other – and I couldn't leave Dick. I love him, too, Richard. It's no good. I've thought it all out and there's just no use pretending – even to myself. I can't go, Richard. And I don't suppose after all this that you'll want me to stay.'

Richard's face told her how wrong she was.

'This is your home, Sherry – for as long as you want it. I shall always want you here – whatever happens now, or in the future.'

'You deserve someone so much better than I,' Sherry said passionately. 'It isn't fair, Richard.'

He smiled a little at her words.

'Life never does seem fair,' he said. 'But it has a way of turning out for the best. Sherry, are you – quite sure about Tony? I mean, you don't know each other very well, do you.'

'I know it seems crazy, but I am sure – as sure as anyone can be. It just happened, Richard.'

'Sometimes it's hard to distinguish between love and infatuation. Don't think I'm trying to influence you in any way, Sherry, but I must ask this: are you sure Tony's the right person for you – in every way? He's not – well, not exactly your type, is he?'

'I don't know what you mean, Richard. And what is "my type", if it comes to that? As you yourself said, one can't choose the objects of one's affections.'

'Well, I'm not arguing the point. Only I've known Tony a good deal longer than you. He hasn't got a very serious attitude to life.'

'But he's never been in love before – this way!' Sherry defended Tony wildly. 'He wants to marry me, Richard. He's never asked any girl to marry him before – never wanted to settle down.'

'No, I know that's true. I'm not doubting his sincerity. Or yours! If you are sure – then we must find some way out for you, my dear. I'm certain something could be arranged about the children. Naturally, I would hate to lose Anne, just as you would hate to lose Dick. Maybe it wouldn't be necessary. They could both stay here with me while you're abroad – and when you come home on leaves, they could go and stay with you.'

'But, Richard, who'd look after them?'

'I could get another housekeeper,' Richard said, and, seeing her expression, he smiled. 'The kind I meant to get – fat and homely. You could choose someone suitable yourself. Children are fickle little beasts. They'd miss you for a while and then get used to anyone who loved them and looked after them decently. Look how quickly Dick grew used to being without his mother, and he worshipped her.'

'But I couldn't bear it if they forgot me!'

Richard looked at her pitying.

'You'd have to make that choice, Sherry – not as far as Anne is concerned, because if you wanted her to, she could go with you – much as I should hate to lose her.'

'But I couldn't leave Dick either – nor could I separate them.'

'If you love Tony enough, you could do without the children! In any case, I doubt if the climate in the part of Africa where Tony lives is very suitable for children.'

Sherry looked at him helplessly.

'I couldn't leave them – I just couldn't!'

Richard bit his lip. He wanted to make things easier for her so that she could judge the whole affair clearly and calmly, but the situation wasn't an easy one to solve. Sherry was very maternal. She adored the children – and her sense of duty was very strong. He took hope from the fact that anyway as yet, her love for Tony was not sufficient to sweep her off her feet – exclude her mind to all else.

It might after all be only a passing infatuation from which she would in time recover – especially if they were not torn apart before she could see for herself that it might not be a lasting affair. And Richard couldn't believe that it *would* last. He felt it strongly now. It was too unlikely a match, too sudden to be based on reality. Sherry was domesticated, maternal, home-loving. Tony was none of these things. He liked a gay, varied and haphazard existence, uncomplicated by ties of any kind. Of course, he might change. Sherry might change him. Richard could remember saying those very words to Sherry, that the right woman might make Tony settle down. *Was Sherry the right woman?* Certainly she had the necessary strength of character, firmness of purpose; and her influence was all for the good. But would Tony be all that *she* needed – both husband and child, as well as lover?

'She doesn't really know him at all,' he thought. 'If she knew him better, she might change her mind.'

But how could that be done as matters now stood? There was a false sense of time for them both here in this house – it was impossible for them to be alone, even if he, Richard, were not around to act as a break to their natural behaviour. Their emotions were constantly being fanned into a blaze by the very necessity to deny their feelings. Richard was psychologist enough to know that it is so often the way that people must want the one thing that seems unattainable.

'Sherry, I have a plan. I think it is a good

one. The best thing for everyone. Why don't you go to town for a week or two – with Tony. You could put up at some hotel or with Susan and see Tony every day – all day – really get to know him. The children can go to my parents. Mother has been asking for some time if Dick could go and stay, and she wants to meet Anne, too. Dick always enjoys a short time there. A change of air would do them both good. Come to think of it, I might go with them. I can get up and down from Sussex every day, just as I do from here. We'll close up this house for a little while. You can forget all about it – or should I say, find out if you can forget.'

'But Richard–' She broke off, unable to find an argument against his idea. Two weeks in London – to see Tony every day, to find out the truth about herself; to discover if she had the courage to break away and start a new life for good – with Tony. And Richard was making it possible for her – Richard who of all people should be considering *her* wishes at a time when she was contemplating ruining his life.

'I just don't deserve your kindness,' she said weakly. 'Why *are* you so good to me, Richard? I don't understand.'

'My dear, I love you!' The words were wrung from him against his will. He wanted so much not to add pity to her feelings for him. If she stayed with him, came back to him, it must be of her own free will and not for his sake. He could no longer expect that she might one day love him, but he might still hope that they would grow closer as the years went by.

'I can't go, Richard. It wouldn't be fair to you.'

'It would be the fairest thing you could do for me,' Richard argued. 'If you let Tony go now, you will always regret it, and I shall know you are thinking of "what might have been", however hard you try to conceal it. I'm staking my future on the fact that two weeks with Tony might change your mind about wanting to marry him. If you discover that for yourself, then there is still hope for me – for us both. So, you see, it's as much for my own sake that I am suggesting you go.'

'May I think about it, Richard? Let you know tomorrow? It's all so unexpected. So much has happened that it all seems to be beyond me tonight.'

'You're tired, Sherry. Try to get some sleep. Don't think about it any more now. And don't worry. It'll all work out somehow or other!'

She had never felt nearer to loving him than she did at that moment, when he was trying to set her free. By his very kindness he had strengthened the bond between them.

'Thank you for – for everything, Richard,' she whispered.

He smiled at her from the doorway.

'Good night, Sherry. Sleep well, my dear.'

Then he was gone.

CHAPTER 12

'I've brought your breakfast up for a treat.'

Susan smiled down at her friend and waited with the tray until Sherry was sitting up in bed and able to take it on her hunched knees.

'Susan, you are a dear! Whatever is the time?'

'Only nine, but I thought you'd like to be woken – there's a letter from Richard. At least, it's a Sussex postmark, so I presume it's from him.'

Sherry held out her hand eagerly.

'Yes! There'll be news about the children.'

'I'll leave you to it,' Susan said, but Sherry caught her hand.

'No, please stay, Susan.'

While Sherry read her letter, Susan watched her friend's face. Sherry was without make-up and yet she was very beautiful with the flush of sleep still rosy on her cheeks. She showed little physical signs of tiredness and looked far better than when she had arrived only three days ago. Since then she had been out most of the day and until late at night with Tony. There seemed to be nothing they had not done together, lunches, dinner-dances, night-clubs, theatres, concerts, matinées – a continual round of gaiety.

It was obvious to Susan that Sherry was madly in love with Tony. She radiated happiness which only disappeared when she paused the hectic round of gaiety long enough to remember Richard and the children. She worried about them with a deep and very real concern – particularly the children.

Sherry had confided in Susan that Anne had departed by car with Richard and Dick without a trace of tears or misgivings; but that she had been afraid that once night-time came – Anne had never been parted from her mother before at night – the child would fret. It was only Richard's promise to telephone her immediately in such an event, that Sherry had finally agreed to their going to his mother for two weeks while she came to stay in Susan's little flat once again.

'It'll finish the Tony affair for good if the children are moping,' Susan thought and knew a sudden wish that it should turn out this way. She had liked Richard from the first meeting with him and felt instinctively that he and Sherry were ideally suited. Their wedding had been a great personal thrill of satisfaction for her. The astounding news that Sherry had fallen in love – not with Richard but with his cousin – had seriously shaken her views. She had imagined that inevitably, Sherry would fall as much in love with Richard as he was in love with her.

Susan had not met Tony until three days ago when he brought Sherry up from the country in a hired car. She had been undecided in her views about him then and was still undecided now. That he had a great deal of boyish charm was indisputable, that he was gay and amusing and obviously very attached to Sherry was also indisputable. But somehow she could not rid herself of the feeling that he was unreliable. It was purely an instinctive feeling as she knew little about him – except what Sherry had told her – and naturally such confidences had been very much biased in his favour. He had made himself very charming to her, Susan; and Gerald, who was at the flat one evening when Tony called for Sherry, had thought him 'quite a nice chap'. But still Susan couldn't understand why Sherry should fall so madly in love with him that she was considering throwing up her home, Richard, the children – everything, to go back to Africa with him – a man she hardly knew.

She had said as much to Sherry.

'But that's why I have come up for this fortnight – to get to know Tony better. Don't you realize, Susan, that I'm terribly serious about him? I haven't felt like this about anyone – since Bob. It's the same hopeless, helpless feeling as if everything inside me were out of control. I'm in love, Susan.'

Of course, there was that to it – Tony's resemblance to Bob, Susan told herself. The two men were unalike physically, but they were the same 'type' – happy-go-lucky, boyish, charming; maybe it was this resemblance that was causing her to question whether Tony were not also as unreliable as Bob had turned out to be.

'Oh, Susan!' Sherry's cry broke into the other girl's reverie. She looked at Sherry in concern.

'Something wrong? Anne missing you?' she asked, seeing Sherry's face sad and woebegone.

'No! They aren't missing me at all – either of them. There's a pony down there and apparently the children are so delighted with it that they don't want to come home. Richard was down there with them until yesterday and says he left them as happy as ever and, apart from asking for me once, Anne hasn't mentioned my name. Oh, Susan–'

Susan laughed.

'My dear old thing, you really are impossible! You worry yourself sick in case they do miss you and when they don't, you're nearly in tears! What a girl!'

'But, Susan – my own daughter! I know she loves me.'

'Who said she didn't? Children are like that, Sherry, darling. They're independent by nature – like puppies. As soon as they can tumble, they crawl off in the opposite direction to their mothers. As long as young things are fed, warm and loved, they don't need much more to keep them happy.'

'That's what Richard said,' Sherry cried bitterly. 'I know I'm being selfish – but my own child, Susan. It seems awful.'

'Nevertheless, Sherry dear, it may turn out the best thing in the circumstances. After all, if you mean to go with Tony, you'll have to leave Anne behind. It wouldn't be fair to split the children up and you told me yourself that the climate isn't suitable for them, even if you did want to take Anne away from Dick and her home.'

A tear slid down Sherry's cheek and splashed on to the toast.

'I know I'm being silly! Don't take any notice of me.'

Susan put an arm around Sherry's shoulders.

'You're being over-emotional. It's all this love – plays the devil, doesn't it! Never mind, no doubt Tony will be here shortly to cheer you up.'

'Susan, life is terribly hard, isn't it? Why can't I have Tony *and* the children?'

'Maybe you'd like Richard, too?'

Sherry flushed.

'That was unkind, Susan. You know I hate the idea of hurting him.'

'Yes, I suppose you do. After all, he's been

very good to you – too good.'

'What does that mean?'

Susan raised her eyebrows thoughtfully.

'Only that if he hadn't been quite so kind all along the line, you might have felt differently. Some women like to do the chasing. I think you must be one of them.'

'That's horrible, Susan. I'm not like that at all.'

'It isn't horrible – it's nature. You can't help your feelings. I dare say if Richard hadn't fallen in love with you first and had seemed quite disinterested in you, you'd have been head over heels in love with him by now, and then you wouldn't be in this predicament. Sherry – what *are* you going to do?'

'About Tony? Honestly, I don't know, Susan. I love him – that's the only thing that seems to make sense these days. Every moment I am with him I know I can't be happy without him. But without him, I wonder if I can ever be really happy with him. If only I hadn't got a conscience–'

'About Richard? I don't see why you should have. If you really love Tony, you'll never be able to make Richard happy. He deserves far more than second best. It would be kinder to leave him now than to stay and make his whole life unhappy. He'd probably get over you in time and marry again.'

Sherry was silent and thoughtful. Watching her, Susan knew that her practical and matter-of-fact summing up of the position had not made her friend particularly happy. But she herself felt it was high time Sherry stopped being over-romantic and started to look at her life practically. The trouble with people of Sherry's temperament was that, sensible in everyday life, they went haywire when they fell in love.

For herself, the position was reversed. A scatter-brain most of the time, she only became logical, thoughtful and sensible with Gerald.

'Gosh, I'm meeting Gerald in half-an-hour,' she said. 'I'll have to rush, Sherry. You'll be all right?'

'Of course!' Sherry said, smiling at Susan with a reassurance she was far from feeling. 'Tony's calling for me at eleven. See you tonight, Susan. We're going to dine and dance somewhere so I'll be back to change.'

After Susan had gone, Sherry put down the untouched breakfast tray and picked up Richard's letter to read a second time.

My dear Sherry, he had written,

I know you will be worrying about the children even although I have not had occasion to telephone and our arrangement was 'no news good news'. This is just to reassure you that they are both well and perfectly happy. We arrived about tea-time on Saturday, and Mother had a huge meal waiting for them, with all kinds of special 'treats'. Anne took to her at once and Dick excelled himself 'looking after her' as you told him to – very proud of the commission, too. She did ask where you were at bedtime on Saturday but since then and until I left last night, there was no further sign of her missing you. (I know you will realize that I'm being cruelly truthful only to be kindly reassuring.)

Please remember me to Susan and Gerald. I hope they are well. Also to Miss Rogers if you see her.

Mary has been taking care of the house and of me since your departure and is her usual self.

Mother has promised to phone me news of the children tomorrow when I will write again. I presume that I am not likely to find you in during the evenings to telephone you, but you can always reach me here after ten should you wish to get in touch with me verbally.

I hope the days are passing happily for you, and that things are beginning to sort themselves out in your own mind. You know that I want your happiness more than anything, and you must feel quite free to determine where it lies. I am well and meeting some friends at my club this evening, so will be late home. I gave Mary the evening off.

Honey is fine – missing the children, I think. I may take her down next week-end when I visit the children again.

Yours, with, as you know, my love,

Richard

It was not a love-letter – far from it, and yet the last line brought a pang to Sherry's heart. If only Richard did not love her; if only she could rid herself of this feeling of guilt. How happy she could be with Tony. These last days with him had been three of the happiest days of her life. Tony was a wonderful dancer and it was heaven to be moving round a dance-floor in his arms, hearing his whispered words of love and feeling that almost-forgotten emotion answering from her own heart that she loved him, too. Every second of time was precious and they wasted none of it. They were the last couple to leave the night-clubs and when Tony took her home in a taxi, it was nearly dawn. Lying back in his arms, careless of the driver's eyes and ears, Tony had held her close against him and kissed her again and again until it seemed as if they could not bear the separation of their bodies.

But much as they longed for a complete union each knew that it was impossible. Richard trusted them both and neither would abuse that trust. He had given them this fortnight together and even if in the end it meant his losing Sherry, they would not hurt him now, however unbearable restraint might be.

'You'll come with me, Sherry? Marry me?

I couldn't live without you now. I love you, darling. I love you!'

How sweet his words sounded to her as she had clung to him, how passionately and fatally she longed to give way to her heart and tell him, 'Yes, yes, yes!' again and again. But she would not say it until she was sure – completely and absolutely sure – that she would leave Richard and marry him. And she wasn't sure – not yet.

Not long after she had had a solitary tea, Minx, to her intense surprise, found herself opening the door of her flat to Richard. His visit was not only unexpected, but inopportune in view of the fact that she had been crying her eyes out and had had barely a minute in which to dab her nose with a powder-puff.

Richard, however, seemed oblivious to her appearance as he made his apologies for turning up uninvited.

'I felt I had to see you – something on my mind I wanted to discuss – please say if it's inconvenient. I can easily come another time.'

'Please come in. I'm delighted to have some company. Make yourself comfortable and I'll get you a drink.'

She escaped to her room and quickly repaired the last traces of tears. When she returned to her sitting-room, Richard was calmer and his face, lined and distraught a few moments ago, was relaxed. He smiled at her.

'There's something very masculine about you,' he said impulsively, and seeing her raised eyebrows, added: 'That was meant for a compliment. I wasn't speaking of your looks, but of your way of making a chap feel at ease and knowing just what he most needs at a given moment.'

'That's the secret of my success,' Minx said laughing, as she poured him a whisky and soda. 'Not that it took much feminine – or masculine – intuition to see what you needed. A moment or two ago you looked as if the end of the world had come.'

For a few seconds, Richard was silent. Then he said:

'In a way, I suppose it has – for me. I felt like that once before – when my wife died – sort of lost and helpless. I got over it – when I fell in love with Sherry, and realized I had never been in love before. Now I've lost her, and it's far more serious because this time it *is* the real thing.'

Minx lit a cigarette and curled up on the settee opposite her companion.

'You don't know that you've lost her – yet.'

'But I will, and the damnable part about it is that I don't feel I have the right to fight for her. If I were to ask her to stay – even let an idea drop that I felt she ought not to go away with Tony – I could keep her. I have all the weapons, but no right to use them. I persuaded her against her will to marry me and the consequences are my responsibility. I wouldn't feel so bad about it if I could put up a fight for her. It's this feeling of utter helplessness to direct the course of things that is getting me down.'

'You're being very magnanimous, Richard – honourable and decent. But surely there's an old saying: "all's fair in love and war"?'

'In a straight fight, maybe,' Richard said wearily. 'But it isn't a straight fight. Sherry would come back to me if I made one move to persuade her, I don't want her to come from a sense of duty, obligation. It's her love I want.'

'And you feel sure she loves Tony?'

Richard looked surprised.

'Don't you?'

'Don't I love Tony, or don't I feel sure she loves him? As to the latter, I'm not sure. It seems to me more of an "infatuation". That's vastly different from love. I think she and Tony are physically infatuated. That can be pretty dangerous, but it has a way of burning out – of going stale, like fashions.'

'You give me fresh hope. If I could only believe that was true–'

'I didn't mean to raise your hopes unduly. I was merely thinking aloud. I may be quite wrong. All the same, I probably ought not to be discussing the subject at all with you. You see, I'm in love with Tony myself.'

Richard put down his drink and stared at Minx who met his gaze levelly.

'Silly, isn't it? I haven't told the others – it would only add to the complications. Tony would be highly embarrassed. Sherry would feel she ought to step out of the picture and leave me the field; and you – well, you can see that I'm not unbiased. Unlike yourself, I don't care if I have to pick up the pieces. If Sherry were to throw Tony over, I'd step in and do my best to grab what was left. Does that shock you?'

'My dear, it surprises me, but it doesn't shock me. After all, who am I to judge anyone else. I don't understand about love. I don't even understand women. I know they are supposed to feel things more deeply than we males, but I suppose it's all relative. Perhaps I'm too idealistic – or too proud. I wouldn't want to force myself on anyone who wasn't at least willing to love me a little. Perhaps I'm wrong.'

'No! It's just that the circumstances *are* different. I believe once Tony was away from Sherry, he would get over her. His nature is more polygamous than your own. He's more fickle – more wayward – more physical than you are. But you probably know Tony better than I do.'

Richard looked down at his hands,

clenching and unclenching them as he struggled to find words.

'That's one of the things that is worrying me – that Tony isn't good enough for her; that he might not be "right" for her. Tony falls in and out of love so quickly – forgive me, I forgot that you–'

'That I love him?' Minx broke in with a wry smile. 'There are no illusions to my love, Richard. But I'm not worth anything better than a man like Tony. I couldn't live up to – well, your ideals. I'm more like Tony – fickle, shallow.'

'I don't believe that for one instant,' Richard said truthfully.

'You don't know me very well. My past is full of events that would shock you if you knew about them.'

'You keep thinking I will be shocked. Damn it, I'm not a puritan or a quaker. I'm just an ordinary man with an ordinary man's ideas about life – too damned ordinary, I suppose, to attract women the way Tony does.'

Minx laughed out loud.

'But surely you know that women always go for "cads"?'

Richard joined in her laughter and then broke off to say:

'That's the first time for weeks that I've felt like laughing. It is kind of you to have me here – shake me up a bit.'

'Well, have another drink,' Minx said, taking his glass. 'Perhaps we should make an evening of it and try to make Sherry and Tony jealous. Might be rather fun!'

'I wish I thought that would work,' Richard replied. 'But I'm afraid it might look a little obvious. Besides, even if Tony were jealous of you, Sherry wouldn't care what I did.'

'I think she's genuine very fond of you, Richard. I mean that seriously.'

'If Tony hadn't turned up when he did – well, there was one evening when I really believed Sherry was beginning to care a little.'

'What about the children?' Minx asked abruptly. 'Is Sherry's little girl fretting for her?'

'Strangely enough, not at all. Anne adores Dick and as long as he is around, she's quite happy. Dick seems to miss her more, but children are fickle little beasts. I promised him a pony next birthday and that's all he cares about now. I think if I found a nice homely housekeeper, they'd be all right. In a way, I wish they *were* clamouring for Sherry. She'd be back like a shot then.'

'But that isn't what you want – or, at least, those aren't the terms on which you want her back.'

'No, that's true. She must come of her own free will.'

'It's hell – isn't it? Waiting for people to make up their minds.'

'They've four more days,' Richard said. 'In a way, I'm fully prepared for the worst – and yet I go on hoping somewhere deep inside me. Now I shall hope all the more – for your sake.'

'Sherry's a fool to throw you over – if she does!' Minx said flatly. 'You're awfully nice, Richard!'

'I'd rather be a "heel" than nice right now,' Richard said, smiling. 'Look, if you're doing nothing, why don't we go to a show? It'll take our minds off everything and I've nothing to hurry home to. What about it?'

'I'd love to go,' Minx said, 'if you really want to take me.'

'I'd really like to!' Richard smiled. 'Do say you'll come. I don't think I could face another evening like the last one.'

'Nor I!' Minx agreed. 'What about the new Terence Rattigan? Or would you prefer a musical?'

But although the next few hours passed pleasantly enough, Richard still had to go back to his empty house, to his memories – and to his hopes and fears.

'Then you will come with me, Sherry? You'll write to Richard – tonight?'

Sherry lay back against Tony's arm and closed her eyes. Her decision had been made – spoken aloud to the man who had been begging and begging for her answer – and was no longer retrievable. She had agreed to marry Tony as soon as Richard set her free. Was she happy now she had decided? Undoubtedly Tony was pleased – his face radiant. But it was easier for him; he had no one else dependent on his words the way she had. He had no cause to feel guilty because of a broken bargain – because he was breaking away from his child. It was easy for him – and, for a moment, crushed against him, her face and body alight with longing and desire, it had been easy for her. Then suddenly, as Tony released her to ask her to confirm those words in a letter to Richard, her assurance had gone and the old doubts were back.

'Sherry, dearest, tell me you do mean it? You'll come away with me – break with Richard for good. We can fly to Africa tomorrow – start a new life there – together. Oh, darling, darling, darling, I want you so desperately.'

She was in his arms again, his lips pressed against hers, his hands setting her body afire. But the mental abandon of a few moments earlier had gone. Irrelevantly, she was reminded of the night she had spent in Richard's arms – the night she had resolved to put Tony out of her life for always – to become Richard's wife in every sense of the word.

She broke away from Tony and passed her hand wearily across her forehead. How was it she could remember Richard's ardent desperate love-making, her own body's response and mind's misery, at such a moment as this?

'Yes, Tony!' she said feverishly. 'Yes, I'll write to Richard tonight.'

They were alone in Susan's flat, Susan having tactfully gone to the pictures with Gerald. A couple of hours ago, they had dined at a little restaurant nearby meaning to go on somewhere to dance, but both had felt that same anxiety to have things settled between them once and for all. Sherry had suggested they go back to the flat for coffee and Tony had readily agreed.

Back in the sitting-room, with only the fire-light to show them each other's pale anxious face, Tony had taken her in his arms and the helpless, unsatisfactory love-making had begun all over again. Every time Tony made love to her, she had felt more hopelessly lost, more and more out of control. Both had agreed from the first that it would be unfair to take advantage of Richard's trust in them, and, however ardent, however swept away they were, the moment had always come when one or other had broken free so that they could master their emotions again. But their resolves were steadily weakening, until this evening Tony had weakened enough to beg Sherry to make up her mind one way or another.

'I can't go on like this!' he had whispered urgently. 'I want you, Sherry – desperately, painfully. Don't keep me in suspense like this.'

The suspense, the pain and longing had been as much her own and so at last she had said yes, yes, yes, she would marry him – as soon as Richard set her free.

There was nothing now to keep them apart except their own moral scruples and Sherry's strange reluctance to believe that she had taken the final irrevocable step and agreed to leave her husband – to marry the man she loved.

Strange that now, of all times, physical desire was dead. It was as if Tony had suddenly lost the magical power to set her nerves and body alight with love.

'It's only reaction,' she told herself, 'and that I'm tired – so terribly, terribly tired!'

The nervous strain had indeed been acute and had had disturbing effects on her sleep as well as her health. For the last few days she had been feeling tired and dizzy, even sick, with continual tension and excitement. Now, like a burst balloon, she felt empty – a vacuum – incapable of thought or movement.

She lay in Tony's arms, only half hearing

his voice as he made eager plans for the future – 'catch the B.O.A.C. plane from... Stay the night at... The bungalow ... black servants ... trousseau...'

'I won't even have time to say good-bye to Anne,' she thought. 'I suppose that's for the best. If I see her, I couldn't leave her. Richard will keep his word – he'll let me have both the children to stay when we come on leave. But suppose Anne gets ill? And I'm thousands of miles away? Suppose–'

Suddenly, she burst into tears. Tony stared at her aghast.

'Don't take any n-notice,' she wept, trying frantically to get herself under control. 'Just being silly – reaction – be all right tomorrow. You go home now – please, Tony. I want to write that letter.'

He brightened immediately. Women often cried, emotional, sensitive girls like Sherry, and she had been under a strain. There was nothing to worry about. She wanted to get that letter over and the whole thing finished with. There were a lot of things for him to see to – tickets, passports – maybe they couldn't go for a few days yet. Sherry would need a passport and time to get a few clothes. Women always wanted clothes.

'I'll ring you first thing tomorrow morning,' he said. 'Now cheer up, my darling. It's all going to be all right now – you'll see.

Sure you want me to go now?'

'Quite sure!' Sherry said, attempting a smile through her tears.

'Then I think I'll pop round and tell Minx the good news. I must tell someone or die. I'm so thrilled, Sherry. We're going to be so happy. Minx will be glad for us both, I know.'

'Yes, do go and see her,' Sherry said, longing for him to be gone. 'Good-bye, Tony. I'll see you tomorrow.'

After the door closed behind him, she cried unceasingly for half-an-hour and then only stopped because Susan had returned and taken her in hand.

'You're absolutely mad, Sherry – stark, staring crazy! I don't believe you love Tony at all!'

'I do, I *do!*' Sherry argued weakly. 'It's just reaction, Susan – and the thought of leaving Anne – and everything.'

Her voice still trembled and her face was deathly pale, with deep violet shadows beneath her eyes, and a drawn look to her mouth that worried her friend.

'What you want now is a good long sleep,' Susan said, firmly and sensibly. 'Too many late nights, my girl. You look worn out. Shall I run a hot bath for you and make you a cup of tea to have in bed?'

'I don't think I could take either of those things. I feel a bit sick,' Sherry said apologetically. 'I suppose I have been overdoing it. Perhaps I *could* drink a cup of tea. But before I got to bed, I want to write a letter.'

'To Richard? Surely it can wait until the morning?'

'No, I want it to go now – to burn my boats. I can't bear the thought of waking up tomorrow morning and knowing it's still to be done. I've made up my mind. Now I must stick to it. Will you be a dear and post it for me, Susan?'

'I've a jolly good mind not to, but – well, I suppose I will. I still think you're making a mistake, Sherry. It's not that I don't like Tony – I do. But I like Richard a lot better.'

'I know, but it's Tony I'm in love with,' Sherry said wearily. 'I wish it weren't. Don't go for me, Susan – not tonight. I must write that letter – now.'

Susan shrugged her shoulders and went off to make a cup of tea. When she came back, the letter was written – rather to her surprise, for she had expected Sherry to struggle for a long time to find the right words.

'I just told him the facts, that my mind was made up and I was going with Tony – to Africa – tomorrow,' she said, seeing Susan's expression.

'Tomorrow? That's out anyway – not that it makes any difference to the letter. But you certainly won't be fit for a twenty-four-hour plane journey tomorrow, Sherry. You're worn out. Have a day in bed and give yourself time to pick up a little. Like this you'll be no joy to yourself or to Tony.'

'But I want to go now, Susan – at least, tomorrow, I mean.'

'Well, what's the hurry? You've got a lifetime in front of you,' Susan said sensibly. 'Anyway, you won't have a passport, so that settles that. Now off to bed with you or I shall have a really sick woman on my hands. I've put a hot bottle in your bed.'

'Oh, Susan,' Sherry said weakly, tears springing to her eyes again, but Susan refused to be sentimental or allow her friend to be.

'If you're not in bed by the time I come back from the post, then I shan't speak to you again – ever,' she said, and marched out of the room.

She was gone barely ten minutes, but when she returned, Sherry was not only in bed but fast asleep, her hair spread across the pillow, her face now as flushed as it had been pale.

'She's going to be ill,' Susan thought, remembering past occasions when her friend had shown just these signs of prelude to sickness.

But in the morning, Sherry seemed quite all right – pale once more and still shadowed beneath the eyes, but perfectly well.

'I suppose you don't feel like talking things over?' Susan asked as Sherry joined her for breakfast.

'But I do, Susan,' Sherry said quickly. 'You see, I was rather hoping you might sort of act as – well, a proxy parent to Anne. I'd rather not see Richard again – to talk to, I mean. There'll be things to arrange for Anne, her school and clothes and a housekeeper and so on. I hoped you might agree to my dealing with all that through you.'

'Sounds a bit cowardly to me,' Susan said bluntly.

A quick flush spread over Sherry's face.

'I know you don't approve of what I'm doing, Susan, but please don't let it come between us. I need your friendship more than ever. And it isn't cowardice – not really. It just seems best. I mean, Richard probably won't want to see me either.'

Susan softened her tone a little. After all, who was she to judge? And Sherry was not doing anything wrong – that is, morally wrong. It was just that she, Susan, could not help feeling that Sherry was making a ghastly mistake. It would be so awful if, after all this, things did not turn out for the best. Not that there was any way of stopping it now. The letter to Richard had gone and Susan, however much she might wish it, did not herself believe that Sherry would go back on her word now that it was written.

'Will you see Anne before you go?' she asked Sherry.

'I'd rather not. I don't want to upset her and she's too little to understand. If she thought I was going a long way away, she might worry. But if she believes I'm staying here with you, she probably won't think any more about it. Later, if she asks, you can tell her I've gone on holiday and, of course, I'll write to her so she doesn't forget me. If only I can find some really nice woman to go and look after them.'

'You haven't left much time to find anyone,' Susan said a little unkindly.

'Oh, we shan't be leaving for a few days. I shall tell Tony when he rings. We didn't really discuss the details last night. I think in about a week's time at the earliest.'

'That sounds slightly more sensible – more like your usual self. Frankly, I was worried about you last night.'

'You used to say I was too sensible – too controlled,' Sherry replied with a faint smile.

'Well, in a way you were. You certainly went off the deep end last night. You're sure you know what you're doing, Sherry?'

'Quite!' Sherry said with a conviction which did not ring true in her friend's eyes. 'Naturally, this part of it isn't very nice, but everything will be all right once we're out of the country – away from it all. Try not to think too badly of me, Susan.'

'Oh, my dear, I don't think badly of you at all,' Susan said, putting her arm round Sherry's shoulders. 'You're obsessed with this sense of duty – to Richard, Anne, Dick. It's not that that is worrying me – only that you may be throwing away a real lasting happiness for a passing one.'

'You mean, you're convinced Tony isn't the right man for me?'

'I suppose if you want to put it like that – yes! I can't help feeling that Richard is far more your type.'

'But, Susan, it isn't a question of "types". I love Tony. I don't love Richard. You talk about my "obsession" but you have one, too. You always hoped Richard and I would fall in love – right from the first time you visited us there.'

'That's true! But I always liked him, Sherry, and as you know, I'm as fond of you as I would have been of a sister. In fact, if I thought Richard would like the idea, I'd suggest taking on the job as housekeeper-cum-nannie myself. But it would mean Gerald coming, too, of course.'

'Susan – you don't really mean that? Why, that's the most wonderful idea. Oh, if only it could be made to work out like that, I wouldn't worry at all. Anne loves you and so did Dick. And Richard liked you and Gerald. I know he did. Susan, do you mean it. Or were you joking?'

'I wasn't really thinking at all. The words just came out. But I suppose I could do it. If I had a small income and a home, Gerald and I could really afford to get married at last. This flat is far too expensive once I give up my job, and I don't want to keep the job on once we *are* married. I don't know what Gerald would say – even if Richard agreed.'

Sherry's face was alight with tension and excitement.

'Please ring him up – Gerald, I mean – and ask him. If he says "yes", I'll write to Richard this afternoon. Oh, Susan, if only this came off, I think I could go away a happy woman.'

'And I shall get the sack before I'm ready for it if I don't push off now,' Susan said, looking at her watch. 'I'm lunching with Gerald so I'll ask him then. He hates the telephone, and it's hardly the kind of thing to discuss on the phone. I'll ring you afterwards from the office. Now for goodness sake, calm down and take it easy, Sherry. And have a rest after lunch. You look dead tired already and you've only been up half an hour!'

'All right, I will – once you've phoned me,' Sherry promised. 'And thanks, Susan. If you only knew what it meant to me.'

'I know! I'll do what I can,' Susan promised, and grabbing her hat and handbag, she hurried out of the flat.

Sherry was not aware that she had eaten no breakfast. She had two cups of coffee and then cleared away Susan's plates and tidied up the flat. When she had finished these few simple chores, she suddenly found that she was exhausted. Susan was quite right – she had been burning the candle at both ends. And this was no time to get ill. It would postpone their departure to Africa and she now knew an unreasoning haste to be off. It was as if she felt the need to put distance between herself and her indecision as a final barrier.

'Oh, if only I could be sure, absolutely sure, that I have decided to do the right thing,' she thought – not for herself, but for Richard and most of all for Anne – her darling, little baby.

Memories of Anne crowded into her exhausted mind and she sat back wearily in one of the armchairs only to be startled out of it by the telephone. Her mind working on the same lines, she imagined that it was Richard to say Anne was ill, needed her; but it was Tony.

'Oh, it's only you!' she said.

'Well, hardly the way to greet your future husband!' came Tony's voice, gently teasing. 'Who were you expecting?'

'I'm sorry, darling. I'm all on edge. If only we could leave today.'

'Yes, I'd like to be off myself, but as I presume you've realized, we can't get away for a few days. All these blasted formalities.'

'Well, I couldn't leave for a few days myself anyway,' Sherry admitted. 'I'll have to see the children are settled. Tony, I suppose you ought to get in touch with Richard – about solicitors and – and the divorce.'

There was a moment's silence.

'Rather tricky! How unpleasant these formalities are! I'd rather hoped I needn't see Richard. Bit awkward. Old friend as well as my cousin. I suppose I'd imagined we could do it all by letter. Still, I don't want to be a coward about it – might as well face him. He won't make any trouble for us, I'm sure.'

His words irritated her faintly but she did not feel able to reason out why.

'You'll lunch with me, of course, darling?'

'Tony, I think perhaps I won't. I haven't been feeling too well – nerves or something. I thought I might have a day in bed and rest. Would you mind very much?'

'Well, I shall miss you, but if you're not well… What *is* wrong, Sherry? Think you ought to have a doctor? Is Susan there?'

'No, it's nothing at all really – just that I'm tired and I'd be poor company. It's reaction, I suppose.'

'Nothing to worry about now. You leave everything to me. I'll be taking care of you from now on. I'll call round and see you later on – tea-time, shall I?'

'All right, Tony. I'll be rested by then.'

'Love me?'

'Of course, I do.'

But why 'of course', she asked herself as she put down the phone. What *was* love? Bob – Richard – Tony – each had moved her in a different way. It was so absurd of Susan to imagine one could fall in love with the person one was most suited to. No one knew better than she did how admirable a character Richard was – kind, good, honourable, decent, humorous, gentle, and he was attractive enough, too. Why shouldn't he have aroused in her the deep-rooted response she felt in all her senses when Tony kissed her, held her in his arms?

Sherry had barely started this train of thought when the phone bell rang again. This time she felt no premonition as to whom it might be – no forewarning of disaster. There was nothing to prepare her for the shock of Minx's voice – calm, too calm, as she said:

'I've been trying to get you for the last five minutes. It *is* Sherry, isn't it? Minx here.'

'Yes! Tony was on the phone earlier. Anything wrong?'

'Yes, Sherry. I'm afraid there's been an accident. Richard is hurt – he's in hospital. I thought you'd want to know.'

CHAPTER 13

Sherry gripped the receiver and tried to keep her voice as matter of fact as Minx's.

'An accident? What happened? Where is Richard? Did he send for me?'

'No! He was driving home last night – he and I had been to a show and had a meal together. Then he left town about ten o'clock. Half an hour later, I had a telephone call from the hospital at Gerrard's Cross. It so happened I'd left my handbag in Richard's car when he brought me home. It had my ration book in it, and as Richard was unconscious, they thought they'd better telephone me and find out who was his next of kin.'

'Then he'd badly hurt?'

'Some fool drove out of a side-turning into the main road without stopping. The driver got a shock and admitted it was all his fault. Richard's car wasn't much damaged, but there was a lot of broken glass – and he had a blow on the head which knocked him out. When he came to he forbade anyone to tell you what had happened. So I got a private car hire firm to take me down there and when they let me see him, he told *me* I wasn't to tell you either. But – well, this morning, the news isn't too good. He's got splinters of glass in or near the nerves of his eyes. They are going to operate later this morning and I felt you had a right to know – are you there, Sherry?'

'Yes, I'm here. Thank you for letting me know, Minx. *Of course* I'd want to hear about it. How silly of Richard to try and keep it from me. After all, I am his–'

'His wife? Yes! But I think Richard was afraid of this accident affecting your decision about Tony. If things go wrong–'

'Go wrong? Minx, Richard isn't – he isn't going blind?'

'That's what I gathered they are afraid of. The doc. I spoke to wouldn't say so outright but he wouldn't deny his sight might be affected. Depends what they find when they operate.'

Sherry held her breath. Blind! Richard? It didn't seem possible. Of course, she must go to him immediately.

She remembered in that instant the letter – the letter Susan had posted. Richard wouldn't have got it yet – couldn't have got it. If she could get it back in time…

Feverishly, she explained what had happened to Minx.

'You mean, this *will* affect your decision to marry Tony?' Minx asked.

'But, of course, *of course*. How could I

possibly go off with Tony now – at a time like this? He'll understand – wait – till we know how Richard is going to be.'

'*Richard* may not be willing to wait. The way you've decided will be the first thing he'll want to know when he sees you.'

'I'll just say I haven't decided – won't decide till he's well again. But I must get that letter back – quickly.'

'There's no hurry – I should imagine he won't be out of hospital for a few weeks at least. You could go home and destroy the letter any time.'

'Yes, of course, how silly of me. I'd forgotten Richard would be in hospital. Is he comfortable Minx – a nice room? Good doctors?'

'Yes! I saw to all that last night. Well, if you're coming down, there's no need for me to stay. I got a room in a hotel down here. Shall I keep it on for you?'

'Thank you! Minx, if it isn't asking too much, could you stay there till I arrive? I'd like to see you – talk to your first.'

'I rather wanted to talk to you, too. I'll wait for you in the lounge. You'll come by train?'

'No, taxi. It'll be quicker,' Sherry said. 'I'll be down in an hour or so's time.'

Hastily, Sherry scribbled a note for Susan telling her briefly what had happened. She decided not to ring Tony until she heard how Richard was. So much depended on Richard's health now. If there were any permanent damage to his sight, she might have to say good-bye to Tony for always – but they could discuss that later. Meantime she must hurry.

By eleven o'clock, Minx and Sherry were facing each other across the deserted, rather dreary lounge of the hotel. Both girls looked pale and tired, but whereas Minx was perfectly in control of herself, Sherry was not. She felt harried and worried to a degree and her mind darted from one anxious question to another – about the accident, Richard's health, his refusal to see her; Tony, the future, the past, the letter.

For a while, Minx was silent, only answering briefly when she could. Then she leaned forward and looked into Sherry's face, her own puzzled, slightly hard.

'You're treating me as a friend, Sherry. I don't know that I should listen to these confidences. I had hoped we could be friends but it isn't going to work out that way. You see, this – this accident – your decision to come down here – it may make a difference *to me*. I've got to come out with it, so I may as well cease beating about the bush. *I'm in love with Tony, too, Sherry.* I thought I was prepared to sit back and wait for him to carry you off. I would have done nothing about it and there may not be much

I can do now. But I want to try. Tony will be at a loose end for the next few weeks. He'll be pretty lonely and probably a bit hurt that you could leave him twiddling his thumbs while you rush off to the husband you're supposed to be chucking up. I might fill in the gap! You see, I feel it's worth a try. But it makes us enemies, not friends!'

She looked both apologetic and amused.

'I never realised *you* loved Tony. I suppose "all's fair in love and war",' Sherry said after a pause.

'Funny! I only said that to Richard last night – when I told him to fight Tony a little harder. But he didn't agree. He wanted you only if you wanted him. I'm not quite so high-minded. I'll have Tony at any price – if I can get him.'

'I – I never realized. How silly I've been. Yet, in a way, I always *felt* you were a rival. I suppose if I were decent, I'd back out now.'

'That would be silly, Sherry, if you love Tony. I wouldn't if I were in your shoes. I don't suppose you've anything to worry about. Tony is mad about you and no doubt he'll just make use of me until he gets you back. But I must try. I'm sorry – I just wanted you to know what was going on.'

'That – that's sporting of you. I still feel – well, that I'd like to be your friend. You were very decent the other afternoon. I don't understand why you did it – if you love him as much as you say you do.'

'Oh, just an attack of high-mindedness!' Minx said, with an enigmatic smile. 'A touch of you and Richard, I suppose. I wanted Tony's happiness more than my own.'

'What made you change your mind?'

'I haven't changed it – at least, only in what I think will make Tony happy. I don't think you would, now.'

'May I ask why not?'

'Because you'll always be bothered by your conscience. And it's bound to repercuss – on Tony. I think you'd end up hating each other. I felt that as soon as you told me you would come down to Richard – even though Richard didn't want you to come. A lot of women in your shoes would have taken him at his word and pushed off with the other fellow quickly. That's the kind of girl Tony wants – at least, I think so. So there we are. Now hate me as much as you can.'

'But I don't – I mean, I can't – hate you – just because of the things you've been saying. It isn't your fault you love him – and I don't even want to ask you to keep away from him. If Tony can stop loving me just because I have to be away from him for a little while, then he isn't in love with me. It's as well to put it to the test now. And I'm grateful to you for warning me. A lot of women in your shoes, to use your phrase, would not have done so.'

They smiled at one another. Then Minx stood up and held out her hand.

'Perhaps we'll meet again – perhaps not. Anyway, I hope it turns out for the best – for both of us. Good-bye, Sherry. Let me know if there's anything I can do for Richard. I think he's a fine guy – too nice to throw away lightly.'

Then she was gone.

For a moment, Sherry sat watching the small, neat, little figure until Minx had disappeared through the hotel doors. Then, more slowly, she followed. As she waited for the doorman to get her a taxi, she could not help wondering if fate were taking a hand in all their lives – finding the obvious solution to all their problems. At least, she wouldn't fight Minx for Tony. It was in Tony's hands now. She herself would have neither the time nor had she the inclination to fight – she was too worried – and far, far too tired.

When Sherry reached the hospital, she was told that her husband had just left the operating theatre. The ward sister seemed reluctant to let Sherry sit with him until he came out of the anaesthetic.

'He specifically asked us not to get in touch with you,' she said, studying Sherry's face. After all, she told herself, her first duty was to her patient and she didn't want him to have any nasty shocks just as he was coming round.

'It was only because I was on – on holiday and he didn't want to worry me. I'm sure he'll want to see me.'

The sister put her hand on Sherry's arm and said more gently:

'My dear – he won't be able to see anything – at least for some days – until we know how the operation has gone. I'm afraid that is rather a shock to you. Come and sit down for a moment. Didn't your friend, the other young lady, tell you?'

'That his sight might be affected – permanently? Yes, she did. I just felt a little faint for a moment. I'm all right now. Please let me go and sit with my husband. I promise not to speak or let him know I'm there unless he asks for me.'

'Very well, then. One of the nurses will be with him now. It's room 231. Second floor to your left.'

The young nurse answered Sherry's timid knock. Sherry explained that the sister had given her permission to stay in the room in case her husband asked for her and the girl gave her the chair on the far side of Richard's bed. She sat down gratefully and turned to look at the man lying so deadly still beneath the white hospital counterpane. His face was practically entirely obscured by bandages. Only his mouth and nose were visible. It did not seem as if there could be anybody alive beneath that mask of bandages.

'He'll be coming out of the anaesthetic soon,' the nurse said, as if to reassure her. 'He may – well, he may be a little sick. You don't mind?'

'No – I don't mind–' Sherry began and broke off, as Richard began to twist and turn. Presently he moaned and turned his head away towards the nurse, then back again towards Sherry. Although he was not yet fully conscious, it seemed to Sherry that he was already aware of the darkness beneath those bandages – was searching for the light. Pity for him welled into her throat and stayed there a hard lump. She sat rigidly controlling herself, never making a sound or a move, watching in turn the young nurse's competent ministrations, and Richard's twisting body.

'Don't go!' His voice, husky, unlike the voice she remembered, broke the silence, making her jump. She bit her lip fiercely between her teeth. 'Sherry – Sherry–'

'I'm here, Richard – here beside you.'

His bandaged face turned towards her side of the bed. She looked quickly at the nurse who shook her head. He wasn't fully conscious yet.

'I love you – don't you understand? Don't leave me – don't go!'

'Richard, I'm here, darling. Don't worry.

I'm here beside you. I'll stay as long as you want me.'

He was conscious now, her voice and her words reaching his brain.

'Is that Sherry?' he said suddenly. 'I thought I heard her voice. Funny thing, I can't see. God, I'm thirsty!'

The nurse placed a feeding cup to his lips and he drank a little and spoke again.

'Thanks! Funny thing, but I can't see you.' His hands came up slowly from beneath the bed-clothes and wandered to his face – felt the bandages.

'You had a little accident, Mr Hayden. Your face was cut by glass. That's why you're bandaged up and can't see very well. But you're quite all right now. I'm the nurse and your wife is here, too. Try not to talk too much.'

'An accident – yes, of course – seem to remember. Minx – the car – hospital – Sherry – are you really there? I thought I asked–'

'Of course I'm here, Richard,' Sherry broke in, taking one of the long, thin hands in her own. 'And I'm staying here until they throw me out – or you tell me you don't want me here.'

'Don't want you – but of course I do. I didn't want to upset–'

'Richard, darling, don't talk. The nurse says it isn't good for you. Just lie still and sleep. I'll hold your hand, shall I? Then you'll know I'm here beside you.'

'Very tired! Nice of you to come – your hand is so small – and soft!'

Only the rigid control she had imposed on herself and the young nurse's presence kept her from crying. She wanted to desperately. But she would not. She sat perfectly still, holding Richard's hand until the nurse said:

'He's asleep, Mrs Hayden. I must just go and report to Sister. Perhaps I could bring you a cup of tea? You look as if you need it!'

'Yes – yes, I think I do. Thank you, Nurse.'

But Richard was not yet asleep. As soon as the door closed, he said:

'Sherry, are you still there?'

'Oh, Richard, yes, of course. I won't leave you.' She pressed his hand more tightly in her own.

'If only I could–' his voice was almost a whisper. 'I want you to tell me the truth, Sherry. I'm pretty badly hurt, aren't I? My eyes, I mean? I remember when they brought me in, I couldn't see a thing. That's why they sent for you, isn't it?'

'No, it isn't true. They didn't send for me. Minx rang me because she knew I'd want to come whatever you said.'

'I'm glad you did – so nice to hear your voice – seems so long since you left home…' He paused for a moment, then, his hands gripping hers, he went on: 'What you just said, Sherry – about wanting to come – did you mean it? It's true that you would have come anyway?'

'Of course, Richard. Now, please don't talk any more or they will send me away. Try and sleep.'

'You've made me so happy,' Richard murmured. 'Perhaps I can sleep now…' His voice trailed away into silence and his breathing slowed and then deepened. This time, he really was asleep.

Sherry leant back in her chair, relaxing her hold of Richard's hand. Only in that instant did she realize that there had been a misunderstanding of the gravest nature between them. 'I'd have come anyway', she had said, meaning that she would have come, as indeed she had, in spite of the fact that Richard had not asked for her. It now seemed more than probable that Richard had interpreted her reply quite differently – to mean that she was coming back to him anyway, had given up Tony and decided to stay with him and the children.

How could she put the mistake right now? She felt a sudden wild impulse to wake him, to tell him that he was wrong, to leave herself some loophole by which she could escape back to her former plans. But even while her body turned towards his, she knew she would not do it – she could not add a further mental hurt to his grave physical pain, for he must be suffering and would suffer so very much more if the operation were not a success and he were to become blind.

'I can't go now!'

The realization struck her so forcibly that she spoke her thoughts aloud. In a way it was almost a relief to know that there was no choice left – at least, for the time being. Her place was here, beside Richard, helping him to get well, giving him the strength and will to get better – something to look forward to and someone to make life worth while.

'I may never see Tony again. I ought to be horrified at the thought, and yet I feel nothing – nothing at all – except this strange sense of relief. Could it be that I don't really love him? No, that can't be true. Only a few hours ago I promised to marry him; wrote to Richard telling him I had made up my mind to leave him and the children. It seems unbelievable that I could have been so sure I was doing the right thing – or at least following the dictates of my heart. Perhaps *that* is the truth – that my heart tells me to go with Tony and all along my mind has been telling me to stay with Richard. I married Richard; I meant to be as good a wife to him as I could – to make him happy, make the children happy. What could I have been thinking of in throwing away those vows so lightly? Anne – Dick – I shall be with them both again – and Richard. What does this man who is my husband mean to me? Why should I feel so terribly shaken because he is lying here helpless – perhaps even going blind? Is it just pity? Duty? If I could only understand myself once more – if only I were not so tired – so terribly tired…'

When the nurse returned to the room, barely ten minutes after she had left it, it was to find Sherry asleep, her head resting on her arm which lay on the edge of Richard's bed.

She turned to the doctor who was following her into the room and said:

'Shock, I suppose. It takes them this way, sometimes, doesn't it, Doctor?'

'Well, more often than not they have hysterics. Let her sleep. The patient won't wake for an hour or two. Put a pillow beneath her head and make her more comfortable – a rug over her. Poor thing – pretty nasty sort of accident to happen to someone you love.'

'They seem so devoted,' the nurse said sentimentally. 'He didn't want us to send for her because he didn't want to spoil her holiday. We wondered at first if the young lady who came down to see him last night was his "girl-friend" but we did them an injustice. He was obviously thrilled to have his wife here.'

'Well, it may help the patient to get well more quickly, and that's all I'm concerned about,' the doctor said, looking down at the still, bandaged face.

'Do they think the operation was a success, Doctor?' the nurse asked.

The doctor shrugged his shoulders.

'They took out several splinters of glass – some very near the optic nerve. But Mr Merrywill is a wonderful surgeon. It really depends whether there is any damage to the nerve too small for the naked eye to have seen. We'll know when the bandages come off.'

'Shall I tell his wife is she asks?'

'I don't see why not. It's usually best to tell the truth in these cases. But keep it from him as far as possible. She'll probably want to say in the hospital near him, but we haven't any spare rooms. Let her visit him as much as she wants. It'll keep his mind off himself. We don't want him worrying. I'll tell Sister myself.'

'It must be pretty ghastly lying there wondering if you're going blind,' the nurse said, thoughtfully. 'Awful for her, too. He'd be so helpless. Still, he's her husband… Would you like this cup of tea, Doctor? I brought it for her, but it'll be cold by the time she wakes.'

It was nearly two o'clock when Sherry awoke, a little ashamed of herself for having been able to sleep and for feeling ravenously hungry. The kind little nurse persuaded her to go back to her hotel for some lunch, since even if Richard woke there would be some tidying up to do before the surgeon's visit and she could not be with him then, anyway. 'Come back and have tea with him,' she said.

'You will be here – to tell him, I mean, when he wakes? Tell him I'll be here by three-thirty at the latest.'

As soon as she had eaten, Sherry telephoned to Richard's mother who had not as yet been told the news. Waiting for the trunk call to come through, she thought how glad she was that Richard had not yet mentioned her affair with Tony to his mother – merely told her that, she, Sherry, needed a holiday and break from the children for a few weeks as she hadn't been too well. Now there would be no need for her to know the truth – and the children need never know that she had contemplated leaving them – no, decided to leave them.

'It's all over,' she thought suddenly. 'In my heart, I know it's finished. I'm glad – strangely glad. I could never have been happy away from the children. I shall always love Tony, now. If I had gone with him, I might have stopped loving him. I shall have to tell him. If only he understands…'

But Tony could not understand this

sudden change of heart. Nor could she bring herself to tell him outright. When she heard his voice, eager, full of love and with the gay note subdued because he had already heard the news from Minx, she began to doubt herself again. But remembering Richard, lying helpless – perhaps blind – in the hospital, she forced herself to say:

'I shall be staying down here – to be near him, Tony. He needs me rather badly. You do understand, don't you?'

'Well, for how long? After all, darling, we're supposed to be leaving for Africa in a few days. I got your ticket today. Do you want me to postpone it for a week?'

Sherry gripped the receiver more tightly and said:

'Tony, it all depends – I mean, on what happens to Richard. I – I might not be able to come – *ever.*'

For a moment there was silence across the wires. Then Tony said:

'You can't mean that, Sherry! After all, you said last night you were going to leave him. It's not as if you knew he was going blind or anything when you decided. You'd made up your mind before all this happened.'

'But, Tony, he'll need me. You can't expect me to walk out on him now? After all, I am still his wife.'

'That's a matter for debate but we won't go into it now. It seems to me it's all a question of duty with you. I'm beginning to wonder if you're in love with me at all.'

She didn't deny or confirm his suggestion. After a moment, he said:

'Are you still there, Sherry? You haven't answered me.'

'Yes, I'm here. I was just thinking, Tony – about us – *you.* Could *you* take me away now, and feel all right in your mind about it?'

'Well, not for a few days – naturally. But once you know he's going to be all right–'

'Suppose he isn't going to be all right? Suppose he does go blind?'

'Look here, darling, what's the point of considering the worst. The thing to consider is what we're going to do if he is all right. You've not changed your mind about *that,* have you?'

'He doesn't understand,' Sherry thought. 'He expects me to go with him whatever happens. Perhaps I wouldn't hesitate if I was really in love–'

'Sherry? Why don't you say anything? I suppose you've got this duty complex again. Minx said you'd stick by Richard in the end.'

'Perhaps she's right,' Sherry said wearily. 'The only thing I'm sure about is that I can't do anything until he's better – until we know what's going to happen. I'm terribly sorry, Tony. I know it must be annoying for you – the way I've been vacillating. But I don't seem to be able to behave differently. I'm just not the kind of person who can walk out on her husband and home and children without a backward glance.'

'Don't I know it!'

His voice was hurt, angry, even a little hard.

'Would you rather call it off now, so you know where you stand?' Sherry said, helplessly. 'I know I can't expect you to hang around indefinitely.'

'That's hardly the point. I'd be quite willing to wait if I knew for sure that you'd be coming with me – you know that. Dash it all, Sherry, I'm in love with you. You seem to have forgotten that fact.'

'I haven't forgotten, Tony. It's just that all this came as rather a shock and I've been so concerned about Richard that–'

'That you haven't had time to think about *me*. Well, it strikes me that's the way it's been all along. I don't think in your heart of hearts you want to leave him – ever did want to. If I hadn't rushed you off your feet you'd probably be plodding along quite happily with him.'

'Tony – that isn't fair. You know I love you – desperately. Why, last night I wrote to Richard to tell him we were going away together, that my mind was made up. It's just that this accident – well, it's changed everything. Surely you see that?'

'What I don't see is the sense in discussing this over the telephone. I'm coming down to see you – we'll talk it over then.'

'No, Tony, don't do that. I may not be here anyway. I shall probably be at the hospital. Besides, Richard might find out and–'

'Find out what for goodness' sake? He knows we're in love. Look here, Sherry, I know this has been a bit of a shock to you and all that, but I just don't get what you're driving at. You haven't told Richard it's all off, have you?'

Sherry bit her lip, trying to fight back the hysteria that she felt was getting a grip of her.

'No – at least, not exactly. But he presumed it from a remark I made. I hadn't the heart to tell him the truth. Tony, do please try and understand. Don't come down. I'll ring you again – when I know how things are going.'

'I think it's all quite crazy. What am I supposed to do – hang around the flat waiting till you ring up?'

Anger replaced the hysteria. Tony was behaving like a spoilt little boy.

'There's no need to hang around the flat, Tony. If you're out when I ring, I'll try again later.'

'And what am I supposed to do when I go out – twiddle my thumbs on my own?'

'Oh, Tony, don't be so childish. You can

find something to do – take Minx to the pictures, if you like.'

'Perhaps that's a very good idea. Perhaps that'll make you a little jealous. I'm really beginning to wonder if you love me at all. I fail to understand you, Sherry.'

'I'm sorry, Tony,' she said weakly, but she could not weaken and tell him she loved him. At this moment, in my case, she was far from loving him. Had he been sympathetic, understanding, considerate – not only of her but of Richard who was, after all, his friend as well as his cousin – she might have felt differently. He was behaving so like a spoilt little boy that she could only be irritated by him.

'I'll ring you this evening when I come back from the hospital,' she added.

'I may not be back myself, but you can try later, as you suggest,' was Tony's childish reply. 'Depends if Minx wants to go on anywhere.'

'I seem to be on Minx's side!' Sherry told herself as she walked away from the phone-box. 'The very first thing I do is throw them together. She'd think me such a fool. Perhaps I am a fool.'

Yet the old feeling persisted – a strange mixture of relief and certainty in knowing that this time she was taking the right road – at least for the time being – that there was no other choice but to stay at Richard's side.

CHAPTER 14

'I'd made up my mind not to talk about the future but Nurse tells me I'm almost certain to be perfectly okay again once these bandages come off, so I *would* like to talk to you, Sherry, if you don't mind?'

For the first time, Sherry was glad of those bandages, glad that Richard could not see her face. She, too, had been talking – not to the nurse but to the surgeon who had operated this morning and she knew only too well that Richard had only a fifty-fifty chance of being 'perfectly okay' again. The ghastly alternative would be that he would be blind for life.

'Of course not – I mean, please talk about the future if you want to, Richard.'

He gave a short laugh.

'My dear, don't sound so terrified. I'm not going to talk about love – at least, only to say that I know you are very fond of Tony, even though you have found out you don't love him after all. You can't be expected to get over saying good-bye to him all in five minutes. But you chose to come back – *to me* – and I realized when I was thinking about it this afternoon, it could only be because you felt there was something after all for us both – our future together.'

'The future – yes. Yes, it will be all right, Richard!'

'I know it! I feel suddenly so terrifically confident about it. You know I love you – and I know you don't love me, but perhaps that will all come right, too. We started off on the wrong foot, didn't we?'

'I can't stop this conversation now,' Sherry thought wildly. 'I can't go on vacillating any more. This is where I throw in my lot with Richard for good and always. It will come right – if I try, too. I'll forget Tony – make a new start with Richard.'

'We'll start again, Richard!' she said softly. 'Forget the past and just live for the present – and the future.'

'I think – that if we tried to make our marriage real – instead of the rather unreal state of affairs that existed before – we would be happier, both of us. But – especially you. You worry too much about things, Sherry. You search always for the ideal rather than for the realities of life. I was thinking, wondering – oh, if only I could see your face, I'd know so much better if I was going to say the wrong thing – I must ask you. Sherry, do you think it would help us to come together if – if we – had a child – one that belonged to us both, I mean?'

His words were so totally unexpected that, for a moment, she scarcely took in what he had said. Her mind swung suddenly to a faint only half-realized concern that something might already have happened. She had supposed vaguely that the nervous tension and emotional upset of these last few weeks had accounted for an unusual irregularity; had put her unusual physical tiredness down to late nights and worry. Now, suddenly, she wondered if these could be the first signs, so similar to the way Anne had started, of pregnancy. There was only one occasion on which such a thing could have occurred – the night she had belonged to Richard – believing by doing so she could forget Tony. Since then, she had been so taken up with other concerns that she had never stopped to consider the possible consequences of that fatal night. Now, aghast, she realized that not only was there a possibility, but taking the time factor into consideration, it was even more than likely that she was to have a baby.

A child – Richard's child! Suppose it were true and she had left Richard – gone to Africa with Tony – what an appalling muddle would have ensued.

'Oh, no, no!' she whispered, unaware that she spoke aloud.

'I'm sorry, my dear. Of course the idea is abhorrent to you. Forgive me!'

The pain and unhappiness in Richard's voice was too much for Sherry to bear on top of all her other worries. The ready tears (perhaps another sign of pregnancy) welled into her eyes and splashed down her cheeks – on to the hand that Richard had placed over hers.

'I've made you cry,' he said wretchedly. 'Sherry, I– Oh, God! I'm such a blundering fool. I love you too much.'

'Richard, you're wrong. Believe me, that's not why I'm crying. I'm just – just tired – and nervy. The shock of finding you here – and saying good-bye to Tony – everything. It has nothing to do with what you – you suggested. The idea – isn't at all abhorrent to me – I – it – perhaps it would be a good thing – I feel…'

But she couldn't go on; she couldn't tell him yet about her suspicion that she might already be carrying his child. She would have to be sure first – not to disappoint him.

'I'm so unworthy of your love,' she whispered. 'You spoke of ideals just now, Richard. Don't idealize me. I'm just an ordinary person – an ordinary woman. You are the unusual one. I've only just realized it.'

His kindness, his unselfishness and consideration for others – they were simple enough virtues but so few people possessed them.

'Sherry, I feel so damned helpless lying

here. I can only imagine how beautiful you look with those large eyes of yours wet with tears.'

'Then it's just as well you can't be disillusioned,' Sherry said, smiling a little for the first time. 'My nose is probably shiny and my hair is all over the place and I know I must look a sight. I think I ought to go back to the hotel, before you start running a temperature. Nurse said you mustn't talk too much.'

'Don't go, please! Stay a little longer. You talk and I'll just listen. You have such a beautiful voice. Did you know that Dick said that to me once. "Mummy's got such a lovely voice, hasn't she?" he said. "It's all hummy-dummy." I think he meant by that that it was melodious and at the same time the soft, sweet voice that bees and mothers have when they're busy.'

Sherry realized with surprise that, for the first time for many months, she was actually relaxed – almost contented. Listening to Richard's slow, deep voice, saying such nice, simple things was restful, curiously soothing after the tempestuous gaiety of Tony's presence. His enormous vitality, his eagerness and enthusiasm, the strain of their attraction for one another and the unsatisfying disturbing kisses had frayed her nerves.

'Was Tony very cut up about you coming back to me?'

Once again, it seemed as if Richard had been sensing the trend of her thoughts. It was so like him to consider Tony, who had shown so little consideration for him.

'To be honest about it, Richard, I think Tony still hopes I'll go away with him. I – I've yet to convince him that – well, that it's all over.'

'And you've no doubts yourself, Sherry? *You're quite sure?*'

She hesitated for a split second. She wanted so much to be honest with him, to be able to tell him the exact truth – about her letter to him, her uncertainty about the future, his blindness, her own feelings. But how could one say to a man, 'I don't know if it is pity or love. I'm not sure if my feelings for Tony were real or only a physical infatuation. I'm confused. I may even be having a baby – your baby.'

No, these were things she couldn't tell him while he was lying there ill or at least seriously hurt. He believed she had given Tony up – had taken it for granted that she had discovered she didn't love his cousin after all. She must let him continue in that belief. For if she failed him now, he would be too proud to accept her help if the worst happened and he were to go blind. He would be so dependent, and far too proud to ask for help from her unless he was sure in his own heart that she cared for him even if she could not love him.

'I'm as sure as I can be, Richard!' she answered his question, thinking, 'As sure as I can be that I'm doing what is right – what is best and fairest for everyone. Tony's pride is hurt, but I don't think he'll grieve for me for long, the way Richard would.'

It seemed strange to compare the love these two dissimilar men had for her, strange to find that the balance weighed heavily in Richard's favour. Supposing she had been in Richard's shoes, lying here hurt, fearing never to see the light again, it would be to Richard she would turn for help and comfort, not to Tony. She had never thought of it that way before. In fact, she had never consciously compared the two men; she had taken Richard for granted and allowed Tony to sweep her off her feet.

'You're very quiet, Sherry. Of what are you thinking? I find it such a nuisance not being able to see your face.'

'Is my face such a mirror for my thoughts?'

'Usually,' Richard said. 'I used to see a little frown on your forehead when you were worried, a smile at the corner of your lips when the children had been good or amusing and you were happy, and sometimes there was a far-away look in your eyes, but I could never decide the meaning of it. Is that how you look now?'

'No, I'm frowning because I'm worried – about you. You really ought not to be talking.'

'But I'm not ill, Sherry. I feel perfectly well – only a little sore where I was cut about, and headachey. In fact, if they'd only take off these beastly bandages, I think I could quite well be at home. I wish we were at home, Sherry – with the children – just the four of us together. The doctor wouldn't give me a date when I can leave here. I asked him this afternoon. I can't understand why he won't. After all, it can't be more than ten days before the scars heal. But he refused to commit himself. I suppose they wouldn't tell you either?'

'I – I didn't think to ask,' Sherry lied quickly. 'I was only concerned with now – I mean, that you were well enough for me to see you again.'

'Well, see if you can get anything out of the powers that be tomorrow. I hate hospitals, and I've a great longing to be home now that I know you'll be coming with me. Sherry, I'm so happy! You've no idea how full of life and energy I feel – because of you! I promised not to talk of love, but I just can't help telling you what you mean to me. When I thought I'd lost you – to Tony – life ceased to seem worth while. I couldn't tell you because I wanted you to feel free to go. I knew I had no right to try and persuade you to stay. There was Dick, of course, and Anne, to live for, but oddly enough, they didn't really count. Nothing else mattered but you. Why, I felt so desperate yesterday evening, I even went to see Minx.'

'I – I gathered as much. She told me she had left her handbag in your car and that was how they got in touch with her after your accident. Richard, did – did Minx tell you that she was in love with Tony?'

'As a matter of fact, she did. I suppose those two will come together now – at least, that would be the ideal solution. Or am I being rather tactless?'

Sherry bit her lip.

'No! It's just that – well, it's not very flattering to one's pride to think Tony will get over me so easily! But I expect you're right. Minx is very attractive – and nice, too. I've always liked her.'

'So have I! Though I never found her particularly attractive – I was too preoccupied with you! There just wasn't room for anyone else.'

'Richard, please don't say things like that. I'm so unworthy of your love. You mustn't idealize me–'

'I'll try not to,' Richard said, soberly. 'You must tell me if I become a nuisance, Sherry. Too much talk of love must become boring, I know, especially as you can't feel the same for me. No, don't deny it. I know you aren't in love with me. I've never dared hope that would happen before. Now I'm beginning to hope.'

'And perhaps I'm beginning to love you at last!' Sherry thought suddenly. It wasn't the kind of love that had existed between her and Tony – an all-absorbing physical passion. What she felt for Richard was a deep fondness and respect; a mature and deeper form of love. She felt again that strange peace and contentment just to be here listening to him, talking as thoughts came into their heads. They had always enjoyed each other's companionship in those early days together. What had spoilt their former intimacy? Was it her fear of letting him down? Of feeling that she could not return the love he had so suddenly declared for her? It had made her awkward, constrained, anxious all the time not to give him any encouragement. She had been afraid, too, although she did not realize it until now, afraid of the natural desires of her body which had answered the demands of his even against her will. Had she foreseen even then that she was going to fall in love with someone else? Was this the reason she had been afraid to give Richard encouragement, hope? Now that Tony had gone out of her life, she knew there would be no other man in it but Richard – and the fear was suddenly gone.

Tony – out of her life! How quickly she had accepted this fact when only twenty-four hours ago she had been wildly planning to go to Africa with him! What had killed those dreams so utterly and permanently? If she were to see Tony again, would he still have the same power over her? Or would the thought of Richard come between them as an impassable barrier?

Well, there was no need now to put herself to the test. She would refuse to see Tony – ever again; forget what had been between them and be thankful that it had not been more. If she were indeed carrying Richard's child, then she could have no doubts as to where her life lay. How glad, thankful, relieved she was that she and Tony had controlled their more passionate moments. It meant that she had never really ceased to be Richard's wife.

For a moment, Sherry could not resist the desire to probe into her heart. Suppose this had been Tony's child! What would Tony have said? Would he have been glad? Somehow, she could not imagine that he would be pleased. It was their honeymoon which he counted above all else. How often he had talked of the time they could be alone together, free from any moral restrictions! 'When you are my wife,' he had often said – but never, 'When we have our own family…' Something he might so easily have said to ease her unhappiness at the thought of leaving Anne. No, Tony was not a 'family' man. He could be husband, lover, but she could not see him as a father.

'And I love children,' she thought. 'I have always wanted a large happy family. Tony and I had nothing in common but the desires of our bodies...'

She drew in her breath as she accepted what she knew now to be the truth about her affair with Tony. It had indeed been nothing more than infatuation. Susan had suspected as much all along. She had had to repress her natural instincts since Bob's death, and Tony had come into her life at a critical moment when Richard had re-awakened her mind to thoughts of love, marriage, sex. Had she never met Tony, she might already be living a normal life as Richard's wife. It had been the thought of *having* to love Richard that had prevented her from doing so. By setting her free to go to Tony if she willed, Richard had broken that barrier down. Now she was freed of that obligation, love might come.

It did not occur to Sherry that she was under an even greater obligation – to remain with Richard because he needed her more than ever before. This chain did not restrict her – as had the emotional chain of their strange marriage.

She turned once more to Richard; and her

face broke into a smile of tenderness, for while she had been lost in self-reflection, he had fallen asleep.

'Tell him I'll come first thing in the morning,' she said to the nurse she met outside the door. 'I'm going back to my hotel now.'

She managed to eat a large dinner, wondering not unhappily about her suspected pregnancy, and then went to telephone Tony. In spite of his warning, she had not really expected to find him out. Her face sobered a little as the phone rang its steady burr-burr. Was he dining somewhere with Minx? she wondered a little jealously, then shrugged her shoulders and went to have coffee in the lounge. It was better this way. It was not her nature to wish him to be unhappy. Nevertheless, she had not expected him to turn to someone else quite so quickly, and her pride was hurt. She reminded herself that she had not yet told Tony her final and irrevocable decision to stay with Richard – whatever happened. Surely Tony could have waited until then to turn elsewhere for comfort? This morning when she had spoken to him, she had believed there might still be hope for them. Now *she knew* that it was over – all over; that she could not bring herself to hurt Richard again, nor gather sufficient courage to contemplate parting with the children, even if she still wanted to marry Tony.

'I ought to feel that my life is over, without Tony,' she told herself, drinking coffee alone in the half-empty lounge. 'Yet I don't! I believe there is a future, a happy one for Richard and myself. I feel placid instead of heart-broken. Perhaps that, too, is merely a sign of pregnancy! How thrilled Richard will be if it's true! I must ring Tony again in an hour and then I shall go to bed.'

But an hour later, there was still no reply from Tony's hotel and Sherry went to bed without speaking to him. For the first time in weeks, she slept soundly without dreaming for ten hours. Waking to the bright sunlight of a new day, it seemed as if the past were behind her and she were on the brink of a new life.

'Let's take a bottle of whisky back to your flat and drink it there,' Tony said to Minx, his face flushed and his voice slurred, as he leant across the table where they had been dining.

Minx bit her lip and her hands clenched beneath the table-cloth.

'Don't you think we've had enough to drink, Tony? I suggest we go to that all night Lyon's and have something to eat. I'm starving!' Her voice was unnaturally gay and bright and did not convince him.

'Oh, for heaven's sake, don't you go

prudish on me, Minx! I know you think I'm drunk. Well, maybe I am – but so would you be if you were in my shoes. It isn't fair!'

She smiled a little at the childish petulance of his remark and tone of voice.

'Perhaps I am in your shoes – in a way. After all, I'm suffering from unrequited love just as much as you are.'

'Don't be so silly! Just who are you in love with all of a sudden?'

'You!' she said lightly.

He stared at her, trying to make up his mind if she was teasing him.

'Rot!' he said at last. 'Shince when, I might ask!'

'Practically since we met – or since that night we had together.'

He shook his head as if to clear it.

'You're not sherious are you? I mean, dash it all, Minx, what an odd time to tell a fellow. You're joking!'

'I'm not, Tony! But don't take it seriously. I'm not going to let myself go to pieces the way you're doing about Sherry. I don't think anyone is worth it and I'm surprised you're taking such a gloomy view.'

'You know as well as I do that she's pushed off for good. I've got to drown my sorrows somehow. Let's have another one – drown both our sorrows!'

'Well, you'll have to drown mine for me. I'm going to that Lyon's to get some breakfast. It's 2 a.m., my boy, and I'm hungry.'

'You can't leave me here on my own – 'tisn't fair. 'Sides, you shaid you loved me!'

'So I do!' Minx laughed. 'But I love my stomach, too, and I want something to eat. Why don't you keep me company? You needn't eat anything.'

'Oh, all right, if you musht! Going to give up women – blasted nuisance, if you ask me. Go back to 'frica by myshelf. Sherry won't come with me. Know it now.'

'Well *I'll* come with you!' Minx said, as she beckoned to the hovering waiter.

'Don't want to marry you – want to marry Sherry!'

'I know,' Minx said calmly. 'You needn't marry me. We'll just have fun together.'

'Not a bad idea – have fun! Not much fun with Sherry – always brooding and worrying – too many – sc – scru – scruples – that's the word – shoopals. No fun at all.'

The waiter put the bill in front of him and he paid it automatically and allowed Minx to guide him out of the club and into a taxi. She gave the driver her own address and they settled back in the seat.

'Thought we were going to Lyons!' Tony said sleepily.

'I changed my mind. A lady's privilege! I'll get something to eat in my flat – and some nice black coffee.'

'Don't want coffee – want whisky!' Tony

said, the cold air making him even more tight than he had been.

Minx felt his arm go around her and he slumped against her. She held herself rigid. She longed to hit him, so wild was she with him for behaving in this way. Yet at the same time, she longed to put her arms around him and pet and comfort him.

'I'm crazy!' she told herself. 'Crazy to love a guy like this! He's weak and unreliable – everything a husband shouldn't be – yet I want him – and I'm going to get him. Sherry ought to thank me for this. Richard is the better man, and she'll find out one day.'

She wondered what Sherry would think of Tony if she could see him as he was a few minutes later, practically incapable of walking as with the driver, she helped him into the lift and up to her flat. She tipped the driver well and, closing the door behind him, pushed Tony into her bedroom, thankful that her girl-friend was still away.

'Shleepy!' Tony said. And, before she had covered him over with one of the blankets, he was out for the count.

Minx made herself coffee and, taking her own pillow and some blankets from the second bed, made up a bed for herself on the settee in the sitting-room. She had a hot bath and went back into the bedroom to take a last look at Tony.

His face looked childlike and innocent in

sleep. The fair hair was curling over his forehead and his cheeks were flushed, the lashes lying long and dark against them.

'He's drugged with whisky,' she told herself sharply, as a reminder, but somehow it did nothing to ease the rush of tenderness that had welled up inside her at the sight of him. 'I'm a fool to love him!' she whispered aloud, but even as she spoke the words, she knelt on the floor and laid her head against his hand.

'Oh, Tony!' she cried. 'Forget her! Please forget her. Love me as I love you. We'll be happy. I'll make you happy. I swear I will. I can be strong for both of us. She needed someone to take care of her, but I can take care of you.'

She wept a little for Tony, for Sherry, but most of all for herself. Not because she felt her quest was hopeless. Tony's affections were, unlike Richard's, not very deep-rooted. He would turn to her in time. The sadness lay in the knowledge that he might as easily turn away from her when some other woman set her cap at him. She could never hope for an all-absorbing lifetime of love from Tony. He was a good-time boy – as she had pretended to herself and her acquaintances that she was a good-time girl. But it wasn't true. In her heart she had longed to love and be loved, to find that all-powerful emotional bond between two human beings one read about in books; which she knew existed in her own heart, but would never exist in Tony's for her or any woman.

But her moment of weakness did not last long. With a little sigh, she stood up, kissed Tony lightly on the forehead, and went back to the sitting-room to her improvised bed. She lay for a long time, smoking and watching the stars until they disappeared and the first bright touch of dawn lit the sky. Then only did she find comfort in sleep.

CHAPTER 15

Sherry's first waking thought was for Richard's health. Everything else seemed to have receded but her concern for his sight. She knew it would be a week before the bandages were taken off and that there was no possible reason for rushing round to the hospital in the hope of gaining fresh information. Yet she felt a need for haste, for urgency.

She ate her breakfast hurriedly and was round at the hospital before half-past nine. An unwelcome surprise awaited her. The young nurse who had attended Richard during the day, stopped her in the passage outside Richard's room.

'I'm sorry, Mrs Hayden – but your husband can't see you this morning,' she said, not meeting Sherry's eyes.

'He's not worse? What's wrong, Nurse?'

'It's just that – well, he isn't feeling quite so well. He said he'd rather not see you. He's resting.'

Somehow, the words did not ring quite true. Sherry bit her lip.

'I'm afraid I don't understand, Nurse. You can speak openly to me you know. Please tell me the truth.'

'I'm sorry, Mrs Hayden, really I am. I don't understand it altogether either. He just told me to tell you he didn't want to see you, and I wasn't to let you in.'

'But for what reason? Did he give a reason? What has made him feel like this? Last night–'

The little nurse looked unhappy. She broke in:

'It seems there was a letter that upset him. He was so pleased when I gave it to him – said it was from you; and wasn't it a nice surprise! Then he opened it and – well, since then he hasn't spoken a word, except to tell me not to let you visit him.'

'I see!' Sherry said, her heart sinking with a dreadful anxiety. A letter from her! It could only mean that somehow or other, by some ghastly mischance, Richard had got the letter she had sent to his home. Oh, if only she had gone home yesterday and burnt it. Who could have sent it to him?

'I must see him, I must!' she told the nurse desperately. 'There's been a misunderstanding but I can put it right. You don't want him worried for nothing, do you? I'm sure the doctor would say it was all right for me to go in.'

The nurse looked doubtful. Then she weakened.

'He ought not to be upset. But I suppose

it's all right. Only, if he seems upset, please don't stay too long.'

'I won't! It'll be all straightened out as soon as I can explain. Just give me five minutes alone with him!'

She sounded so desperate, so distraught, that the nurse wondered if she had done the right thing in permitting Mrs Hayden to see her husband. They had seemed so happy yesterday. Before she had handed over to the night nurse, her patient had actually told her he was 'the happiest man alive', in spite of his accident.

'Let's hope Mrs Hayden can put it right,' she thought, 'whatever it is that has gone wrong!'

Sherry opened Richard's door and closed it quickly behind her. He was lying on his pillow, his face turned away from her. When she remained silent, he said:

'What is it, Nurse? I'm not sleeping.'

'Richard, it's Sherry. I had to see you. I couldn't believe you mean what you said to the nurse – that you didn't want me to come.'

'I did mean it. I'd be grateful if you'd go now.'

His voice was cold and rigidly controlled. He still had not turned towards her.

She took a few steps towards him and put her hand on his shoulder. He stiffened beneath her touch and fear rose up in her again.

'Richard, whatever it is, surely you are not going to let it come between us – now, of all times?'

He turned then, his white bandaged face turned unseeingly towards her.

'Now, because I'm lying here ill, you mean?' His voice was tense with bitterness. 'I don't see that *the time* has anything to do with it.'

'Richard, don't – please don't talk like that. Let's discuss this thing like two human beings. Let's be perfectly honest with one another.'

'Well, suppose you start. I think it's a very good idea if you start telling the truth for a change.'

Her hand went to her mouth. Richard – so gentle, so understanding – speaking in that tone to her!

'Richard, I've never willingly or consciously lied to you.'

'Haven't you? I'm afraid you're lying now, my dear. You see, I had a letter from you this morning – a letter telling me you were going away with Tony. For a moment, I thought "She's changed her mind again" – then I asked Nurse the date and realized you had written it before you came down here – before my accident.'

'That's true, Richard, but I was going to destroy that letter. Since I've been here – yesterday – I decided not to go with Tony after all. It's all over between us. I don't love him. I swear it.'

'I've no desire to be the object of your pity nor the reason for your self-sacrifice. Now please go, Sherry.'

She sat down weakly in the chair beside him.

'Richard, please!' she said desperately. 'Try and understand. It has nothing to do with your accident. After all, why should it? I mean, you'll be perfectly well in a few days.'

'Will I? How are you so sure? It so happens I overheard the doctor and sister discussing me in the corridor. Blindness seems to accentuate one's hearing abilities. I am under the impression that I stand a fairly even chance of going blind. Don't pretend that you didn't know that all along. They would have told *you* – and that's why you thought you should stay with me. No, thank you kindly, Sherry. I don't want you on those terms.'

'Richard, I'm going to be perfectly frank with you – we must get this sorted out. I'll admit that I knew what – what might happen. I'll admit that it might have been a sense of duty, pity – call it what you want – that brought me down here yesterday, in the first instance. But since then, it has been something else. I swear it, Richard. It happened gradually yesterday – a knowledge that I didn't want to go with Tony after all – that I was *glad* this had happened so that I could stay with you.'

'You expect me to believe that? How does it sound to you, Sherry? On Monday you are so much in love with Tony you are prepared to go away with him – divorce me – the children, and fly to Africa with him. On Tuesday, you've not only fallen out of love with him, but in love with me. Don't belittle my intelligence as well as my pride, Sherry. I'm not a complete fool.'

'Richard, it isn't like that – it hasn't happened like that. It isn't even falling in and out of love the way you put it. It's just a feeling – a kind of knowing what I ought to do after days of uncertainty.'

'You were always worried about "what you ought to do", Sherry. But I'm not willing to let you do what you think is your duty this time.'

'I didn't mean that. Richard, why do you persist in misunderstanding, misinterpreting my meaning? You always used to be so perceptive. Can't you see, hear, that this time I'm sincere when I say it has *nothing to do with the possibility that you might go blind.* I swear it hasn't and I'm more certain of that than of anything else I've said so far. Besides, it may not happen – and I still want to stay with you.'

'Naturally you say that now.'

'Because it's the truth, Richard. I was going to ring Tony to tell him last night but I couldn't get him on the phone. I would have rung this morning, but I was so anxious to see you I rushed straight round here, and never gave Tony a thought. Don't you believe me?'

For a moment, silence lay heavy between them. Then, in a quiet, controlled voice, Richard said:

'I'm sorry, I don't believe you. It doesn't add up, Sherry. You weren't in love with me before, and you aren't now – you admitted as much in so many words. You say you don't want to go with Tony. Well, I'll tell you why – because you're worried about leaving me to face this alone. It isn't good enough, I'm afraid. You see, your concern, while being very flattering and all that, isn't born of affection, and I've already said I don't wish to detain you on any other terms. I couldn't put it more plainly.'

Sherry was growing every moment more desperate. She had thought she could convince him, if not easily at least after explaining a little while. Far from being able to do so, the misunderstanding seemed to grow bigger with every word she said.

'Richard, how did you get that letter?'

'Does it matter? Mary forwarded it, if you want to know. I made them send her a telegram when I was brought in here, explaining what had happened. Unfortunate, wasn't it? Or perhaps fortunate. Nobody can be happy living in a fool's paradise.'

'Please don't be so bitter. I know you've no reason to trust me. I so nearly let you down before. *But please try and believe that I'm no longer in love with Tony.* I knew that I couldn't be when I found it so easy to cancel all our plans the moment I knew you needed me.'

The wrong words again! She knew it as soon as that fatal word 'needed' broke from her lips.

'It seems to me you don't understand yourself as well as I understand you, Sherry. Can't you see that your sense of duty is at war with your heart? First one gains the upper hand, then the other. If I had never forced you to marry me and you had met Tony as my housekeeper, you'd be his wife now.'

'But you didn't force me to marry you,' Sherry argued wildly. 'I married you of my own free will. I *wanted* to marry you.'

'Until you met Tony – then you realized the mistake you had made. You cannot expect me to believe you were merely flirting with Tony, Sherry, or that the flirtation should have ended at so very convenient a moment. You are not a flirt and if you were honest with yourself, you would admit that you fell in love with him.'

'But that's just it, Richard. *I only thought I did.* It was a mistake – I see that now. I discovered the truth yesterday. Richard, be fair to me. Give me a chance. You know how confused I've been all along – how full of doubts about leaving you. If I had really been in love with Tony, I wouldn't have had those doubts.'

'Of course you would have had them, Sherry, with your loyal temperament. Now please let us stop this discussion. It is a very painful one for me. I don't wish to seem ungrateful for your – your efforts on my behalf. But at least try to see that I couldn't tolerate the position as it is. I do believe that you are only trying to do your best, but the kindest thing you can do is to go away – now – for a long time. As soon as it is possible, I'll arrange for you to divorce me and then you can marry Tony. Don't deny that this is what you really want in your heart, for I wouldn't believe you. Do me the last service, Sherry, of leaving me my pride.'

Tears were pouring down her cheeks but Richard could not see them – nor see the utter misery expressed in her face. She knew it would be useless to try and convince him when he was so certain in his own mind of the reason for her giving Tony up. But she could not bring herself to go. She had not found it easy to leave him before, when there was so little to lose and, as she imagined, her whole life and Tony's love to gain. Now, when she knew that she did not love Tony, when Richard needed her, when she had discovered the first sweet signs of love for *him* in her heart, leaving him was an impossibility.

'I can't go – I can't!' she whispered. 'Don't send me away, Richard. It's such a waste – just when I am beginning to care as you always hoped I would.'

'Don't – don't torture me!' The cry was wrung from him and his hands clenched tightly on the bed-clothes.

'I don't mean to – but I can't go, Richard, I can't!'

Beads of sweat broke out on his forehead and she knew, seeing them, that this emotional scene was terribly bad for him. Whatever her own feelings, she must consider his health before anything. Perhaps, after all, she should go – at least, for an hour or two – come back when he was rested.

'Richard, if I go now, will you promise to let me come back – this afternoon?'

'What would be the use, Sherry? You cannot alter my mind!'

'But perhaps I can think of some way to convince you that you are wrong, Richard. Give me that chance. I *cannot* go unless you promise.'

'Very well, then. But it can't do any good.'

After she had left, he lay back against the pillows, fighting the weakness that was both physical and mental. He had felt the strain of that scene telling on his vitality and his head throbbed wildly. Not only this, but Sherry's tearful voice, her pleadings had almost weakened his resolve to send her away. Temptation to accept what she offered him was desperately strong. It was true that he had never needed her more than he did now – never longed so much to believe that she did care. At the same time, he had never been so completely certain that she was sacrificing herself for him. If only he could bring himself to accept what she said – even while he knew it wasn't true! But he would not hold her through pity – nor through any sense of loyalty – no matter how desperate his plight.

Blindness! That had been a big enough shock without a second one to follow it. Yesterday he had been so happy – so utterly content. He had felt confidence in the future and had been blissfully ignorant of the seriousness of his accident. Now he knew that his sight might have been affected by the accident and he was tormented with fears – with a horror of this total blackness continuing for ever. Never to see Sherry's face again, nor Dick's; never to see anything – but he would not think about it. It might not happen and there would be time enough to worry when they told him it was a fact. It was so silly to torment oneself with, please God, unnecessary fears.

But the shock of Sherry's letter – nothing could undo that blow. *She had meant to go – to leave him – to marry Tony.* She must have loved Tony to have come to that decision. Girls like Sherry did not fall in and out of love easily. How well he knew it! It was past belief that she could change her heart overnight – as she had told him. He did not understand women very well, but he could not fathom such a possibility. As to the fact that she was beginning to care for *him* – well, that was equally unbelievable. No! It all pointed to the fact that she had been told he might go blind – and had wanted to stand by him – to make up to him for this tragedy.

'If only I need not see her again!' he thought. 'She can't know what it's like – how much strength I need to send her away. I must find some way of showing her I mean what I say – of making her hate me instead of feeling sorry for me. Perhaps if I were to tell her that Minx and I – but that wouldn't be fair to Minx. I must think of something else before she comes back. There must be some way I can show her it's all over – all over– Oh, Sherry, my darling child – over, when I had thought it had just begun!'

Lying on her bed in the hotel room,

Sherry had the self-same words on her lips.

'It can't end like this – just as it had begun to come right.' She thought. 'Oh, how mad, stupid, blind I have been. Susan was right. She always said that Richard should not have shown me that he loved me. I was frightened by his love – thinking I could not return it. Tony was a way of escape. He attracted me and I believed I loved him. I don't – I don't. It wouldn't worry me if I never saw him again! He isn't worth a hair of Richard's head. Oh, Richard, Richard, forgive me – give me another chance. Please God, help me to think of some way to convince him.'

As if in direct answer to her prayer, a sudden fit of nausea shook her. It was the first time she had felt ill – and, as she lay there fighting against it, she realized what it meant. She was having a baby – Richard's child. This was her salvation. He would not send her away when he knew about it. He would have to believe then that it was finished between Tony and herself. Even if he felt the baby was responsible for her return to him, at least it would stop him thinking it was because she pitied him. In time, she would convince him by her actions, her behaviour, that she cared for him – deeply; that she loved him. It was true after all, that she loved him.

'Yes, yes, yes!' she cried silently. 'I'm glad

about the baby – glad that it is *Richard's* child. I could not be glad if I didn't care. Oh, Richard, don't you see? I've loved you all along, but I've been too blind to see it.'

The nausea had passed and she knew that she was hungry again. She hugged the thought to her. Every sign of pregnancy would now thrill her. Feverishly, she thought back again to the night it must have happened – counted days, weeks and reassured herself that everything pointed to the confirmation of her suspicions.

The telephone beside her bed shrilled suddenly. She picked it up and heard the operator saying: 'You're through now'; then Tony's voice, rather taciturn – even angry:

'That you, Sherry? I've been trying to get you all morning!'

'I've been at the hospital, Tony,' Sherry said. 'I did ring you twice last night, but you weren't in.'

'I was on the binge with Minx – got pretty tight, I'm afraid. Look here, Sherry, I must see you. Things can't go on like this.'

'I know! that's why I wanted to speak to you, Tony. I think it would be better if we didn't meet. You see, it is all over. I know it must sound pretty casual to you – and sudden – but I shall never leave Richard now.'

There was a moment's silence before Tony said:

'You don't mean he *is* going blind?'

She bit her lip.

'No, it still isn't certain one way or the other. But it won't make any difference – between you and me. I've decided to stay with him, Tony. I ought never to have imagined otherwise.'

'Look here, Sherry, I don't understand this at all. What's made you change so suddenly? I know you weren't any too happy about leaving your husband and the children, but you said you loved me enough to do that. You do still love me, don't you?'

'Tony, I don't know how to answer you. I – I thought I did. Now I realize that I didn't – at least, that what was between us wasn't love – real love. I'm terribly sorry if I've hurt you. I've behaved abominably to everyone – but I'm trying to put things right now. Try and forgive me.'

There was another pause before Tony spoke.

'I think it sounds crazy!' he said petulantly. 'I would hardly have thought you were just flirting with me.'

'I wasn't, Tony. That's not fair. I *thought* I loved you. It was very real – while it lasted. It's just over, that's all. I can't feel the same any more.'

'So this is the brush-off?'

'Tony, don't put it like that, please! I know I've hurt you and I'm desperately sorry. But you'll get over it. I'm sure you will. I think you'll be glad – later. We wouldn't have been happy.'

'At least you could have given it a chance!' Tony said. 'You really mean this, Sherry? You've changed your mind pretty often over this affair, you know.'

'I really mean it, Tony. There is another reason, too, beside the one I've told you, but I can't speak of it now – on the phone. I'll write to you. You'll see then, why even if I hadn't changed my mind, you would have changed yours.'

'I don't get it,' Tony said. 'But I suppose you know what you're doing. This is all a bit of a shock. Dash it all. I'm in love with you, Sherry. I suppose you realize you've ruined my life?'

The words were so petulant, so dramatic and childish that, in spite of the gravity of the situation, Sherry smiled. She was glad Tony could not see her.

'Tony, don't take it too badly. I hope one day we can be friends. Just forget all about me – and don't think too badly of me.'

'Hang it all, I don't think badly of you, Sherry. I'm just damned hurt about it. You won't even give me a chance to get you back. Why can't I see you? I'm sure we could straighten things out again. What has happened to make you change your mind if it isn't this accident of Richard's?'

'Tony, it was the accident – in a way. At least, it showed me I was on the wrong track. I'd see you, Tony, if it would make any difference – but it can't. This time I really know what I'm doing – what I want. I know it sounds terribly selfish – everything the way I want it – but I'm equally sure that it's best for you, too. Try to believe that.'

'Well, what's this other thing that's going to make me change my mind? It's all so damned mysterious!'

'I can't say now. I'm not even certain about it, but I'll write, Tony, tonight. You'll get the letter tomorrow. Be patient till then, please!'

'I haven't much alternative,' Tony said. 'Oh, well, it just shows how wrong one can be, I suppose. Minx only said last night that you'd stick to Richard in the end. I swore you wouldn't. Seems she knows you better than I do. And I thought I understood women!'

There wasn't much more she could say – and nothing she could do except write and tell him she thought she was going to have a baby. It seemed as if he had already turned to Minx for company in her absence. She recalled suddenly that it had happened before – the last time she had sent him away. Knowing Minx's intentions towards Tony, it seemed more than likely that she would be only to willing to make up to him for any hurt she, Sherry, had caused him.

'Don't be unhappy, Tony!' she said, before she rang off. But deep in her heart, she didn't think that he would grieve for her long.

While she was in the phone box, she telephoned to Susan.

'I know you'll be glad about part of my news anyway,' she said to her friend, as she gave her details of the last twenty-four hours. 'All the same, I'm terribly worried about Richard. The doctors won't commit themselves until the bandages come off. It's such a ghastly possibility, Susan. Richard – blind.'

'Let's hope for the best, Sherry, dear. At least, he'll be comforted by your presence.'

'I'm afraid he's not at the moment,' Sherry said. 'The letter I wrote that night – the one you posted – was forwarded to him at the hospital. Since then, he's had a bee in his bonnet about my coming back to him because I felt sorry for him. I spent over an hour this morning trying to convince him it isn't that – and it isn't, Susan. I love him – I've only just discovered it. It sounds absurd, I know, but when I realized he was trying to send me back to Tony, I knew I didn't want to go – couldn't leave him.'

'I'm not in the least surprised,' Susan said calmly. 'I always suspected there was something pretty big between you two – but you were all wound up the wrong way and couldn't see the wood for the trees! You'll talk him round, I'm sure. He'll want to believe you.'

'I'm hoping to convince him this evening, Susan. I think I may be going to have a baby – Richard's – and I know he'll be thrilled. It'll all come right when I tell him and I'm practically certain.'

Susan's voice was warm and thrilled.

'I'm so glad, Sherry, dear – and now I think about it, even that news doesn't surprise me a great deal – you've been pretty seedy this last week, looking deathly tired and always bursting into tears! I thought it was the emotional upheaval, but it was probably the baby after all.'

'I do hope so!' Sherry cried. 'I can't be sure for another two weeks, but I felt sick this afternoon – not the usual kind of bilious attack – the real thing. You know, Susan, it horrifies me to think that I might actually have flown to Africa with Tony and not discovered anything about the baby until we were there.'

'Well, don't worry about what hasn't happened. Go and settle things with your Richard, and give him my love. Gerald and I will visit him if he's stuck there for long and would like to see us. We always liked him.'

It was with renewed hope and confidence

that Sherry made her way back to the hospital. This time, there was no nurse waiting in the passage to prevent her seeing Richard. He was obviously expecting her for, as she opened the door, he said:

'Is that you, Sherry? These blasted bandages. I find myself guessing my visitors by their footsteps.'

She sat down by his bed and resolved to talk as sensibly and unemotionally as she could.

'Richard, I do hope you've thought better of sending me away from you. I want you to know that it's all over between Tony and myself. I spoke to him on the phone about an hour ago and it's finished – quite finished. Please believe that I want to stay now – not only for your sake, but for my own.'

He steeled himself against the appeal of her voice and his own desperate longing to believe her.

'I'm afraid I can't change my mind, Sherry. I'm sorry. I know you mean to be kind – but it's useless to go over it again. I'm sorry you brought matters to a head with Tony, but I've no doubt the damage can be repaired.'

'You're still convinced that I – I'm only doing my duty?'

'Briefly, yes!'

So now she would tell him. She would

have preferred to convince him some other way, but she had no alternative now.

'Then perhaps you'll believe that my motives are not so unselfish when I tell you this – Richard, I'm practically certain that I'm going to have a baby!'

For one swift moment, hope sprang to his heart, but it was followed immediately by disbelief. It couldn't be – it was too much of a coincidence. There had only been that one occasion when it could have happened and – no, it wasn't really possible. She had made this up as a last effort to talk him round. She hadn't even been able to say it was definite. She had left herself a loop-hole for later – when she would be forced to tell him it wasn't true. If she only realized how much he longed with all his heart to believe all she had told him was the truth – but it wasn't – it wasn't – and he must find some way to put an end to this torturous business of forcing her to leave him – some way...

He clenched his teeth and bit hard on his lower lip – there was a way – *a way to make her hate him.*

'A baby?' he said, his tone carefully casual, faintly derisive. 'Whose baby, Sherry? Mine – or Tony's?'

CHAPTER 16

'How could he? How *could* he say such a thing!' Sherry wept. 'Susan, how could he?'

'I'm sure he couldn't have meant it,' Susan said comfortingly. Since Sherry had arrived in the flat an hour ago, she had not stopped crying and Susan was worried – not only about her health, but about this new misunderstanding, for she could not believe it to be more than that. It sounded so unlike Richard to say such a thing. It had been with difficulty that she had wormed the whole story from Sherry.

'He did mean it! He went further than that – he said he could hardly suppose that it was his child and could only assume that it was Tony's.'

'Well, surely you could convince him that it couldn't have been?'

Sherry raised her tear-wet face to Susan's. 'I tried, Susan – I tried. I ought to have had more pride than to argue about such a thing. I couldn't believe he meant it at first. I said that if it *had* been Tony's baby, what reason had I for coming back to *him*.'

'Well, that was reasonable enough. What was his reaction to that?'

Sherry buried her face in her hands and said in a shamed, muffled voice.

'He said that Tony wasn't the paternal type – that no doubt he in turn was wondering if it was his, Richard's, child, and that Tony probably hoped to get me off his hands!'

She broke into a fresh bout of weeping and Susan looked at her in concern. Her face was deathly white with two brilliant spots of colour on her cheeks. Her eyes were red-rimmed and swollen with crying and were deeply shadowed with violet. That Sherry, so controlled and sensible, should give way like this, indeed indicated that something was wrong. It was a pretty safe bet that she was pregnant, Susan thought wryly – and this hysteria wouldn't be doing her any good.'

'Into bed with you, my girl,' she said firmly. 'We'll talk about it in the morning.'

'Susan, no, I couldn't sleep! How can you expect me to?'

'You will – and you must. I'll send for the doctor if you don't promise me at least to go to bed and lie down. I'll bring you a hot drink.'

'I couldn't sleep,' Sherry argued weakly.

'Then I'll come and talk to you – we'll try and sort it out. I'm certain you're worrying unnecessarily. If there's nothing else I'm sure about in the ghastly muddle, I *am* sure Richard loves you. Now run along to bed,

Sherry, dear, please!'

Tucked up in bed, with a hot drink and Susan sitting beside her, Sherry felt calmer and her voice was more normal as she said:

'It was so awful, Susan, the tone of voice he used. It was hard and bitter and as hurtful as it could be. It didn't sound like Richard at all. I know I've behaved pretty badly to him – hurt him. But he trusted me with Tony because he knew he *could* trust me – and we never once allowed things to go too far. It wouldn't have occurred to me to be unfaithful to Richard. He must have known that or else why did he pretty well throw us into each other's arms?'

Susan reached for a cigarette, but she had scarcely taken a few puffs before Sherry's face went white and she said apologetically:

'I'm terribly sorry, Susan, but the smell of smoke makes me feel ill. I suppose that's conclusive proof – I felt that way with Anne, and I haven't wanted a cigarette myself all day!'

Susan stubbed out the cigarette with a smile.

'So that's that! What a thing to happen at a time like this!'

'I was so thrilled and happy about it this morning,' Sherry said miserably. 'I thought Richard would be glad, too. It never occurred to me he'd–'

'Now, don't let's start all that again,' Susan

said firmly, seeing the tears come back to Sherry's eyes. 'Let's try and think *why* he should have said those things. Do you think he could have believed them himself?'

'I don't know,' Sherry replied wearily. 'He sounded completely convinced. There's no way to prove him wrong – not until the baby is born and looks like him. Besides, I wouldn't degrade myself trying to prove such a thing. It's insulting – in spite of anything I might have done to hurt him.'

'I suppose if Richard believed you loved Tony enough to agree to go away with him, that you might well have considered yourself free to do as you wished.'

'But I wouldn't do such a thing – not unless Tony and I were married. Even if I had wanted to, I'd have waited until then. Susan, I almost hated Richard when I finally got up and walked out of the room. I kept thinking that he knew about Anne – knew I wasn't married to Bob, however much I believed myself to be Bob's wife, and that he was trying to make out the same thing was happening again.'

'You mean that because you had had one illegitimate child, you might well be having another? No, Richard isn't like that. He's not vindictive and he loves you, Sherry. You know he does.'

'I only know that he did love me. He couldn't be in love with me now and have said those awful things. It's all over, Susan – I know it. I found out how much he meant to me too late.'

'My dear old thing, I refuse to believe it is too late. You must remember that love and hate are very close. Once this wretched affair is straightened out, and he sees how much you care, then he'll love you again. You must believe that.'

'I shall never see him again,' Sherry said hopelessly. 'I never want to see him again, Susan. I couldn't face him – listen to anyone in the world – even Richard – saying such things to me again. I humbled myself to him – pleaded with him – even argued with him about something that should never have been mentioned. I won't do it again – ever! You couldn't expect me to, Susan.'

'No,' thought her friend, 'I couldn't expect it of Sherry, so upright and proud and self-sufficient.' Richard had gone too far. Whatever had he hoped to gain by such words? Or perhaps *he had meant to lose her* – put an end once and for all to their strange marriage. If so, he had certainly gone the right way about it. Sherry was distraught and hysterical and desperately miserable at the moment, but when she calmed down and became her normal self, she would close her heart to Richard – stamp out the new love that had begun to grow there. Is this what he had meant to do? And for what reason? Because his love for her had turned to hate? Or because he believed he was going incurably blind and must break the last tie between them?

'I'll go and see him,' she said aloud, seeing a glimmer of hope left.

'No, I forbid you to do so,' Sherry cried wildly. 'I will not have you pleading for me, Susan. I hate him – I hate him.'

But the angry avowal gave way to a flood of tears, and Susan knew that as yet Sherry was far from hating the man it had taken her so long to learn to love.

'Sherry, my dearest girl, don't be so silly! I have no intention of pleading for you, as you put it. I merely want to find out what was behind all this. After all, there are other factors to be considered – the children, Dick and Anne, I mean. What is to happen to them now? Will Richard still want to keep Anne with him? Are you willing to leave her with him? I presume you have no intention of going back to Tony?'

'No, no, never! It's all over!' Sherry said without a moment's hesitation.

'Then what is to happen? Are you going to divorce Richard? Let him divorce you? Will you each take back your own child and start a new life apart?'

'But we couldn't part the children from each other. They're devoted!' Sherry cried.

'Well, that will all have to be discussed,

won't it? And if you won't see Richard, someone must. I promise not to bring up any personal matters unless Richard does. If he should ask me if you love him, I presume I may tell him that you do?'

Sherry leaned back against the pillow, her tears dried and a feeling of acute fatigue numbing her brain.

'I don't know! I can't think. Oh, Susan, what a blind, silly little fool I've been. I've thought only of myself – and I've hurt Richard, Tony, perhaps even Minx indirectly. She loves Tony.'

'Well, don't start worrying about her. From what I hear of her she's quite well able to take care of herself – and Tony, too!'

'All the same, if it hadn't been for me, she and Tony might have made a go of it from the beginning.'

'He'll get over it, Sherry. Men of his type don't take long in finding consolation elsewhere – and Minx is very nicely to hand.'

'You never liked Tony, did you?' Sherry said curiously.

'I didn't dislike him. I merely felt he wasn't the right type for you. You're the serious intellectual, homely type, Sherry. I suppose opposites invariably do attract one another, but I do think that married couples should at least have some common interests. As far as I could see, you and Tony had none – unless you count a fondness for dancing!'

'It – it was a – a physical attraction,' Sherry admitted. 'I've never analysed it before but I think it had something to do with Bob. Tony's the same type. I suppose I believed I would never fall in love with Richard because *he* was so unlike Bob. Oh, I don't know! Looking back on these last few months, everything I have done seems crazy! I shouldn't have married Richard until I was in love with him. That was the first mistake.'

'But, Sherry, if you hadn't married him, you might never have known *he* loved *you*.'

'And what good has that done?' Sherry countered. 'Now I'm going to have his baby and he never wants to see me again – any more than I could bear to see him.'

'Well, if you won't think of your own health, at least think of the baby's,' Susan suggested. 'You need sleep and to relax, Sherry. You don't want to lose the baby, do you?'

'Perhaps that would be the best thing!' Sherry said helplessly. 'What kind of a life will my baby have? At least Bob admitted he was Anne's father.'

'My dear, you brought Anne up alone and without help; you can do the same with this baby if needs be. You know you will always have a home with Gerald and me. And if nothing else, at least Richard is legally the child's father.'

'Perhaps he'd like a paternity test to prove he's not the father,' Sherry said hysterically. 'Isn't there a blood test or something?'

'Sherry, we mustn't forget that there may not be a baby. You can't be certain yet. Let's worry about it when we know. Meantime, to please me, try and sleep. I want to go and see Richard tomorrow, and I can't leave you if you're ill or overwrought.'

'All right, I'll sleep,' Sherry said, and, putting her hand on Susan's arm, whispered: 'Forgive me for being such a nuisance. I've ruined your evening with Gerald.'

'Gerald understands,' Susan said. 'Now I'm going to put the light out and leave you. Don't worry, Sherry. I'm sure it will all come right.'

But she had not convinced herself, far less Sherry, and it was a long time before her friend finally fell into an exhausted sleep.

Susan's visit to Richard was not very reassuring. She went down immediately after work and obtained permission to see him out of visiting hours.

'I've several urgent messages from his wife,' she told the sister. 'You know she came back to London – she isn't very well.'

The sister looked unimpressed.

'Seeing that you are her close friend, perhaps it would not be out of order for me to say that I understood she had left for other reasons. Mr Hayden's nurse told me she thought there had been some sort of a "row".'

Susan resisted her impulse to make a feminine and catty remark about spies. Seeing the expression on her face and guessing the reason, the older woman added:

'Please don't misunderstand me. It is the nurse's duty to tell me anything that she feels affects her patient's health, however personal it may be. Such confidences wouldn't go beyond me – in fact, I would not even have mentioned it to you except that I am hoping you will be able to put things right. As the nurse feared, Mr Hayden is running a temperature this evening – not very high – but we particularly want him to keep calm and be unworried.'

'I understand,' Susan said. 'And I came here to try and put things right. Mrs Hayden is probably having a baby, you know. It's made her nervy and over-emotional. I'm hoping to straighten things out for them both.'

'It seems an odd time to worry her husband, whatever the condition.'

'On the contrary, it is he who is worrying her. I understand that he has realized what serious consequences his accident might have and that he is under a misplaced idea that his wife will be better off without him. Naturally that is quite absurd, but I suppose he's only trying to think of her happiness.'

'I'm sorry. I must have misjudged Mrs Hayden. It will be all right for you to see him. Try and calm him down. We want him to have all the sleep and rest he can. His general health is important and that includes mental health. He must as far as possible have an easy mind.'

It was obvious that Richard was far from restful when Susan went into his room. His head jerked round, and he said:

'That you, Nurse?'

'No! It is I, Susan. Is there anything you want?'

Richard turned restlessly on the pillow.

'Not particularly. Nice of you to come. I get pretty bored lying here, you know. Can't read – and I hate the wireless!'

Susan sat down beside him and paused for a moment before saying:

'I haven't come from Sherry, or at her request, Richard. She made me promise to tell you that first of all. But I have come to talk about her – if you'll let me.'

'She's all right – not ill, I mean?'

'Not ill. Only a bit upset, nervous, and very, very unhappy!'

'Hasn't she made it up with Tony?' His tone was harsh, abrupt.

'Richard, she won't ever make it up, as you

put it, with Tony. They say that there is nothing deader than a dead love. Well, whatever she felt for Tony is finished – for always. I know Sherry pretty well – perhaps better than you do and I can promise you that. It's all over.'

For a moment Richard did not speak. Then he said wearily:

'I don't understand it, Susan. It doesn't make sense to me. I've lain here for hours trying to reason it out, but I simply cannot believe that she's in love with Tony one day and not the next. She told you about the letter, I suppose?'

'I posted it for her,' Susan admitted. 'And when she wrote it Richard, she was very distressed and still desperately uncertain. She dashed it off in such a hurry that it was perfectly obvious that she felt she had to make up her mind one way or another. Tony held all the trump cards, you know. For ten days he was doing everything in his power to persuade her to go away with him. You never made one move to keep her.'

'But how could I? She knew I loved her. It wasn't up to me to try and hold her back if she loved him.'

'Oh, I know what you must have felt, Richard. As a matter of fact, I've always been on your side – believed that she would be happy with you. I did my utmost to dissuade her from marrying Tony. But to get back to that letter, can't you see that it was the prevailing influence that counted at that moment of crisis? She was worn out with indecision and worry and felt she must make up her mind for everyone's sake as much as for her own. If she had had one word from you, a phone call, even a post-card, I don't think she would have written that letter.'

'But she *knew* I loved her!' The words were wrung from his lips.

'Certainly she did. That's all she was sure of – yours and Tony's love. But the moment she heard from Minx that *you* needed her, she flung up all her plans as if they were so much cotton wool. If she'd really loved Tony, she'd have come here to see you, yes! But she would have told you herself that she intended to go back to Tony when you were better.'

'And suppose I don't get better?'

'I don't think that would deter a woman who really loved a man as much as Sherry could love someone. She'd merely have waited to find out how you were going to be. There would have been no question of throwing Tony over even before she knew if your injuries were permanent or not.'

Richard turned his face towards her.

'I wish I could believe that. I wish I knew what to believe.'

'She told me what you had said about –

about the baby,' Susan said gently. 'It was very cruel of you, Richard.'

'But surely *you* understand why I said it – and it isn't as if it were true – that she's having a child, I mean.'

'It's almost certainly true,' Susan said simply. 'She can't be completely sure yet, but it's fairly obvious, you know.'

'It can't be true! I never believed her for one moment. I thought it was just another effort on her part to get me to agree to her standing by me.'

'And if it is true, Richard – do you still mean what you said to her – about it's being Tony's child?'

Richard swallowed.

'It was an unforgivable insult, but please believe me, Susan, I only said it to make her hate me – to make her leave me once and for all. I couldn't stand her pity. It was her love I needed – not her unwilling presence for my sake.'

'I'm glad you don't think it's Tony's child. Will it alter things, Richard, if it is true?'

'Yes, yes, I suppose so. That is, if she wants to come back to me, naturally I shall continue to be responsible for her – and the child. But I don't think it would be a very happy state of affairs. We tried it once–' His voice was very bitter. 'It was my idea, too. How incredibly stupid of me – husband and wife in name only! Though this time I may not be much use to her – a helpless blind man.'

'Richard, don't please say such things. You don't know you are going blind and there's every chance that you won't. Even if you did you would not be helpless. Blind people aren't nowadays. And as to the rest of it, can't you believe that Sherry loves you? She does – I know it as surely as I know you love her.'

She waited a long moment for his answer. When it came, it was a bitter disappointment to her.

'I can't believe it – much as I want to. It's too much of a coincidence that she should suddenly discover it is me she loves at the self-same moment that I'm rushed into hospital. Would you believe it was coincidence if you were in my shoes, Susan?'

She bit her lip.

'Perhaps not. I don't know. I do think that sometimes people who have been confused as to where their affections lie need a jolt – a shock, if you like, to show them the truth. I think that is what happened to Sherry. She was swept off her feet by Tony at a pretty psychological moment – a pretty tricky moment in your own relationship with her. She knew you were in love with her and I think she was afraid of falling in love with you. Or perhaps I should say, of falling in love with anyone, but the fear centred round *you* because you were the first person to wake her out of the apathy of Bob's making. With Tony, it was different. He offered escape from your love, from the past; he offered a new life and a complete break, along with a very plausible charm of manner.'

'This sounds very Freudian to me. Frankly, from what I heard of Bob, he resembled Tony rather than me. Surely, therefore, she should have been more afraid of him, than of me?'

'I know it sounds odd, but I think it was Tony's very resemblance to Bob that attracted her to him at all. She never realized it, of course.'

'I wish I could be sure you were right. I believe that Sherry didn't send you, but you are her friend and naturally want to help her. Can't you see that even if all you say is true, and I *can't* believe it, then it isn't going to help her or make her happy to be tied to me?'

'You're thinking of your blindness again – something which may never happen. Richard, let's suppose for a moment that you are going to be perfectly all right. If she still wants to come back to you then, will you believe that she loves you? After all, there would be no strings attached then, would there? No need for you to feel that she was sorry for you or felt she must stand by you?'

'Yes, I suppose I'd believe it then. Unless she were doing it for the sake of this child.'

Susan gave a little sigh of exasperation.

'You're a masochist, Richard. This time I can answer you pretty conclusively. Sherry has already brought up Anne without any help, and she could have had as much financial help as she wanted. She chose to manage on her own. I'm certain that she would and could do the same thing again if the need arose.'

'You don't suppose I'd let her–' Richard began when Susan broke in:

'You may find that she will refuse help from you, Richard, if things go on the way they are. She told me she could never forgive you for suggesting it might be Tony's child. I don't think it is too late yet to put things right, but it might be if you go on like this. Pregnant women can be very touchy, and their instinct is so often to turn against the mate they no longer need. Her new-found love for you might get lost again, Richard. Don't forget that when you stand on your pride.'

'If I could only believe she does love me,' he said again. 'If it were only true.'

'Then since I can't convince you, perhaps time will,' Susan said firmly. 'I refuse to believe that you are going blind, and I won't believe it till it happens. Then, when you know you were fussing about nothing, I'll try and get Sherry to tell you she loves you. If she does, and especially after the things you've said to her, you'll *have* to believe her. She has her pride, too, you know.'

'Don't think too badly of me, Susan. It isn't just pride that makes me behave this way. It's because I love her – her happiness has always been more important to me than my own. Look after her – and please let me know immediately you are sure – about the child.'

'I will, Richard, and – don't worry. If you want anything, please get one of the nurses to ring me. You know my number and, no matter how trivial, I'd like to do anything I can.'

So her interview with Richard ended. On the way home, she resolved not to tell Sherry all that had been said – only that Richard did still love her, and his reason for insulting her so terribly. The rest must wait, for she did not want Sherry to start worrying about the future, asking herself what would happen if Richard were to be blind and refused yet again to have her back.

There was nothing more she, Susan, could do now except hope and pray for the best.

CHAPTER 17

'I've finished with him for ever! If Richard were to go down on his bended knees and beg me to go back, I wouldn't!'

Susan looked down at Sherry's flushed face with a mixture of irritation and amusement. It was so obvious that Sherry had been fretting dreadfully during the last fortnight. The doctors had postponed a decision about Richard's sight although the bandages had, in fact, been removed once and he had claimed to be able to see reasonably well. But they would not commit themselves to promising complete success until the full fourteen days were up.

Meanwhile, Sherry had been to see a doctor in London who had been her medical practitioner when she lived here with Anne and Susan, and he had definitely confirmed her pregnancy.

She had arrived back in the flat in tears.

'I would have been so glad – so thrilled about it,' she wept into Susan's consoling arms. 'Now it's only going to make things more difficult all round. I wish I'd never been born!'

Susan had not worried too much about

these slightly hysterical statements. She knew that they were merely symptoms of her condition, aggravated by her upset emotions. She had refused point-blank to go to the hospital, receiving Susan's report of Richard's progress with no outward show of emotion. But Susan knew her friend well enough to judge the inner relief she was feeling. Sherry was hopeful not only for Richard's sake but because she loved him, and because in her heart she believed that the only chance of a reunion between them was Richard's complete recovery.

It therefore seemed so silly for Sherry to make the remark that she would not go back to her husband even if he were to beg her on bended knees.

'I don't suppose Richard would go that far again, Sherry, in any case. He humbled himself once before and you turned him down. He's hardly likely to risk a second rebuff.'

'I don't care what happened in the past anyway. I don't *want* him to humble himself. I don't want him back.'

Susan sat down in the armchair beside Sherry and prepared herself for an argument which she felt to be quite stupid since she was convinced Sherry did not mean a word she said, but essential if she were to make the girl behave sensibly. (That she, Susan, should be preaching common sense to Sherry, of all people!)

'From my two conversations with Richard, I am under the impression that it isn't a question of him returning to you, but of you returning to him.'

'Don't split hairs!' Sherry said sharply to hide her secret desperation. Suppose Richard still refused to have anything to do with her. She needed him so badly now – not only his mental support and the security of the home he always gave her and the care he took of her, but she needed his love! How desperately she craved the knowledge that it was not too late – that he did still love her! And here was Susan hitting below the belt with remarks like the last one – that Richard might indeed refuse to take her home. But she would not let Susan see her fears.

'The question of who makes the first move is irrelevant,' she added. 'I want nothing more to do with him – or any man.'

'It sounds as if that cable from Tony has piqued your vanity a trifle,' Susan said caustically.

Sherry flushed a dark red.

'I wouldn't mind if Tony married Minx fifty times over – and fifty other wives as well. I'm not interested in Tony, only–' she broke off, aware that she had been about to give herself away. She glanced sideways at Susan who was looking at her with raised eyebrows.

'Only in Richard? Sherry, why do you try

and hide your real feelings from me, of all people? I've stood by you all through this, and you've confided in me right up to the last. And now this. *You* know, and *I* know, that you're head over heels in love with Richard. Why not admit it to me?'

Sherry covered her face with her hands.

'I'm such a fool – such a ghastly little fool,' she whispered.

Susan gave a little sigh of exasperation.

'Now don't sink into a state of maudlin self-pity and remorse,' she said firmly, trying to keep Sherry from giving way to this upsetting state of over-emotionalism. 'People can't *make* themselves fall in love, and it wasn't your fault you were too blind to see what Richard meant to you when *he was* in love with *you*. And I suppose you couldn't help imagining yourself in love with Tony. But you can help yourself now. You know you love Richard, and you know as well as I do that he loves you. If I've talked occasionally as if he didn't love you any longer, it was only to try and shake you out of this perfectly stupid attitude you're now adopting. How many times must I explain to you that he didn't ever mean for one single instant that he believed you were having Tony's child.'

'Then why did he say so! It was unforgivable. I shall never forget it. I was so ashamed–'

'Sherry, for goodness' sake make a few allowances for Richard. Heaven knows he's made enough for you. You knew yourself that he was scared to death you were only returning to him because you thought he was going blind and would need him. No self-respecting man would want his wife back on those terms. He *tried* to make you see this and when you arrived with your story about the baby, it sounded too darned much of a coincidence for him to credit. After all, you must admit that this baby happened at a very opportune moment – just when you had run out of reasons for throwing Tony over.'

'But the real reason had nothing to do with the baby. I found out how much Richard meant to me,' Sherry said wearily. 'Why couldn't he believe the truth.'

'Would you have believed the truth – coming at such a time, and after that letter you wrote him? No! Be reasonable, Sherry. It was too much to expect him to swallow in one dose. So he magnanimously decides to give you a last firm and final outlet – by insulting you so that you will never forgive him or want anything more to do with him. And what happens? Your love is so weak that you play into his hands and take exactly the attitude he meant you to take!'

'Oh, Susan, you know that isn't really true. You know I love him – that I'd do anything

– *anything* – to be back at home again with him – to be given a chance to prove my love. It's just that I can't stand this suspense. It has seemed more like two years than two weeks, and I torture myself with ghastly fears that he *will* go blind! They said at the hospital they would know for certain after a week – ten days at the most. Now they say they can't tell before a fortnight. It may go on and on and be months before they know.'

Susan refrained from lighting a much-needed cigarette. Nicotine still had the power to bring poor Sherry to a pitiful state of nausea. She sighed.

'My dear, you must have faith. The doctors aren't magicians. They are doing all they can – and, naturally they have to be one hundred per cent certain before they pronounce a complete cure. Imagine the shock to Richard if they did so and then things started to wrong. At least now, Richard is prepared for bad news – has grown gradually accustomed to the idea of what might happen.'

'*I* haven't grown accustomed to it. I never could. Richard, of all people. He loves life so much, Susan, and beautiful things. He's one of the most observant people I know. When we used to take the children for walks, he was always pointing out views, landscapes, colours of trees and flowers. And he'd sit for hours watching the children playing, and laugh at their facial expressions and attitudes. Everything, his work, his whole life, would be ruined.'

'It's just as bad for everyone else who goes blind,' Susan said. 'The only difference is that you and I have never had anyone we loved robbed of sight and so we haven't stopped to consider how dreadful it might be until now. But I think you're being unduly pessimistic. The doctors seemed quite cheerful when I spoke to them yesterday. Even that little nurse who looks after Richard was chirping around him like a robin in spring. And she's been pretty "snarky" lately. I think she thought you'd walked out on Richard *because* he was going blind. Shows that a little knowledge about people's private lives can be a dangerous thing. She positively hero-worships Richard – says he's the bravest patient she has ever nursed.'

Sherry smiled for the first time.

'I know you aren't trying to make me jealous, Susan, but you are doing so all the same.'

'Well, about time, too. Sherry, you must stop mooching around and think what you are going to do tomorrow when we hear the verdict.'

'But there's no about what I shall do – if he's – if he's reprieved!' Sherry cried swiftly. 'I'll be down there just as soon as I can get there after you've rung me.'

'And if he isn't "reprieved", as you put it?'

'Then what can I do? You said yourself that he wouldn't believe I loved him until I could prove it by showing I still wanted to go back to him when he didn't need me. That is what has been worrying me so terribly, Susan, that he should go blind and never let me near him. Then, more than ever, I would want to be with him.'

'I know. I've thought about it myself. I think Gerald had a good idea when we were discussing it last night. He suggested that *I* talked to Richard – told him that I had agreed to telephone you the news and that if the verdict was against him, it would only be fair to give you some way to prove you meant every word you said; so I would tell you it was all right, whatever the verdict. Later, when you turned up, Richard could break the bad news to you himself. By then, he'd know that his blindness had nothing to do with your coming, since you believed him cured.'

'Would he trust you to tell me a lie under the circumstances?'

'I don't know. I'd give him my word of honour. If he didn't trust me, he could get the little nurse to telephone you. But I don't see why he shouldn't trust me. After all, he wants to believe you do care, wants you back, Sherry. He's as hopelessly and incurably in love as you are, you know!'

A soft, sweet smile spread over Sherry's face and the tautness in her body relaxed as she allowed Susan's words to give her the courage she needed so much. If it were only true that Richard hadn't stopped loving her, they would come together again somehow. If he did go blind, she would spend her life trying to make him happy in spite of such a tragedy. There would be the new baby to take his mind off himself. If he could not see it, he could hold it, feel it, hear its cry. And the two older children, Dick and Anne, would give him *their* picture of life – describe things to him. They would take his blindness for granted after a little while until he, too, could do the same. And she would not ever let him know that she wanted to help him. She would stay quietly by him, loving him, there when he needed her.

'We could be happy – whatever happened,' she said aloud. 'But pray God, for Richard's sake, that it isn't to be the worst. He'd suffer so terribly and his suffering would be mine, too.'

'Let's not think about that any more,' Susan said reasonably. 'It's useless to get upset about something which may not happen. Time enough to worry about that tomorrow. I'm so relieved you are being sensible at last. I told Gerald last night that I was afraid you were going to mess up your life for good and always if you went on as you have been doing these last few days. You've had me worried, you know.'

Sherry looked remorseful.

'I've been so terribly selfish,' she said. 'It's not easy to see it at the time things are happening to you. They seem to push every other thought out of your mind – thought for other people, I mean. First Tony, then Richard, then the baby. It's hard to believe that six months ago I was calmly discussing with you the possibility of becoming Richard's housekeeper! It seems a lifetime ago.'

'Life is like that,' Susan said philosophically. 'Let's hope you don't get bored with the many settled years to come.'

Sherry laughed.

'Bored! Me? I don't think I have ever been bored, Susan. I've never had time. And if – well, if things do work out as I hope, then I'll be far too busy with a family of three to find life quiet. As to being settled emotionally, there's nothing I would rather be as you know. I'm not polygamous, if that's the right word; by nature, I cleave to one person. The trouble is I've never had a chance to stick to one man, unless you count Richard and I wasn't ready to marry him when I did, as you know.'

Sherry leant her head against the back of the settee and closed her eyes. She was quite oblivious to the picture she made – her face pale but touchingly young and tired. Susan felt a moment's deep affection for her friend. Life had not treated Sherry too kindly, but the future looked so rosy, provided the problem of Richard's sight worked out right. Sherry may not fully have understood how difficult life might be with a man who lived in total darkness. To begin with, he would probably have months, if not years, at St Dunstan's, and Sherry would be left quite alone with the three children. When he came back, it would take all her love and tact and understanding not to make him feel inferior, a handicap, a nuisance…

Susan pulled herself up sharply. Here she was doing just what she had forbidden Sherry to do – worry about the future until they knew for certain that it was necessary. She felt her own impatience to know one way or another matching Sherry's.

'Let's go to a cinema,' she said abruptly, and seeing Sherry's expression, added: 'It would do us good, both of us, – take our minds off tomorrow. Come on, Sherry. We'll join the rest of the world in a nice hour or two of escapism.'

Sherry smiled.

'All right! It might be a good idea. What shall we see?'

'You choose,' said Susan cheerfully.

'Well, it may sound crazy, but Tony

promised to take me to see *African Queen.* He said the local colour was so good and I'd made up my mind to see it, prior to the real thing. Now I never shall know what Africa is like – except through books and films. Let's go and see what wild and torrid excitements I have exchanged for a nice domestic life in rural England!'

Susan hugged Sherry impulsively.

'You've no idea how good it is to hear you talking like that, Sherry. It shows that Tony doesn't mean a thing to you any more. Aren't you glad he married that girl, Minx? You've no need to worry about him any more. He's obviously not suffering from a broken heart.'

'I'm glad – terribly glad,' Sherry said sincerely. 'I always liked Minx – and she loved Tony from the start. Not that I knew, then, of course. She only told me when I went down to the hospital – as a warning that she was going to put up a fight for him. I'm glad he turned to her. I know she's far more his type than I am. I think they'll be happy.'

'Come on, Sherry – no more reminiscing. If we hurry, we'll be in time for the first house.'

'It's wonderful news, the best in the world,' Susan said to Richard as she sat by his bed, her face glowing. 'I'm so glad for you,

Richard – and for Sherry, too. You know, she has been in a frightful state of anxiety, longing for your sake that it would turn out like this, and at the same time, realizing that things would be so much harder for *her* if they didn't. You don't question her love for you now, do you?'

Richard looked at Susan's kindly face, his own filled with a bright tenderness.

'No! I don't question it – and I can't think now how I ever dared to risk losing her – at any price. You know, I used to lie here, trying to picture her face – those beautiful, expressive eyes of hers – wondering if I would ever see them again. Now I shall, and I feel like a condemned man must feel when he is reprieved. Life's wonderful, Susan, and I'm so tremendously grateful to you for being such a good friend to us both.'

'If I were acting in Sherry's interest, I'd rush to the phone this minute and tell her the good news. She's all ready and waiting with a taxi to bring her down as soon as she hears from me.'

Richard shook his head.

'No, don't let her do that, Susan. It may sound crazy, but – well, I've been thinking about it all morning. When we are next together again, I want it to be for always. If she came down now, we'd have to part again so soon. I'll be out of here in a week, the doctors say. I'll have to come back periodically for a check up but I can go home in seven days. Susan, do you think she'd mind? I'd so much rather go home and find her and the children waiting for me. Would she be horribly disappointed, do you think? Would she understand?'

'I'm sure she would!' Susan said, thinking how lucky Sherry was to have married a man who bothered about romance. He wanted their reunion to be in the right setting – their home. How could any woman fail to understand! 'But I can't wait to tell her you're passed as okay. I'll tell her not to take that taxi down, and that I'll explain why as soon as I get back.'

'I don't want her to worry,' Richard said thoughtfully. 'She might think I don't want her for the old reasons.'

'I'll tell her that's all right, too, and that you sent your love. That should be enough for her.'

Richard walked across to the window and stared down into the hospital grounds.

'Spring has really come to stay,' he remarked eagerly. 'I can't wait to get home. It should be so lovely there now. During this last fortnight, lying here alone, in darkness, I've dreamed about such sights so often, wondering if I should ever look on them again. Such little things – one takes them for granted as a rule – Dick's grubby little face and mischievous grin, Anne's quaint little smile, Honey's crumpled jaw! Does that sound very sentimental to you, Susan?'

'It sounds – I don't know, Richard, but I think I can understand a little of all you have gone through. Sherry, too, has thought of little else. She has been so utterly miserable, Richard! I've worried about her health. She looks so pale, and painfully thin, in spite of the baby.'

Richard looked at her aghast.

'You don't mean – that there really is to be a baby!' he exclaimed.

Susan stared at him.

'But I thought you *knew!*' she said.

'Only that Sherry thought she might be having one. As you know, I didn't believe her at all at first. I never really took the idea seriously – it seemed so improbable. So it is true?'

Susan nodded, watching Richard's face as it changed from surprise to great pleasure.

'But that's wonderful – wonderful!' he said at last. 'There is no doubt about it?'

'No! Sherry saw her doctor the day before yesterday. She told me it should be born early in the new year. That will be 1953, Richard. I wonder what will have happened to the world by then!'

'It may sound selfish, but I couldn't care less at the moment what happens to the world. I shall be a father again, and this time it will be *our* baby – Sherry's and mine –

Sherry – Susan, she's going to be all right, isn't she? She's not really ill? Oh, how can I have been so brutal to her? Whatever must she have felt like. That I should have treated her as I did at such a time!'

'I don't think it has done her any harm, at all, Richard,' Susan said comfortingly. 'It never does a woman any harm to be a little unsure of the man she loves, especially if she's in any doubt as to her own feelings for him. As to her health – well, she's strong enough to bear anything, I think, and once you are home – well, she'll be so placid and contented that she'll put on pounds overnight!'

'I must see her,' Richard said. 'I shall never be able to wait a week now. Yes, I will! I so much want our reunion to be perfect. Oh, Susan, I wonder what the children will say – Dick and Anne – when they hear about the new baby. I wonder if it will be a boy or a girl. I don't think I really mind *which* it is! Tell me, Susan, Sherry does want the baby, doesn't she?'

'She will now!' Susan said smiling. 'She only needed your approval to give way to her own secret delight. She's a very maternal person.'

'She's everything a woman should be,' Richard said warmly. 'Please telephone her now, Susan, give her all my love and tell her I'll be counting the hours till next week.

Then I'll tell her in person how I feel about the baby.'

At first, Sherry sounded bitterly disappointed that Richard should not want her down there immediately. Then, as Susan explained the reason, she said:

'He's right! That's the way I want it, too. I'll go home tomorrow morning and get the house in order; then the day after I'll go and collect the children. Oh, Susan, I'm so happy! Did he really say he loved me?'

'How many more times must I tell you,' Susan chaffed. 'I don't know which of the pair of you is the more tiresome, you when you "glow" about Richard, or he when he "radiates" about you!'

Sherry laughed, a warm, deep laugh of happiness.

'You and Gerald are just as bad,' she said, 'only you "gush" in private. Please tell Richard that I shall telephone his mother right away to give her the good news and tell her I'll be fetching the children tomorrow. Tell him – tell him that I love him very much – please, Susan, no joking! And how thrilled and happy I am that he's going to be all right.'

'I'll tell him,' Susan said. 'I should be home for lunch, so try and come out of your clouds of rosy dreams sufficiently to cook an omelette or something! I'm hungry after all this emotion.'

‘So am I!’ Sherry laughed. ‘I’m starving! And don’t make that crack about having “two to feed now” or I shall brain you.’

‘You might as well get used to it,’ Susan said calmly. ‘I think Richard is going to fuss over you as if you were one of the crown jewels.’

‘I shall like being fussed over by him,’ Sherry replied. ‘I shall wallow in it. So he knows about the baby. You told him?’

‘It just slipped out without my thinking,’ Susan said apologetically. ‘I’m sorry, Sherry, I should have left it to you to tell him.’

‘I don’t mind, Susan – not as long as he’s glad about it. He is glad, isn’t he?’

‘Thrilled to the core,’ Susan sighed. ‘Blissful – glorying in his coming paternity! Now I’ve run out of superlatives as well as cash for this call box and I’m going to ring off. Don’t do anything silly before I get home.’

‘But I will,’ Sherry sang. ‘I’m so happy – I could dance on the roof! Oh, and Susan, tell Richard I shall will the baby to be a boy. Men always want lots of sons. And, Susan–’

‘I’m not giving any more messages,’ Susan said firmly. ‘You can possess your soul in patience until next week and tell him yourself. See you later, my dear, mad, love-sick girl!’

And she rang off, leaving a starry-eyed Sherry alone in the flat.

CHAPTER 18

Richard garaged his car and walked round to the front door. As he reached for his latch-key, he thought of Dick's shining happy smile of welcome he would receive the moment he opened the door. Although so many months had passed since he had believed he might go blind, he still could not take such simple delights for granted. Life had opened up new enjoyments by forcing him to realize the privileges of good health.

He felt for his key with hands that were numb with the cold of January winds and shivered in anticipation of the warm fire that would be glowing brightly in the sitting-room; he looked forward, too, to the whisky and soda he would enjoy before dinner. He had a quick mental flash of the brief half-hour when he would say good night to each of the children, tell them a story, answer their innumerable questions, hear their prayers.

This was always a precious time of day for him. Sherry, face warm, rosy and contented from the exertions of bath time, would turn out the lights in the two little bedrooms, then go to their room to tidy and beautify herself for him. Presently she would come down to the drawing-room to sit with him while he had his drink and tell him the funny things the children had said, what they had all been doing, the domestic trifles which made up so great a part of family life.

But, other than Dick's radiant face as he opened the door, his pleasant anticipations were not to be realized. The little boy came helter-skelter down the staircase and flung himself upon his father.

'Daddy, it's come, it's come!' he shouted.

To Richard's surprise, Anne's small figure came hurrying down the stairs behind Dick. By this time she was usually tucked up in bed.

'It comed this afternoon,' she told him gravely.

Richard searched his mind for the reason for their excitement. It couldn't be the new baby, for it was not due to be born for another fortnight. Could it be some belated Christmas present they had been expecting?

He took off his overcoat and hung it in the hall and concentrated on the children's gabbled sentences.

'It was all bare!' Anne was saying.

'Nuffing on *at all!*' Dick told him. 'But it's got something on now, 'f course.'

'An' it cried ever so,' Anne told him. 'I 'spect it was cold, don't you, Daddy?'

'Just what are you two talking about,'

Richard demanded.

The children looked at him in surprise.

'Why, our new little sister,' Dick said. 'It was magic, Daddy. Mummy was going to the hospital to get it and now she needn't go.'

'It camed all by itself,' Anne supplemented. '*I* think the fairies brought it.'

'Pooh!' said Dick. 'Silly sort of fairies not to put any clothes on it. It might have caught cold. *I* think it was magic – real magic.'

Richard did not wait to hear any more. He bounded up the stairs and nearly collided with Susan who had heard his voice and was coming down to meet him.

'Susan – it's true? The baby's arrived? Is Sherry all right?'

Susan grinned and brushed the hair off her forehead.

'It's true all right! And mother and daughter are doing fine! It was all so unexpected, we hadn't time to let you know. By the time the baby had come and I had a moment to ring you, you had already left the office. My dear Richard, go and have a drink! You look as white as a ghost. If Sherry sees you like that, she'll have a relapse. You men – anyone would think having a baby was a matter of life and death. It was all over in three hours and Sherry had such an easy time of it, she hardly believed the doctor when he said it – I mean she – was there.'

Richard sat down weakly on the top step. The children climbed over him and Susan shooed them quickly off to the nursery.

'Those kids!' she said. 'They're so thrilled I can't do a thing with them. It's high time they were in bed. Goodness knows when you'll get a meal tonight, Richard. We're all upside down.'

'But you, Susan! How did you get here?'

Susan sat down beside him and accepted the cigarette he offered her.

'Sherry telephoned me soon after lunch – said she had a hunch things might be going to happen – asked me to come down just in case. I thought she was flapping a bit because she was still as right as rain when I arrived an hour later – apologized for getting me here for nothing and, before I could answer, the baby was well and truly on the way!'

'But two weeks early – and she was to have gone to the hospital! You're sure she's all right?'

Susan smiled.

'Fast asleep at the moment, and thrilled to death with the baby for all it's a girl rather than the boy she promised you.'

'As if I minded!' Richard said.

'The kids can't contain themselves, they're so excited. They haven't seen the baby yet – Sherry wanted you to be the first. You know, it – I mean, she – was only born two hours ago! I haven't known whether I was coming or going. The nurse hasn't been gone long. She'll be coming back later this evening.'

'And the baby – there's nothing wrong – early?'

Susan laughed.

'Good heavens no! She weighs eight and a half pounds and has a mass of fair curly hair and looks about six months old already. She's like you, Richard. Except that she hasn't any signs of your patience. I never knew any baby in such a hurry to be born.'

Richard took a deep breath.

'I can still hardly believe that it's all over – the baby's here – and that Sherry won't have to go to hospital after all. I'm awfully glad about that. I know things will be difficult with the two older children in the house, but they could go to my mother if necessary.'

'Nonsense! We'll cope!' Susan said. 'Mary will carry on with the house-work and cooking and the nurse will be here for a fortnight to see to Sherry and the baby, so I'll have nothing to do but mind Dick and Anne. We'll be nicely organized by tomorrow, you'll see!'

'You don't think Sherry will worry – the noise – that kind of thing?'

'My dear boy, she's had such an easy time, she'll probably be up and bossing us all round in a day or two. Seriously, though, I think she's glad she needn't leave you all. There's nothing she likes better than to have the whole family within earshot. And she hated the thought of being parted from you – even for a fortnight!'

'When can I see her?' Richard asked.

'I think she ought to have her sleep out,' Susan said. 'The nurse said she'd probably not wake for an hour or two, so she went home to pack her things. She left her home in such a hurry she didn't have time to bring anything. But you could see the baby if you want to. She's yelling her head off.'

'No – no, I'll wait till Sherry is awake. I'd like her to – to be the one to introduce me to our daughter. I think I'll go down and have that drink, then I'll come up and help you put the kids to bed. You'll probably need a hand if they're over-excited. Father's strong arm can do wonders at a time like this.'

He looked tired and still a bit white, but Susan felt it would give him something to think about while he was waiting for Sherry to wake. Naturally he would be impatient to see her and it would help to pass the time quickly.

The children were put to bed with difficulty. They talked of nothing else but the new baby.

''F course, it's a pity it's only a girl,' Dick told his father as he climbed into his pyjamas. 'But I dare say I won't mind much. I've got sort of used to girls with Anne – and we can always get another one, can't we? Then next time we'll make it a boy.'

'Next time!' Richard exclaimed, shooing his young son into bed. At this precise moment, he hardly wanted to consider next time.

'Well, we *can* get another one, can't we? How *do* you get babies, Daddy? What's being borned mean?'

Fortunately for Richard, Dick did not wait for an answer.

'You know, I don't believe in fairies, Daddy – that's girl's stuff, but, all the same, if the fairies didn't bring it, how *did* it get here?'

'Maybe Father Christmas brought it!' Richard said, thinking that Dick would soon be old enough to know the truth. They had decided to let Honey have puppies in the summer. Maybe that would be a good time to give both the children an idea of the greatest miracle of nature.

'Well, he jolly well might have put some clothes on it,' Dick said vehemently. 'It was so cold, it cried and cried. Anne 'n I heard it.'

'Never mind, I expect it's all tucked up warm and safe now,' Richard said smiling. 'You and Anne shall see her first thing in the morning. So you'd better hurry up and go to sleep now so the morning comes quickly.'

Dick snuggled down in the bed-clothes and said with a contentment which he tried to hide:

''F course, it is only a girl, but I rather want to see what an absolutely *new* baby looks like. If she's nice, I might give her a ride on my rocking-horse.'

'Well, not quite yet,' Richard told him, as he turned off the light. 'She'll be too small to play very much to start with.'

'How small?' Dick asked. 'As little as Anne was when she first came here to live with us?'

'Oh, heaps smaller than that,' Richard said, hiding a smile. 'Not much bigger than your Teddy.'

'Gosh!' said Dick sleepily. 'That's teeny! Oh, well, 'spect she'll grow pretty quickly. I've growed two inches last term, Daddy–'

'Hey, no more questions! Time you were asleep. Good night, son, and remember to be a good boy tomorrow. I shall need your help you know. We men have got three girls to look after now.'

'Don't worry, Daddy,' came his son's voice. 'I'll look after them while you're at the office. I've got my cap gun to 'tect them if a burglar comes.'

Richard closed the door softly, thinking how very dear this little boy was to him. He was not Sherry's child, but he felt a very special love for the child of his former marriage – as if there were a double quota of love in him because he had never really had his mother's love. Not that Sherry did not love Dick every bit as much as she loved her own little daughter – and Dick was deeply devoted to her. It was wonderful the way they had become such a united and happy family!

Anne was already asleep when he crept in to take a last look at her. She lay with her dark hair framing her small face, a faint smile on her mouth, her lashes curling darkly over the rosy cheeks. One small hand lay curled with perfect grace across the pillow behind her head. She looked almost a baby again.

Then, for the first time, he heard his new daughter's voice, little gasping angry cries that came from down the passage. He hurried into the bathroom where Susan was mopping the floor.

'The baby's crying!' he said, anxiously. 'She's not choking, is she?'

Susan smiled.

'No, just hungry! And I expect you are, too, poor man. Mary should have a meal on the go by now. As soon as I've cleared up, I'll go down and see.'

Richard hesitated.

'You don't think Sherry will have woken up yet?'

Susan smiled.

'I doubt it, but you can go and see if you want. Having babies may not be dangerous these days, but it certainly must be tiring–'

She broke off sighing, for Richard was already on his way to Sherry's room.

He opened the door quietly but Sherry, lying half-awake, half-asleep, turned her head towards him. She had realized he must be home – heard his voice in the background of her dreams – and was waiting for him.

'Richard?' she asked softly.

In a moment he was beside her, staring down at the beloved face. She looked white and tired but so deeply contented and happy that he caught his breath at the expression in her eyes.

'Oh, darling,' he said huskily. *'Darling!'*

She put up her arms and drew his head down to hers, so that they lay cheek against cheek.

'I love you so,' he said softly.

'You're not sorry – that our baby is a girl?'

He held her hands more tightly in his own.

'I'm thrilled to the very marrow – and horrified that I have been carrying on at he office as usual and never had a moment's worry, while you were going through it all alone.'

Sherry smiled, a deeply maternal smile, and her hand went to Richard's hair, smoothing it from his forehead.

'I wasn't alone, dearest Richard, and I didn't have very much to go through. It was all so wonderfully thrilling and exciting that I scarcely noticed any pain. Susan says she's beautiful. Do you want to see her, Richard?'

'In a moment,' he said gently. 'Just for a few seconds, I only want to see you.'

'I'm so happy!' Sherry said softly. 'Almost too happy. I hardly dare breathe in case anything should spoil our life.'

'Nothing can spoil it while we are together,' he told her. 'And nothing can ever come between us again.'

'The past – those dreadful days – they seem so unreal, so impossible now!' Sherry said dreamily. 'If only we could have had a glimpse into the future, they would never have happened.'

'They were meant to happen, I think,' Richard said gently. 'They taught us really to appreciate each other.'

They were silent for a moment in the close, intimate silence of people who are deeply in love. After a little while, Sherry said:

'I never did ask you, Richard, but I've often thought about it. When you had that accident – suppose you *had* lost your sight. Would you have let me come back to you?'

'My dearest, how could I have helped myself? I should have needed you so badly – your love and your help. I was going through an absurd and juvenile state of hurt pride, I think. I know I could not have kept up our separation for very long – not once I knew you really did love me.'

'I was so silly!' Sherry said. 'I never knew what love meant before. I shall never forget the day you came home from the hospital. I kept the children by me all morning because I felt too shy to meet you alone. I worried myself stiff what to say to you – what you would say to me – how I could tell you all that was in my heart. Then, when the moment came, you shooed the children into the garden and took me in your arms. Do you remember, Richard? I didn't have to say a word and you made that moment perfect for me – the most perfect of my whole life – until now.'

'As if I could forget!' Richard said. 'You looked so very beautiful, my dearest Sherry – standing in the doorway with your hair and skirt blowing softly in the breeze, a child on either side of you. You were symbolic of all women waiting for their men to come home. Yet when I saw your eyes – you were nothing but a small, shy little girl – a little afraid, yet eager – oh, Sherry, Sherry, I still cannot understand why you should love me! Yet I know you do and the knowledge glorifies my whole life.'

'As if I could ever love anyone else!' Sherry said tremulously. 'You hold my heart, Richard.'

Richard stared down into the eyes that looked so trustingly into his; saw the violet shadows of fatigue beneath them and tenderly drew away from her.

'You must sleep again, my darling,' he said. 'But I'll ask Susan to bring the baby in first. I so much want to see *our* child – our little daughter. I want *you* to show her to me. Later, tomorrow – we shall have to think of a name for her. None of those boys names will do now!'

But before he could reach the door, Susan opened it and came in with a bundle in her arms.

'I guessed Sherry was awake when you didn't reappear – and that you'd want to gloat over your joint creation! Here she is – bless her little heart!'

Sherry took the baby from her and Susan slipped quietly out of the room. Richard bent forward as Sherry drew back the shawl from the tiny fair head.

Sherry's eyes were wet with tears of happiness as she said:

'Oh, Richard, she's so absurdly like you!'

He stared down at the tiny crumpled replica of his face. Then, dropping to his knees beside the bed, he pressed his lips reverently to Sherry's hand.

'Thank you – thank you for everything, my darling wife,' he said.

, for people
nal print,
auspices of

OUNDATION

oyed this book.
Please think for a moment about those who have worse eyesight than you ... and are unable to even read or enjoy Large Print without great difficulty.

You can help them by sending a donation, large or small, to:

The Ulverscroft Foundation,
1, The Green, Bradgate Road,
Anstey, Leicestershire, LE7 7FU,
England.

or request a copy of our brochure for more details.

The Foundation will use all donations to assist those people who are visually impaired and need special attention with medical research, diagnosis and treatment.

Thank you very much for your help.